I0627708

SEVENTH SEAL

A Reverse Harem Tale

Lovin' the Coven
Book 7

Jacquelyn Faye

∞ Untold Press ∞

SEVENTH SEAL

A Reverse Harem Tale

Lovin' the Coven, book 7

ISBN: 978-1-945893-18-6

Published by Untold Press LLC
114 NE Estia Lane
Port St Lucie, FL 34983

www.untoldpress.com

PRODUCED IN THE UNITED STATES OF AMERICA

10 9 8 7 6 5 4 3 2 1

Dedication

This book is dedicated to Porn Hub

Thanks for all your help with "Research" and getting me through "self-Isolation"

Bow chicky wow wow

Chapter 1

The stone door slid open, the sound of granite on granite echoing slightly in the damp smelling hallway. My heart started pumping faster as the darkened room beyond came slowly into view. The guards parted and ushered me into the dryer, warmer section of the Temple of Night. The only piece of furniture visible was an ancient table of black wood covered in scrolls and tomes. Seated on the other side of said table was Delron, poring over an open scroll and jotting notes down on a separate sheet of vellum.

"Lord Delron, she has come."

He looked up and his eyes met mine as a small smile splayed across his face. "Lady Dorothea, welcome." He stood and walked around the table, his feet shuffling beneath a hooded, heavy black robe, pausing in confusion as Yuki stepped between us and handed me a five-dollar bill over her shoulder.

"You win."

Delron stopped and blinked in confusion.

"Don't mind her." I laughed and took the money, stuffing it in the front pocket of my jeans and walking the rest of the way to greet the dark elf. "She was convinced this was a trap."

Delron chuckled and knelt before me, kowtowing in respect. When he stood, he rushed forward, closing the final distance between us, pulling something from his robe and stopping when my vampire familiar had him in an armlock, shaking it until the loose sleeve flopped down enough to expose the glowing red jewel he held in his hand. He stared at her in shock. "I mean her no harm," he said innocently.

Yuki turned her head to me, resigning herself to my judgement.

"Let him go, Yuke."

She did and stepped aside, but not before Delron rubbed his wrist and shot me an apologetic look. "You have to know, my lady, I would never intentionally harm you?"

"No. I've become jaded as of late. It seems that everybody wants to harm me."

Sadly, he nodded. "Well, from the *unseleighe* court you have *nothing* to fear. You are our goddess."

"I'm no goddess, I just want to give you back yours. God, not goddess. You know what I mean."

He nodded. "Sit, please."

"What is it you were trying to give me?" I nodded at the jewel in his hand.

"A token of thanks for resurrecting our lands and bringing back the night." He smiled and offered me the jewel.

"It's just a jewel, right? It didn't go so well the last time I touched one of these." My fingers hovered over the surface, waiting for an answer.

"It is whatever you make of it. We gifted one to your father millennia ago. He chose it to be the receptacle of his power when the higher planes called for his imprisonment."

I nodded and took it from him, holding it up in front of me. Letting my magic flow through it, I saw he wasn't lying. It held nothing, but I could feed whatever I wanted into it. Memories, magic, or power. I tucked it into the other pocket of my jeans.

"Sit, please," he motioned toward the two empty seats on the closest side of the table and went back to his. He stood until I parked my butt.

"That was a neat trick with the unicorn," I said drolly and crossed my legs in front of me.

He beamed proudly. "It was the only way to get him to you. I hope Lord Jaeren wasn't too distraught that his Yule gift was actually from us?"

Yuki snorted.

I smiled in appreciation of the entire situation. Jaeren had been so proud, but when the unicorn introduced himself to me, he shimmered and morphed into a stallion of the purest shimmering black, eyes of red, and two horns of matte ebony. He wasn't technically a unicorn, but a cousin of sorts. A bicorn of unseleighe stock. The seleighe king sputtered and began a tirade of elvish curses that lasted until Dar and Shea dragged him inside the house and got him calmed down with a glass of wine and a box of crayons.

Yuki had been convinced the entire thing was a trap and had even bet me we were going to be met with swords.

Delron sat back in his seat, clasped his hands, and positively beamed at me.

"You said you found a way for me to get to Tartarus?"

He nodded and smiled before motioning toward the guards by the door. The same grinding noise told me they left and when their footsteps returned, Elleslyn of Willowmere was between them.

"Ellis?"

"Greetings, my lady." He gave me the same reverent display as Delron and practically prostrated himself on the ground behind me.

"Rise, Lord Elleslyn. Join us." Delron waved his fingers and one of the guards grabbed a chair from somewhere and set it next to mine.

I was a little surprised when only Delron sat on the opposite side of the table, but I shrugged in resignation. I would have sat on Ellis' lap if it got me some answers. "You were saying?"

Delron lifted his hands and put them under his chin, smiling at me and nodding toward Ellis.

I turned toward him. "You can get me to Tartarus?"

He shrugged and looked at Delron for an explanation, just as in the dark as I was. I didn't let go of him with my eyes. He was even more handsome when he thought I wasn't looking at him. I probably stared a little too long. It wasn't until Yuki pinched me that I turned back to Delron who was practically grinning at me.

"How is Ellis supposed to get me to Tartarus?"

"The same way your father made his way there."

"My father was dragged kicking and screaming by a horde of pompous angels. I fail to see how Ellis can accomplish that?"

His grin broadened a little.

I stared at him blankly until realization reared its ugly little head. "You want me to have a *baby?*"

"Aww, hell no. Come on, Master." Yuki stood and started tugging my arm from the rest on my chair.

"That was your whole plan? Get me pregnant and piss off the higher planes enough that they tossed my ass into Tartarus?"

"Can you think of a simpler solution?"

"There's gotta be a bus or something. Taxi? Charon? Anything but producing an offspring? Plus, what makes you think it would even work? I'm not a god, I'm just a Dot."

He scoffed. "Your father used his jewel to pass his mantle onto you. You give birth, put his godhead back into the gem, and pass it back to him upon your arrival. Do you not see the beauty of this plan?"

"I don't want to have a child! Not now, probably not ever! And if I do, it's going to be with a mate of my choosing, not yours!" I glanced over at a very meek looking Ellis. "No offence."

"None taken, Lady." He scowled at Delron, too. "This is what you discussed with mother?"

Delron nodded, not sorry in the least.

"Your mother was in on this, too? Why am I not shocked by this revelation?" I scoffed.

"I am truly sorry. Had I known, I never would have agreed."

I narrowed my eyes at him. "Agreed to what?"

"Becoming your *Aiqua*."

"Her what?" Yuki pulled me and my chair away from Ellis.

"*Aiqua*. I do not know the word in the common tongue?" He looked at Delron for a translation.

"The closest word you would have in the mortal realm would be…everything?"

"You want to be my everything?" I blinked at the absurdity.

Ellis looked thoughtful and said something to Delron in elvish.

Delron looked at me and nodded. "Everything or anything. It is a position of honor among us. He would be whatever you *need*. Friend, guard, servant. Confidant, counsel, kin. Lover… Or perhaps even husband. His role is determined by your need."

"Pardon?"

"I devoted my life to you, Lady. In whatever capacity you would have me." He lifted himself from his seat and prostrated himself on the floor beside me.

Yuki lost it and started giggling.

Delron *beamed*.

I wanted to run. "Ellis, stand up. Delron, you're insane. Yuki, let's go." I stood up and walked between her chair and mine, not wanting to step on Ellis in my haste to retreat.

The guards didn't know what to do as I practically ran for the exit. They kept waiting for Delron to say *something*. "Lady Dorothea," he called softly.

I slowed but didn't stop. "What?"

"Think about it. You know my plan is the only way."

"Bullshit. It's the only way you can think of. I'll find a way to free my father, with or without your help."

"By your leave, my lord," Ellis said to Delron with a small bow as he hurried toward Yuki and me. When we were out of the room, I stopped and turned toward him.

"Go home, Ellis."

He sighed and shook his head. "I cannot. Upon my oath I am now bound to you heart and soul."

"But I don't want you."

It was one of those moments when I realized I said something hurtful and stupid as soon as the words flew out of my mouth unfiltered. His face fell and turned to shock as the tears flowed from his eyes. "If that is your wish."

"I want you to go home, find a nice spidery princess, get married and have lots of dark elf spider thingies." I shuddered at the thought.

"Had I known before I made the pledge, I would have been happy with that. But, alas, that is not what the stars have written for me now."

"Whatchu talkin bout, Ellis?" I squinted in confusion.

"An *Aiqua* without a *Varni* has no purpose. My life is forfeit."

"Say that again? Slowly."

"If you will not have me, I have no purpose. I shall go. I am sorry for the subterfuge on part of my mother. Lord Delron is his own creature and I make no apologies for him. As for me, I am sorry to have troubled you, Lady. I shall take my leave." He turned and headed back toward Delron's study.

"Master?" Yuki hissed.

"Don't look at me. I didn't fucking know." I turned and looked at the broad shoulders slumped in defeat as he trudged away. "Ellis, come on. We'll figure it out. Later. Away from here."

He stopped walking but didn't turn back toward us. "You will have me?"

"Just come on. Let's go. This place gives me the willies."

12

He nodded and turned back toward us. His expression unchanging. "There is no later, Lady. Either you will have me or not. Do you accept my oath?"

"We'll discuss it back at my house."

"Lady…"

"*Master*." Yuki actually sounded worried.

"What?" I glanced down at her.

"Say yes. Or he's going to off himself."

"What? How do you know?"

"Because I can feel it coming off of him. He's already resigned himself to his fate. It's like a vampire swearing fealty to a lord. Fuck, it's like being a familiar. If the master doesn't want you, you die. Say yes!"

I looked up at Ellis who seemed a little shocked to have an ally in my court. Shocked but hopeful. He tore his eyes from Yuki and slowly lifted them up until his met mine.

You already have a Jaeren. He's in the same boat as Ellesyn. What's one more? Yuki's pleading argument in my head was worse than her words.

I found myself nodding at Ellis. "Fine. I accept your oath. Now can we go home?"

"Yes, my *Varni*." He practically skipped in excitement to me and got down on one knee, bowing his head.

"Oh, get the fuck up. Come on. I need a drink."

Turning, I strode back the way we came and didn't stop until we exited the temple and found Delanir milling about the entrance majestically, as only a unicorn could. Even an evil one.

You seem distraught. His mindspeech made me wince. Out of all of the ones who could talk to me in my head, he was by far the loudest. Kind of like a deaf uncle who spoke at thirty-times the normal volume because he spent too much time around exploding ordinance in the military. Only it wasn't because Delanir wasn't deaf, it was because he was a friggin' unicorn. It was like asking a dragon to whisper.

I am distraught. Could you take us home, please?

As you wish, Master. Though, I do not think I can carry three.

Take them, then. I can find my own way home.

Through the shadows?

I nodded. *I might as well. Please take them home. I think I need a drink.*

And when the vampire has a fit of shits when she realizes you will be alone as you drown your sorrows, what excuse should I give her?

None. Just stop her from looking for me. Not kidding, I need some me time here. And it's a shit fit, not a fit of shits. That's what happens when you get bad tacos.

He bowed his head.

"Get on Delanir. I'll shadow walk home."

"Yes, Master," Yuki answered and gingerly stepped on the bicorn's offered foreleg, settling herself neatly behind his neck and gently running her fingers through his silky mane.

"Be careful, my lady," Ellis answered and deftly hopped up behind her.

"What does he mean be careful?" Yuki shifted, intent on getting off the bicorn just as he slashed a portal home through the air with his horns and stepped through.

Maste–

Her mindspeech was cutoff as the portal closed behind them.

I lifted my hand to take myself back to Cedar Falls, but I knew if I did, I'd just end up sulking at the diner. I needed something way stronger than that, and I knew just where to find it. Which worked out perfectly with my mother still in Cedar falls. The chances of running into her were nil. Maybe not nil, but certainly greatly reduced.

Calling the shadows to my hand, I pulled myself into the shadow realm and stepped out into the alley between the Daystrum Cleaners and Tir Na Nog, the biggest Irish pub in Ashville. I had puked so many times in that alley in my youth, I knew it by heart. And smell. It brought back so many *happy* memories, I found myself smiling from

14

nostalgia as I walked around the corner and pulled open the heavy oak door with the brass handle.

The smell of corned beef was the first thing that assaulted your nose as you walked in, then the smell of beer and polished wood warmed your heart. Waving at the hostess, I pointed at the bar. You needed to wait to be seated for booths and tables, but not the glorious, majestic oak bar with the hammered copper top.

"Dorothea?" The burly bartender stared in shock as I ambled up to his domain.

"Heyla, Mr. Connors." I smiled at his mustache, still wondering after all the years I had been going to the pub, how he managed to eat or drink anything without swallowing a half a pound of hair. He had just started growing it the first night he had taken over as bartender from his father. That had been twenty years ago. Now, it dangled long enough to brush his shirt. It was no wonder he was so fond of it. It was the only hair gracing his head.

"Still as beautiful as ever."

I grinned at him.

"Usual?"

"Yes, please. And make it a double."

"Rough day?"

"Rough couple of months. Rough, but good."

"Good. How's your mother?" He whispered the question.

"Fine? Why?"

He set my whiskey sour in front of me and frowned. "Well, it's not every day the High Priestess steps down without someone in mind to take over. Everyone thought it was going to be you, but you hightailed it out of town first."

"Excuse me?" I gripped my glass and stared at him in shock. Mr. Connors wasn't a witch, but his wife was. He was as human as they came, but between his wife and the number of drunk witches that got blabby-mouthed after a few dozen beers, he was almost as bad as Marge in the gossip department.

He stood up straight, realizing I didn't have a clue. "She didn't tell you." He wasn't asking, he knew.

"Tell me, what?"

"That your mother is an asshole." A drink slopped down on the shiny metal bar beside me, and a very drunk Nestor Flume slopped down in the seat next to me. Mr. Connors started wiping down the bar, quickly polishing his way away from the conversation.

"Nestor? What the hell is going on?"

"You tell me. The coven would fucking *looove* to know." He clinked his glass of straight whiskey against mine and poured the rest of it down his throat before leaning against the bar and holding his head up with his hand.

Several more witches got up from the surrounding booths in the bar and circled around us. I guessed old Nestor wasn't the only one who wanted answers.

Sighing, I sucked down some of my drink to steel my nerves. "Mother came for a visit. As far as I know, she should be leaving any day and coming back here."

"That's not what her letter said." Nestor pulled out a folded piece of stationary and slapped it down beside me.

Gingerly, fearing the worst, I picked it up off the bar and scanned the contents. The letter was addressed to Nestor. I'd known they'd been lovers, but seeing the graphic and detailed address to Nestor, I felt my drink rising in my gullet as it threatened to make its escape. I did *not* need to know Nestor was endowed like a bull elephant. He was creepy as fuck enough already. How Mother found him attractive was beyond me. But, then again, she found most of the male members of her coven attractive. Probably why she bedded half of them.

After the disturbing greeting, she basically said she quit and that her troublesome daughter needed her. She was resigning the coven to the witches of Ashville to decide on leadership going henceforth.

Nestor was right.

My mother was an asshole.

"Fuck me." I handed Nestor back his letter. "Don't look at me. She showed up and kept going on and on about how she was leaving any day. Then she agreed to stay through Yule. This is the first I'm hearing about it."

The other witches grumbled an understanding, but Nestor was scrutinizing me, gauging if I was telling the truth. "Why? Did you really need her that bad?"

I opened my mouth to deny it, but I couldn't. Not after how much help she *had* been. Her and Nana both. "I did. And I won't lie to you, Nestor. I might need her for a bit longer, but I'll send her back as soon as she's done."

"Don't bother. We don't need her." He got up from his stool and wobbled off toward the bathrooms.

There was one thing for sure as shit. I didn't want her, either. She was my mother, and I loved her, but I would be much happier with her several states away. Plus, Ashville needed her, despite Nestor's proclamation.

Gulping down my drink, I tossed a twenty down on the counter and waved goodbye to Mr. Connors. I needed to get my shit together and get her back where she belonged. For both our sakes and my sanity. And for the safety of Cedar Falls. Having her and Nana in the same city was never a good idea, no matter how much they pretended to get along. They had to be up to something...

Chapter 2

Yuki was glaring daggers at me over the back of the couch while the coffee maker sputtered behind me. Jaeren and Ellis, both coloring, were looking intently at the books sprawled out on the table in front of them. That was their excuse not to look at the impish vampire glaring daggers at me, and me pretending not to notice. I was sorting through the mail like there wasn't an absolute fucking thing wrong in the world.

"Anybody want ice cream?" I asked without looking up from the stack of mail on the counter.

"What is ice cream?" Ellis whispered the question to Jaeren.

"Frozen milk from cattle with fruit mixed into it. Or sometimes chocolate. It is quite delicious."

"What is chocolate?"

"A sugary confection made from the nuts of a tree."

"Yes, I'd love to try some," Ellis called to me over Jaeren's head.

"Rocky Road?"

"What is–"

Jaeren silenced Ellis with a wave of his hand. "Yes. For both of us, please, Lady."

I chuckled under my breath. Maybe Ellis would be good for the overbearing king. Hard to be an asshole when you're stuck teaching elves about the mortal realm. Ellis had taken to him like the older brother, even though they were as different as night and day.

Jaeren didn't seem to be harboring any open hostilities toward his *unseleighe* cousin, either. I was shocked and pleased, almost crying when he offered him some of his color sticks and books.

"I'll be back in a little bit," I said to them, grabbing my purse, and heading for the door.

"There's seven different flavors of ice cream in the fridge, Master." Yuki got up and walked into the kitchen, pulling out the freezer door and showing me our stock.

"Huh. No Rocky Road. I'll be back in a bit."

"There's fudge nut brownie. Put some of the little marshmallows in it."

"Not the same."

"It is and you know it."

"You want to go with me?" I asked as a peace offering. She had been more than pissed I'd traveled halfway across the country, unsupervised and without her.

"Can I drive?"

"I've seen you try. Let's go with no, you can't."

"Oh, come on. I'm getting better."

"Tell that to the seven squirrels."

"I can't. They're dead."

"Exactly."

"They weren't people."

"Had there been any by the road, I'm sure you would have found some way to get *them* caught up in the wheel well. You coming?"

"Fine." She huffed and headed for the front door.

"Hey, Yuki?"

"Yes?"

"Want some hot cocoa?"

Her frown turned into a grin and she ran out the door.

Emo vamps were so easy. I laughed and grabbed my keys, tilting my head as a realization came to me. My little Yuki wasn't so emo anymore. She was even wearing a bright, lime green shirt. Her hair was still purple, but it wasn't spiked, and she had forgone the heavy black lipstick and eyeliner for a while. I sniffed as I walked out the door, pleased. My little Yuki was turning into a lady.

"Did you really want to buy me a cocoa, or are you just checking on the store because you haven't been there all day?"

"Little bit of both," I said as I got into the car. "It's the day after Christmas. The place should have been a madhouse. I want to survey the damage."

"Think there's a body count?"

"I doubt it. Jason is one smooth ass talker when he wants to be."

"If the customers were female. Betcha there's ten dead guys stashed in your office."

"I'll just reanimate them and send them home. Their wives might appreciate the silence. Hard to fight when all you can say is, Glaaaaah."

Yuki giggled. "I miss Squishy."

"I don't miss the smell."

"No."

She flicked on the stereo and we danced in our seats to K-Pop for the five minutes it took to the bookstore. Even from outside, I could tell it was still busy, even though they were closing in an hour. "We should check to see if they ate. Or if they even had time to eat."

Yuki wasn't looking at the bookstore, she was staring at the diner and frowning. "Go ahead. I'm going to pop my head into the CFD."

"What's wrong?" I already knew it had to do with the town's vampire population. That worried me, and I wanted specifics.

"Nothing's wrong… I don't know what it is. But I'm going to find out."

"Want me to go with you?" I pulled into a spot in front of the police station and put it into park.

"No. Not sure how the vamps will react. I'm going in cautiously and planning on running if I have to."

"Keep me posted."

"Yes, Master." She got out of the car and weaved through the moving traffic on Main like a ballerina on speed. Hopefully, nobody noticed her display.

Showoff.

Worried.

Okay. Be careful.

Getting out of the car, I stood there for a moment just to make sure nobody came flying through a plate glass window. When I saw Yuki's head as she sat down at one of the occupied tables, I relaxed.

You good? She didn't look like she was in trouble, I just wanted to make sure.

Yes.

Keep it that way.

I felt her mental chuckle more than heard it and headed for the bookstore. Chief was standing by the front desk of the station but talking on the phone. Smiling and waving, I headed past.

The bookstore was even more crowded than I thought. The registers were packed, but the aisles were even more so. "What are you doing here?"

I narrowed my eyes at Jason. "Is that any way to greet the lady who signs your paychecks?"

"When she was expressly forbidden from showing up on Boxing Day, yes."

"Boxing Day? Did we move to Canada?"

"We're close enough." He chuckled and spared me a smile, stepping a little closer and giving me a quick hug.

"Who are the new kids?" I motioned to the pair manning one register while Shea ran the other.

"That's Peter," he said and pointed to the kid scanning books and punching keys. "And the other one is Suzy. This is her first day so she's learning and bagging. The two of them together can't keep up with Shea. I don't think I would have made it through the day without him."

"Have you guys eaten?"

He grinned.

"What?"

"Worked it out with Herb. There's food in the back." He motioned toward the stock room, giving me a gentle push.

"Don't try to feed me, I already ate."

"Just showing off my brilliant idea and making sure you don't mind."

I pushed through the heavy swinging plastic door and whistled in surprise. "You had food catered?" There were four steam trays with Sternos on a longer table against the back wall.

"Yep. Already paid for a week. They deliver after lunch and after the dinner rush. Which works out good since we don't open until ten and the second crew comes in at five."

"You're brilliant."

"And because we are repeat customers, they're not charging us even half of what they should be. Just wanted to make sure this was okay with you. We're working everybody to the bone–"

I silenced him with a kiss. "This isn't just my store. Not anymore. It hasn't been since the day you started working. If *you* think it's a great idea, I think it's fucking genius. You never need to ask me about shit like this."

"Can I ask you for another one of them kisses?"

"Tell you what, why don't you," I paused and put my lips next to his ear and whispered the rest. "Stop by the house and I'll kiss you where it *really* counts." I pulled away and ran my hand over the front of his jeans.

"Ooh. A bonus."

"No. A bone me." I gave him a saucy smile and squeezed, nearly groaning as he swelled under my hand.

"I'll see you tonight. Can I use your shower?"

"Since that's where I was planning on giving you those kisses, absolutely."

A dizzy, dreamy grin spread across his face and Dar snickered behind us. "Can I get some of those, too?"

"You gonna be home tonight?"

"Well, I wasn't, but maybe I can talk Shea into having a sleepover at the boss' house."

"Don't. I may come spend the night with you guys tomorrow."

Dar and Jason's eyes narrowed. "Is everything okay, Master?"

"Yes. Just picked up another stray."

Jason tilted his head and Dar scrunched his eyes in worry. "Stray?"

"Remember the dark elven prince?"

"Elleslyn?"

"Yeah. Long story, but he's kind of in the same boat as Jaeren. Sworn to serve me." I sighed heavily and almost dropped to the floor. Anger, doubt, and frustration making my head hurt. I didn't need another servant, and I sure as hell didn't *want* one. "All right. I'm supposed to be on an ice cream run, not ruining everybody's mood with my problems. Gonna check on the girls and go grab Yuki from the diner." Giving them each a kiss on the lips, I left them standing there staring at me in shock.

I made it about three feet from the backroom door when the shakily asked question stopped me in my tracks. "Excuse me, Miss? Do you have any books on hydroponics?"

I almost laughed at the elderly lady browsing the gardening section. "I'm not sure, but you're in the right section if we do." The door behind me swung open and Jason stepped out. "But the guy to ask just walked through that door." I waited until he got a little closer. "Hey, Jay. Books on hydroponics?"

"Yep. Several of them. Here," he answered and bent down to find them. I caressed his shoulder and gave the old lady checking out his ass a smile.

Leaving them, I headed for the coffee shop. It was running like a well-oiled machine. Josie was running the register and Candace was conducting a symphony of younger vamps manning the espresso machines, blenders, and coffee makers. The three of them were flipping cups, ducking under each other, and not spilling a drop. The people in line were applauding their barristacrobatics and stuffing tips in their jars. When an order was filled, it was handed off to Candace who got it to the appropriate customer. It was almost mesmerizing to watch.

I couldn't take my eyes off them as I pushed my way through the line and walked around the side of the counter, slipping up behind my sister. "Holy shit," I said behind her back in awe.

"Brilliant, huh?"

"Hiring vampires? Fuck yeah."

"You can thank your little princess. She hooked us up."

"She did?"

"Janay, cover for me for a minute?"

"Sure thing, Miss Josie." One of the vamps broke from the pack and slipped behind the register. The other two vampires sped up a little to cover the missing person and keep the production going. They weren't a well-oiled machine, they were a fucking Tesla Model S.

Josie motioned for the back room, letting me lead the way through the swinging door. There was another vampire back there grabbing a snack. "Hey, Miss Josie."

"Karl."

"Need some privacy?" He motioned to the bag of blood in his hand.

"Please. Give 'em a hand for a minute."

"Sure thing, Boss." He grinned at her, fangs on display as he bowed almost reverently to me. I caught a whiff of fear coming from him and I shuddered in ecstasy.

"You okay?" My shiver didn't go unnoticed by Josie.

"Yep. Peachy. Nice to meet you, Karl."

He blushed and shot through the door, leaving the two of us alone. I rolled my head over my shoulders and felt my neck crack. The stock room was quiet. The first actual silence I'd had all day. I almost didn't want to start talking.

Too bad that wasn't a trait of my sister. "Yeah, it was Yuki's idea hiring the vamp kids."

"Brilliant. What about paperwork? Some of those kids have been around for ninety-something years. Don't you need social security numbers and shit?"

Josie blushed.

"What?"

"They have them."

"How?"

"You can thank your buddy, the mayor."

"Sherry?"

Josie giggled and nodded. "Remember Georgie Blake?"

"Your seventh-grade crush?"

Josie nodded. "He moved to town and since he worked at the records department in Ashville... Sherry gave him a job at city hall. He's been working diligently magicking birth records and helping the kids in town apply for social security cards. A whole flock of 'em ranging in human ages from sixteen to nineteen."

I leaned against the wire shelving behind me. "Holy shit." I blinked at the implications.

"Yep. Cedar Falls is turning into Ashville."

I blew out a breath of appreciation. Things were moving along nicely, much faster than I'd expected. Now if we could just stop some of the townsfolk from rounding us up, tying us to stakes, and burning us, things would be great. At least we didn't have to worry about the three major ones anymore. Hard to stage a witch hunt when you'd been reduced to zombie kibble. I felt bad. Not for their deaths. They were almost zealot level in their hatred of witches, but because I'd inadvertently caused their demise. The zombies I'd accidentally created had eaten all three of them to protect me. Personally, I would have felt much better turning them into horny toads.

"You sure you're okay?" My sister was staring at me intently.

"Yes. You can stop asking now." I blew her a kiss for her concern.

"You just seem..."

26

"Preoccupied?"

"Yep."

"Lot of shit happening. Store, mother quit the coven, we picked up a dark elf houseguest, the vampires think I'm going to eat them, Yuki is at a vampire town meeting at the diner. The usual."

"Wait, what?"

"Which part?"

"Uh, all of it?"

"Stopped by Ashville to get a drink. The witches are pissed at Mother because she skipped town to come help me. Left her letter of resignation."

"Are you serious?"

"As a heart attack."

"Don't tell my mother." Josie started fidgeting with worry.

"Okay. Why?"

"Because she'll head back there and try to take over."

"And that would be bad, why?"

"Could you imagine what that scatterbrain would do to Ashville?" She shuddered.

So did I. "Okay, mums the word."

"Dark elf?"

"Long story."

"Eat vampires?"

"Longer story."

"Vampire town meeting?"

"Gonna go find out what all that's about now."

She chuckled and leaned over, giving me a hug. I almost sobbed in her shoulder. I wanted more than anything in the world to tell her right then and there how much she meant to me and who she really was to me, but I bit my lip. It wasn't the time. Once I sorted out everything with my father, then, and only *then,* would I spill the beans.

"Dot?"

"Yeah, Jose?"

She pulled back and looked me in the eye. "There's something I've been wanting to ask you."

27

"What?"

"Will you marry me?"

"Huh?"

"Candace and me. Sorry, I should have said will you marry *us?*"

My heart started beating again and my stomach settled back down. "Of course! Have you picked a day yet?"

"It's kind of soon, but the next day the store is closed is New Year's Day…"

I smacked her on the head. "You are not planning a whole wedding in a week. Don't make me smack you. I will marry the two of you, but you're going to do it right, with beautiful dresses and food and friends and a band." Mustering the sternest look I could manage, I booped her on the nose. "We'll plan it together, all of us. In the meantime, treat your lady right. She's not going anywhere, and neither are you. And don't worry about coordinating around the store being open or not. We can close for such a momentous occasion."

She started crying.

Master… Yuki's voice didn't sound panicked, but it was close.

What?

I need you. Now, please.

"Gotta run. Yuki."

"Go!"

Hugging her one more time, I ran back through the door and out of the store.

Chapter 3

Enter slowly.

Okaaay?

Trust me.

Always. I slowly pulled the diner door open. The chime above the door even seemed to ring slowly as I took one step into the diner and surveyed the situation. The vampires had pushed three of the tables in the far corner of the diner together and were angrily staring at Yuki, who sat across from her cousin George.

The rest of the diner was business as usual, nobody seemed to feel the tension in the air, except for Marge who was glancing at me nervously from behind the counter. I made a stay motion at her and slowly sat in my booth.

Good. George and I are coming to sit with you.

As if on cue, she and he stood and slowly marched their way across the diner, weaving through the tables between us. Almost with a strained look on their faces, they slid into the booth, Yuki first.

"Greetings, Lady Dorothea."

"Hey, George. Long time no see."

The door chimed behind me, and I felt another vampire enter the diner. More familiar than the others. It was Amir, the very first vampire I'd seen in Cedar Falls. I'd saved him and his sister from a vampire-hunting band of witches. Amir was one of the good guys. Without looking, I slid in further to give him enough room to sit. "Hi, Amir."

"You knew it was me?" He didn't sound shocked, he seemed pleased.

"Yes?"

He sat down and smiled. "Could you tell me how?"

"I don't know. I could feel it was you when you came in."

"See?" He made a gesture at an incredulous looking George.

"That does not prove anything. She could have smelled your cologne."

Amir sighed. "Lady Dorothea, could you tell me where Yvette is right now?"

"What?"

"Just see if you can *feel* her like you did me."

I hated parlor tricks, but I did as he asked, rolling my eyes as I closed them and felt around for Amir's sister. She was gone. A scene flashed through my mind of the battle between Lord Abernathy and me. Yuki's father had kidnapped her to marry her off to another clan of vampires. It had turned into an all-out war between me and the vampires. Amir had refused to fight out of loyalty to me, but his sister chose Lord Abernathy's side. Evidently, she had been torn to shreds by the undead, wounds grave enough that even a vampire could not have survived. I hadn't even known. "Oh, Amir. I'm so sorry."

I blinked up at him through the tears.

"You saw her death?"

"Yes. Not a way to go."

"Do not worry. She chose to follow him into his insanity. Those who followed their own hearts are alive to this day. She put too much faith in a man who did not deserve it. If only he could have been more like his daughter."

I smiled at Yuki, but she was staring at me nervously. "What?"

George stopped her from answering. "How many vampires are in the diner at this moment?"

Without closing my eyes, I knew the answer. "Three at this table, twelve in the back and one in the bathroom?"

"Count the number of people at the other table."

Lifting my gaze, I did as he asked. There were fourteen heads. "Fourteen. But only twelve vampires."

"Are you sure?"

I knew without a doubt that I was. "Positive."

"How can you tell?"

"Beats the hell out of me, George. I just can. The blonde girl on the end and the guy in the middle closest to the wall. They're human."

George turned to his cousin and nodded. "You were right."

"Yuki?"

"I'm sorry, Master."

"For what?"

"Before I answer, can you do something else?"

"Depends on what that is," I answered her honestly, narrowing my eyes at my familiar.

"Tell me how many vampires are in town?"

"What? Come on, Yuke, I can't do that."

"Try? Please?"

Sighing, I rolled my eyes again before closing them, picturing Cedar Falls in my head. One by one, little red dots appeared on the map in my head. I counted each one as they appeared. Three of them appeared outside of the city limits. "Forty-eight in town and three just outside of town," I answered, surprised at myself.

"Holy shit." George's forehead hit the table. "It's not possible."

"What isn't?"

"One more thing?" Yuki nervously tore the napkin apart that had been beside her hand. Marge was gonna smack her.

"What? No more parlor tricks, Yuke. Tell me what's going on."

"I will. Can you feel the vampires in Amersville?"

Wanting the weird conversation to end, I did as she asked and closed my eyes. "None that I can see."

"So, it is just the local vampires you can feel?' George lifted his head from the table.

"Yes? Wait. No." There was a tugging on my consciousness. Closing my eyes, I followed the pull to the southeast. "No. I can see them in Ashville, too. Eighty-seven of them. Yuki, call your mother. She is worried about you and angry at herself that she didn't warn you about your father. George, your father misses you and regrets what he said to you about your sexual preferences." I opened my eyes and stared at the two of them with their mouths hanging open. Amir chuckled beside me.

"And the two of you doubted me."

Yuki looked at Amir. "How did you know?"

"Since I wasn't at the graveyard and had already sworn my loyalty to Lady Dorothea, I felt it as soon as he died."

"Who?" I was behind on the conversation, but I had a feeling I knew who he was talking about. I just wanted him to say it.

"Lord Abernathy. When you sent him to the earth, you took his power."

"No, I didn't. I had a vampire side before that. It's what got those sweet kids killed."

"You had vampire powers beyond belief," he answered. "Almost on par with a vampire lord."

"Yes. They thought I was one. Abernathy didn't like his power being questioned."

"*Exactement.* But when you killed him, you tied all of his line to you."

"Huh?"

"You're not just *my* master, Master." She motioned to the vampires behind us and then spread her hands and included the rest of Cedar Falls into her quantification. "Ashville, too. Apparently. It's how you know what my mother and uncle are feeling."

"No. Not possible. I'm not a vampire, I'm a witch. A witch who needs a fucking cup of coffee and some aspirin." I motioned at Marge and made the universal symbol for 'I need some fucking coffee' by pouring an imaginary pot into an imaginary cup. Either she would know what I was talking about or get a good laugh at my

32

mime skills. She grabbed four mugs and a fresh pot and headed toward us. Apparently, I didn't suck at charades.

"You're more than that, and you know it, Master." She said the words almost reverently. I didn't like it. Not one bit.

"I'm just Dot."

All three of them laughed. It was probably a good thing. I could feel the vampiric tension leave the room. Thankfully, I wasn't sitting close enough to the others to smell their fear. The fear I could feel. Luckily, the feeling didn't set off my fangs and hunger.

"So, what does this mean?"

"It means that you have a lot more on your plate than you thought, Lady Dorothea." Yuki bowed her head.

"Oh, you just knock it the fuck off, Yuki." I reached across the table and bopped her over the head with the tips of my fingers. The calmed vampires' fear swelled inside my head as they backed the whole table a little farther away from us, scrunching against each other like minnows in a bucket. "Relax," I shouted across the diner. "That was a play tap. I'm not going to hurt her or any of you."

Marge dropped the pot of coffee.

The rest of the diners, the human ones, stared at me like I'd lost my mind. Which I was about three seconds from doing.

"What's goin' on, Darlin'?"

"They want to make me the leader of their youth production of Romeo and Juliet but think I'm too mean to be a good director."

"Yeah. Sure. Let me get this cleaned up and get another pot of coffee. Sorry, you scared me!"

"Sorry, Marge."

"Hungry?"

"Pie. Double."

She nodded in understanding. If I had a drug addiction, it was pie. At least I only indulged when the shit hit the fan. With the way my life had been going, I was running a serious risk of getting fat. "I'll have it right out."

33

She left us sitting there, Yuki trying very hard to stifle her giggles. Miguel brought a broom and swept up the glass and then cleaned up the coffee with a mop.

"This is just perfect."

"I know this causes you discomfort, Lady Dorothea. Some of us were afraid, too. Some still are." Amir nodded at an uncomfortable looking George. "But this will be a good thing."

"What will?"

"Having a lord who will do right by us, not exploit us or others for personal gain."

"I'll speak to your mother and my father," George told Yuki and stood up. "I shall inform the others, as well. My lady," he said to me, bowed low, and headed back to the table of vamps.

"He's pissed," I said, not caring if he could hear me or not.

"Well, his father or my mother should have become the next lord of the clan."

"To have a witch is probably a little insulting."

"Not so much insulting as it is a financial nightmare."

"What?"

She laughed and Amir patted my arm in sympathy. "You don't understand," Yuki said with a sad smile.

"Understand what?"

"You get it all."

"All what?"

"Everything. The houses, cars, boats, and limos. Hell, even the blood banks will go to you."

"I don't want them," I answered adamantly just as Marge returned with a pot of coffee, pouring cups for all three of us.

"You don't get a choice, Lady Dorothea."

"Yuki, if you call me that again, I'm going to flog you with spaghetti. Dot. My name is Dot."

"Yes, Master."

Marge giggled. "Pie will be done in a minute. I'll bring it out. Carry on."

Covering my face with my hands, I rubbed vigorously. Shadow walking to the far side of the moon seemed like a better and better idea every minute. Every time I turned around, I was in charge of something, or someone, else. My mother had one coven and it turned her into a raving lunatic. Nana, too. I had a coven, a dark elf, an elf, a couple of races, and a godly sphere. There was no way I was going to get through everything with my sanity intact. I'd be drooling by Wednesday.

I didn't realize I was staring at the teal Formica top of the table until there was a piece of pie blocking my view. "Thanks, Marge," I said without looking up.

Then a thought nudged its way into my brain.

"Wait, if I'm the head bitch in charge, I can do what I want, right?"

Yuki and Amir exchanged a glance but nodded slowly.

"Good. Tell your mom to stay right where she is in that big assed house. George's father, too. And first order of business once the blood banks are in my name is every vampire in the clan no longer has to pay for blood." I grinned and took a bite of my pie.

"What?" They asked simultaneously.

"You friggin' heard me. When I heard your father was charging them, I wanted to kill him." My heart stopped when I realized what I said, but Yuki didn't seem fazed by my outburst at all. In fact, she smiled at me. "I can do that right?"

"You're the boss," she answered with a snicker.

"Enjoy your pie. I'm going to go spread that little bit of news with my brethren. That might make all of this a little easier." Amir patted my leg and got up, rejoining the other vampires.

"Think they'll be happy?" I ran my fork through the crust of the pie, opening its juicy entrails and letting it mingle with the vanilla ice cream.

Their cheer was answer enough.

"What's that all about?" Chief slid into the booth next to me. I hadn't heard the *ding* of the door over their cheer and he sat down before his aftershave made an appearance in my nose.

"Their team won the world cup. Hey, sexy." I leaned against him, stealing some of his calm and warmth. Happy for a moment until he picked up a spoon and stole a piece of my pie. The bastard. "Get your own!"

"Big Bird says share." He stuck his tongue out at me.

I tried to steal it back by kissing him. Our tongues fought for a moment before he swallowed with a chuckle.

"I'm going to fucking throw up now." Yuki got up and went to sit with the others.

"Poor kid. Can't stand to see the grownups fight over a piece of pie." He looked back at the table of vampires. You gonna tell me why they're so excited to be sipping coffee in a diner? And don't tell me it was about soccer. The world cup was a few weeks ago."

"Damnit. I knew I heard something about it. Figured it was a good excuse."

"Why were they all happy? I thought they were supposed to be broody."

"Do you really want to know?"

"I wouldn't have asked if I didn't."

Sighing, I took another bite of pie before he ate it all. "Apparently, I'm the new vampire lord. Lady. Whatever."

"Woah." He huffed and stole another bite.

"Like I needed more on my plate."

"What are you talking about? There's plenty of room. The pie is almost gone."

"Quit eating it, and you know that's not what I meant."

He kissed my temple. "Well, if anybody can handle it, it's you."

"Gee, thanks."

"You're welcome. Need a pep talk about anything else?" His grin was infectious, and I found myself smiling alongside his goofy ass. Then I frowned. "What?"

"Picked up another roommate today, Bill."

"I know. I met him when I stopped by your house. Thanks for telling me, though."

"Don't look at me, I didn't know until today, either."

"You misunderstand. I was actually thanking you for telling me. I figured it would take you a couple days to build up the nerve." He grinned to soften the blow, even though it was accurate as fuck.

"We fight enough without outside help. Figured I'd nip it in the bud."

"Is he another mate or boyfriend...?"

"No." I sighed, still appreciating his lack of jealousy.

"Well, he thinks the world of you."

"Huh?"

"You were all he talked about once he found out you were my girlfriend."

"Oh. Yes. He is very friendly for an evil dark elf." I chuckled. Ellis didn't have an evil bone in his body. His mother on the other hand... Noble but psycho.

"Well, how about I pick you up for dinner tomorrow and you can hide out at my place?"

I dropped my fork. It clattered against the plate and flung tiny bits of pie over the table. "What?"

"I'll pick you up for dinner and you can spend the night at my place if you want," he reiterated slowly for the dumb witches.

Since we'd been dating, I'd been at his house *once*. One time. Didn't even stay that long. It was almost a monument to his late wife, and I didn't feel comfortable there. Whenever Chief and I got together it was at my place, for him to invite me to his and spend the night was... It was kind of monumental. The last thing I wanted to do was ruin the moment. Swallowing my discomfort, I smiled and nodded. "I'd love that."

"Good."

"Hey, Bill. Coffee?"

"Yes, please. And two more slices of pie." He turned to me. "You want anything?"

"You're a shit."

"Yep. Yours."

Chapter 4

I knocked my phone off the nightstand trying to get the ringing to stop. When I bent over the edge of the bed and cracked my eyes open, Chief's name was flashing across the screen. Picking it up off the floor, I answered it quietly and snuggled back into Jason's arms.

"It's," I paused to pull the phone away from my ear and looked at the time, "six in the fucking morning. There better be a body or I'll make damn sure there is one."

"You read the paper yet?"

"You assume too much. One, that I could comprehend words at this ungoddessly hour. And two, that I read the paper."

"Grab a copy sometime today."

"Just save me yours. Give it to me at dinner."

"You might want to read it before then."

"How about you just give me the Cliff's notes version so I can go back to sleep?"

Jason's hand slid down my stomach and two of his fingers slipped between my thighs, gently rubbing me in his sleep. Maybe he was awake, it was hard to tell with him. Until he started nibbling my shoulder.

"How about I just read you the headline. Local witch threatens children in restaurant. Sound familiar?"

"Yeah, kinda. I wasn't threatening them, I was telling them I wouldn't hurt them. And they weren't kids, they were vampires."

"Yeah. I know. I was there, remember?"

"Vaguely." I let out a hiss of pleasure as Jason's fingers dipped inside me and spread my wetness over my rapidly hardening nub.

"And you're okay with this?"

"That I vaguely recall your presence at the time of the incident or that the paper is slandering my good name."

"Both." He chuckled.

I moaned as Jason's nibbles turned into him gripping the flesh of my shoulder between his teeth as his morning wood prodded my entrance. Bending at the waist, I exposed myself to him, easing his access. Without releasing me, he lined himself up and plunged into my depths. My moan turned into a groan as he filled me.

"Is somebody there with you?" From Chief's voice I could already tell he knew the answer to that.

"Maybe."

"You're getting fucked right now, aren't you?"

"That's a bigger…maybe." I managed to get the words out between thrusts as I closed my eyes.

"That's really fucking sexy," Chief said with a little catch in his breath.

"You like…fuck…hearing me?"

"Yes. What are you wearing?"

"What I usually…oh goddess harder… What was I saying? What I usually wear to bed. Nothing."

"He's behind you, isn't he?"

"Yes."

"Hand cupping your breast, pulling you against him?"

"No. He's fingering my clit and biting my shoulder."

"Holy fuck."

"Are you hard, Chief?"

"What do you think?" There was the tiniest of groans as he pictured me getting railed while talking to him. He'd been spending a little too much time with Jimmy.

"Pull your cock out. Stroke it." I grunted with each thrust as Jason increased his rhythm.

"I'm at work."

"It's six. I sincerely doubt anybody is at the station but you. Shut your door, you're on an important phone call."

There was a moment of silence, but then I heard the door click shut. I couldn't hear him lowering his zipper, but

I could picture it easily. Seeing him struggle to get his cock out of his pants was easy to imagine, too.

"What's he doing now?"

"He's fucking me harder, Chief. Oh wow. I think you listening excited him. He's palming my clit and spreading my lips with his fingers." I lifted my leg and threw it back over his, giving him more room to work my pussy with his fingers.

"Are you going to come soon?"

"Are you?"

"Yes."

"Good thing you have that drawer full of towels, huh." My grunting picked up pace as Jason frantically tried to push me over the edge. "Come for me, Chief. Like you did when you cuffed me on your desk."

"Oh, Lady," he whispered, and I could faintly hear him beating his meat over the connection.

Jason slammed into me, held himself for a moment, and then did it all over again. I could feel his cock spasming inside me, throbbing as he filled me with another load. Between that and knowing Chief was masturbating as he listened to our love making, my sanity didn't stand a chance as I cried out as I came.

"I'm coming…"

And I heard his grunts as Chief came over the other end of the phone. "Where?" I had to ask.

"All over my fucking desk."

I chuckled as I imagined the sight.

There was a rumble as he set the phone down. Jason kissed my neck and shoulders as I lay there panting. Every few seconds, he'd pull back with his cock still inside me, and then push himself back against me. It sent micro spasms through my whole body with each slow thrust.

The phone rumbled again as Chief picked it back up. "Fuck that was hot."

"Still is. He's still slowly fucking me."

"He didn't come?"

"Yes. I'm very squishy right now."

"Don't say that name."

I chuckled. "Mmm. This feels good. You should come over and feel how wet I am."

"I'd rather feel how wet I'm going to make you tonight."

"Deal."

"Is it the dark elf or Dar?"

"Neither."

"Tell Jason I said good morning." He chuckled.

"How'd you know?"

"I'm a cop."

"Tell me?" I smiled at nothing, relishing at how cute Chief could be sometimes. Some. Times.

"If it's not the elf or Dar, then Dar is at Shea's. Jimmy and Dennis went fishing this morning. Ergo, Jason."

"You're so brilliant sometimes it scares me."

"You gonna add the dark elf to the mix?"

"Feeling cute, might fuck him later. I assume you like that idea since you keep bringing it up."

"The more the merrier. I'd be okay with Jaeren, too. Just be careful. He's probably into crayon play…"

I snorted into the phone. "See you tonight, sexy."

"Tonight," he said, and the line clicked dead.

"He sure is lightening up in his old age."

I tossed the phone on the nightstand, reached behind me, and swatted Jason on his ass. "I'm older than he is, pup."

"But you're so much hotter. And younger *looking*." He nibbled my ear as he whispered.

"Go back to sleep. You gotta get up in an hour."

"Oh, I'm wide awake now."

"Well, I'm not. Have fun. I'm going back to sleep." Pressing my ass back against him, I stuffed the pillow under my head and covered myself back up with the blanket.

∞ ∞ ∞

Jason unlocked the front door of the bookstore, pulling it open and letting Josie and Candace slip inside. I followed behind them and trailed them all the way to the coffee shop, waiting while they flipped the lights on, and Candace started a pot of regular old coffee for me.

"You look like hell, Lady," she said quietly as the machine slowly bubbled itself to life.

"Good. Then I look like I feel."

Josie went back out the front door to grab the stack of newspapers the delivery truck dropped off. When she came back and cut the tie, only then did I remember the real reason Chief had called that morning.

"Let me snag one of those for a minute, Jose."

"Since when do you read the paper?" She handed one to me and stacked the rest on the wire rack beside the trash can.

"Since I'm in it." I unfolded the paper and looked at the headline. Sure enough, it read exactly as Chief had said. There was even a picture of the front of the diner under the headline. Against my better judgement, I read the article.

The reporter, a Jake Bloom, hadn't even lied in the piece. He'd twisted the entire context and made me sound like a threatening monster, but he didn't lie. The rest of the article questioned the existence of witches and gave a brief history of facts and fiction about witches in general. Most of it was garbage, but incredibly well-written garbage. Scowling, I folded the paper and stuck it on the rack on top of all the others. Except for the one Josie was holding next to Candace as they read the article.

"Uh… The coffee is done."

They ignored me. Even Candace. She shot me a worried look when she finished reading. Josie would probably need a few more minutes. Without a word, Candace grabbed a cup and filled it, deftly slapped a lid on and a sleeve around it before she held it out for me. "Want a shot of espresso in it, Lady?"

"No thanks. I'll be in my office if you need me. Jason needs me to approve a few things." I waved over my shoulder as I headed for the checkout area and slipped behind the counter into the office. I couldn't even really call it my office. It was Jason's more than mine. He didn't even need me to sign the checks anymore since I'd proudly added him to the business account.

I glanced at the security monitors, there were people lining up outside the door and we still had fifteen minutes until the store opened. Shaking my head in confusion, I pointed at the screen.

Jason smiled as he lifted his head from the paperwork in front of him. "Want to know something funny?" He grinned at me nervously.

"Jason, I love you, but if you tell me you put a spell on the bookstore to bring in customers, I'm going to kill you."

He shook his head. "No. That's what's so funny. I *almost* did. Could you imagine what this place would have been like?"

"You're sure that nobody else did?"

He laughed. "I thought that, too. Ran my fingers over every inch of this place to make sure. There isn't one spell on this place other than your shields. I can't explain it and your guess is as good as mine."

That wasn't good enough for me. Considering the financial situation of the entire region, *something* had to be dragging the townsfolk into the store. Leaning against the wall and closing my eyes, I let my magic flow into the wall behind me and spread out through the building.

The only spell on the place was my barrier ward. The one that kept out ghosts and people intent on harming anyone or anything in the store. First Moon Books was probably the safest place in Upstate New York. I needed to up the defenses on my house to match it. I whistled in appreciation at the fortress it had become, but there was nothing amiss. No spells that filled my pockets while emptying those of the customers. It didn't make *any* sense, but I guessed it would remain a mystery. Pulling my magic back into myself, I finally felt it.

I had searched every inch of the place, but not the store as a whole. Leaving my magic where it was, I took in the big picture and smiled as I realized what it was.

The bookstore wasn't alive, but it was close. When objects were filled with enough love, hate, or any other emotion, they tended to take on the traits of those emotions. Humans did it every day with their cars. Call it a broken-down piece of shit every day and scream at it, the odds of it starting every morning were slim to none. Tell your car it is the bestest, most beautifulest car in the whole world, and that puppy would gladly take a freight train for you. It was a constant shock to me that humans didn't realize it.

The bookstore was loved. I loved it. Jason loved it. Candace and Josie loved it. Everybody that worked there loved it. But most importantly, the people of Cedar Falls loved it. They saw it as a change in the luck of the town. Five years ago, a store like this would have gone out of business in a week. It had become a bastion of hope. So, they lined up outside the doors to spend a little time in its warmth, grab a cup of coffee, read a few magazines or the paper and bask in that glow. It made them feel alive. Like the town had gotten a heart transplant. It made me smile and it made me cry.

"You okay?"

I nodded at Jason. "Hope."

"What?"

It was hard, but I managed to express everything that I had realized and when I finished, Jason's grin was bigger than mine.

"That's fucking amazing," he answered.

"Don't look at me. Most of this was you, buddy."

I wasn't the only one crying and he kept wiping at the corners of his eyes so I wouldn't notice. I kissed his head and left the office to give him a moment of privacy. We'd all come a long way. Some of us more than others. But none of us as far as Jason.

Sipping my coffee, I wandered around the bookstore just to breathe in the smell. A few minutes later, Jason unlocked the front door and the crowd rushed inside. Half of them went for coffee, the other half for the books. Smiling, I realized they were more than likely going to switch places shortly.

Shea and Dar waved as they walked through the door, smiling at each other as Shea headed for the register and Dar toward me. "Good morning, Master. For what momentous occasion do we owe such a smile this early in the morning?"

Grinning like a fool, I held out my hand for him, just to feel the warmth of his hand against mine and to recharge his battery a bit. Since he practically spent every night at Shea's house, I'd noticed he touched me a lot more when I was near. He needed my energy as a familiar and being apart was rough on him. It made me happy he thought Shea was worth it. "Nothing. Just happy."

He brought my hand to his lips and gently caressed the back of it with them. Then he sniffed my skin. "You smell stronger…"

"I showered before I came here?"

"No. Not scent. Power. Cold and dark."

Pulling my hand from his grip, I frowned. Damn him and his hellhoundy nose. "Long story."

"The vampires?"

I nodded.

"Something else, too. Vaguely like Shea?"

He was way too fucking good at this game. "Dark elf. Elleslyn. He's staying at the house."

"In your bed?" He grinned at me.

"No. On the couch."

"Odd place for a lover to sleep."

"Not my lover."

"Yet."

"Gah! What is with all of you and your obsession with me collecting guys like baseball cards?"

"I sincerely doubt any of us wish to be stuffed in a plastic sleeve and stuck in a book."

"You know what I mean." I frowned at him.

He pulled me to the side of the aisle to give the elderly lady behind me room to pass. "Thank you." She grinned at him before turning to look up at me. "If the others look like this one, keep on collecting them!" She cackled and ambled down the aisle.

"Oh, I will!" I smiled at her retreating back. "Okay, seriously. Why is it whenever a guy shows up, you all keep badgering me about them?"

Dar at least had the decency to blush. "Because."

"Why?"

"We want you to be happy."

"And you don't think I am with all of you?"

"Yes. But if another lover makes you that much happier, it makes us happier. Does that make sense?"

"Vaguely. But I don't think my vagina can take much more happy. I'm completely happy. Any happier and I'm going to get friction burns."

"Might I suggest lube?"

"You know what I mean. You guys give me so much love and loving, I don't need any more."

"And if that makes you happy–"

"Finish that sentence and you're not going to be happy. All of you need to quit worrying about me so much and be happy yourselves!"

I hadn't realized my voice had risen in volume out of frustration. The rest of the bookstore did. They were openly staring. Hopefully, it didn't sound like a threat and I wouldn't end up in the paper again.

Dar grabbed my arm and started pulling me toward the front of the store. "Come with me, Master."

"Where?"

"To the diner. You need some food."

"I'm not cranky! I was happy until a minute ago."

"And I intend to rectify that." He grinned at me in apology.

47

"Well, I am a *little* hungry. I mean I *could* eat..."

We stopped at the curb until there was a lull in the traffic long enough for us to get across the street. The diner seemed to be as busy as the bookstore, but not busy enough we had to wait. I just didn't get my table but managed not to snarl at the couple sitting there as we passed.

As soon as we sat down, Marge made a beeline for our table, coffee and menus in hand. "Did you see what that shit rag printed about you?"

"I did."

"You gonna sue? I'd sue. Slanderin' you like that."

Dar shot me an inquisitive look across the table.

I shrugged at him and sighed before answering Marge. "Technically, they didn't print one thing that was a lie. They totally twisted the context of the situation, but there's nothing to do. I'm not worried about it. None of the..." I paused to look over where the vampires normally sat when they were hanging out in the diner. "None of the people that I was talking to filed a complaint, so it's just one of those things."

"Still. Those kids were petrified of you until you did whatever you did. First time I ever seen 'em that happy."

That brightened my mood a little. "Thanks, Marge."

She waved my thanks off and pulled out her order book from her apron and her pen from her hair. "Whatcha havin?"

"Steak and eggs," Dar answered with a grin.

"Coffee? Coke? Both?"

"Coffee and a water, if you would, please." She smiled and turned to me.

"I'll have the same." When I was with Dar, my craving for red meat skyrocketed exponentially. I didn't want the eggs, but asking for a steak for breakfast might have seemed a little odd. He could have mine if he wanted.

"Scrambled, too?" She knew his preference for eggs from him ordering just one time. She amazed me sometimes.

"Please."

"Erky derky," she answered and started walking away.

"Erky derky?" I laughed as the words slipped from my lips.

Marge started giggling. "A few days ago, this little Asian girl came through here, cute as a button. She said some of the strangest things. That was one of them. I must have picked it up from her!"

"I say enough weird shit. If you catch me saying anything like that, have Herb smack me with a skillet."

Marge chuckled and headed for the counter. "Herb! Two eggs and legs, extra moo and whip 'em!"

"Aye, aye." Herb waved at me through the window into the kitchen.

"So, how did your foray into the elven lands go. I mean beside your consolation prize elf."

I snorted. "Consolation prize. I wish it were that simple. Delron's entire plan consisted of me getting preggers and cast down into the fiery pits of hell to rescue my father."

"That isn't the best of plans."

"Oh, and he gave me a jewel to shove my father's gifts into to give them back to him. Like the one that gave them to me in the first place."

"That is the better part of the plan. Where is the gem?"

"In the lockbox on my dresser. I'm going to get a pouch to carry it around in or something. Doesn't seem very safe leaving it where it is. I'm going to need it."

"You just need a way into Tartarus."

"Yep."

"Dot…"

"You know a way?" My eyes narrowed and I leaned closer.

"No. That's just it. It is the literal bottom of the planes, far below Gehenna. Only those from the adjacent planes can access it. There is no way to get there anymore. You either have to be an angel or a devil."

"Devil?"

He sighed and leaned back, sipping his coffee. The plane above Tartarus is called Cania. There was one sole inhabitant."

"Who?"

"Mephistopheles He was rumored to have a stronghold in Tartarus as well."

"So, he can get us into Tartarus?"

"He could if he wasn't eradicated by the angels."

"So, only the plane below can get us to Tartarus? Wait! I thought you said Tartarus was the *lowest?*"

"It is. But everything comes full circle. Instead of thinking of the planes above and below, think of them side by side, but when you're on the plane, down takes you to the left." He tried to explain by having his hands one above the other and then twisted them together until they were side by side. It hurt my head.

"Okay. I kind of get it. So, the one below is actually the highest?"

"Precisely! So, the angels can get to Tartarus because it is above them, but on the bottom."

"I need a fucking drink."

"Got some whiskey behind the counter. Need a snort in your coffee?" Marge looked at me seriously as she deposited the plate of steak and eggs in front of me.

"No! It was a figure of speech. Dar hurt my head."

"Silly boy. Hurt her ass, not her head." She cackled and dropped the plate of food in front of him alongside a glass of water.

I blushed as I picked at my eggs.

"Let me know if you kids need anything else."

"Will do, Marge," I grumbled slightly, unable to look her in the eye.

"Perhaps she meant by spanking it?"

"You're gonna be spanking something else if you don't stop talking, Dar."

"Yes, Master."

Chapter 5

"We should totally have a New Year's party," Yuki said as if she was some sort of genius and tossed a four pack of Red Bull into the cart.

Reaching in, I lifted it out and put it back on the shelf. "You need Red Bull like I need another boyfriend." I kept walking and grabbed a case of Coke. By the time I got it into the cart, the Red Bull was back. At least she had tried to hide it under the stack of coloring books I found by the entrance to the Amersville Walmart. "Sneaky little shit," I said with a chuckle and pretended not to notice.

"Did you say something, Master?"

"Nope. Head for the coffee aisle. We need to stock up."

"Should I grab another cart?"

"Har, har."

My phone dinged in my pocket. Pulling it out, I rolled my eyes. I had texted my mother before I headed for the bookstore. I told her to call me when she got up, but I doubted she had slept in until after lunch. She was ignoring me, but finally caved and texted instead of calling.

What can I do for you, daughter?

I hit the call button. It rang four times and went to voicemail.

I am indisposed at the moment. What do you need, Child?

Therapy. We need to talk.

I shall be home for the remainder of the day. Feel free to stop by.

You're still at Nana's?

Of course. Where else would I be?

"Oh, I don't know, Mother. Building a candy house to lure children into your oven?" I wanted to type it, but my fingers wouldn't let me. Sometimes, my fingers were smarter than I was.

"What?" Yuki was staring at me like I had lost what little of my mind I had left.

I shook my head at her. *I'll see you this afternoon*, I texted to my mother and stuffed my phone back in my pocket. "Let's get the coffee and get out of here. I have a hag to banish."

"Banish?"

"Yeah. She needs to get her ass back home before she doesn't have a home to go back to."

"I'll pretend I know what you're talking about if you buy me an iPad."

"My mother, but I'm not buying you an iPad," I said with a laugh, thinking she was joking. She might have been, her face was all smiles, but I could feel disappointment wafting from her in waves. A scene played itself out in my mind. Yuki, in an effort to defy her father, cut off her beautiful, waist length hair and bleached the tips to hold the purple dye better. In a fit of rage, he had destroyed everything in her room, including her first-generation iPad. The one she had saved for and bought on her own. It had happened just before he had sent her to live in Cedar Falls in disgrace.

"I know. I was just kidding, Master."

We turned down the coffee aisle and she ran ahead to replenish the three boxes of coffee we'd gone through since the last time I made it to the store. By the time I made it to her, she had them stacked in her arms and set them on the floor, shoving them on the bottom rack of the cart one by one. "That's it. To Grandmother's house we go."

"One more thing." I pushed the cart and headed to the back of the store instead of toward the registers.

When she saw we were headed for electronics, she started getting antsy. When I stopped in front of the Apple display, she growled, shook her head, and started pulling on my arm. "I told you I was kidding! You're not buying me an iPad. I was really joking!"

"I know you were, but then I saw what your father did."

She hissed and stepped back away from me. "No."

"Yes," I said sternly and started looking around for one of the sales associates. Two of them were hovering around another female employee with pink pigtails stocking the DVD rack. "Can I get some help over here?"

"Coming," the older of the two headed in our direction. "What can I get for you?"

I pointed at the largest tablet on the display. "One of those, please."

"Sure thing."

"That's an iPad Pro!" Yuki stared in awe, clearly having a vocal debate in her head about shutting her mouth or continuing to protest.

"Yep."

"Seriously, Master. You can't!"

The associate unlocked the sliding glass door on the display and pulled out the matte white box. "You want it?"

"Yes," I answered.

"No," Yuki protested.

"I'm paying." I ignored her, and after my proclamation, so did he.

He stepped behind the kiosk and rang it up, and I held out my card before Yuki could utter another word.

I had seen something else in the brief moment I'd been in her memories. Something I didn't know about Yuki. She *loved* to draw. Her dream had been to become a graphic artist. The fight between her and her father had boiled down to one thing. She wanted to go to night school. He had adamantly refused. And then made her life a living hell when she rebelled.

The associate stuffed the purchase into a bag and handed me the receipt. "Come on. Let's go pay for the rest of the stuff and go torture my mother." I handed her the bag and leaned in close to her, whispering in her ear,

"Draw me something pretty." I kissed her cheek and ruffled her hair, and then dropped the whole topic.

"Thank you, Master." She was shuffling her feet and I barely heard the words that escaped her lips.

"Don't thank me. I'm going to put you to work."

Clearly confused, she asked, "How?"

"Well, first I'm going to find you a local art school. I'm going to get you enrolled. And then, you're going to pay off your tuition by creating all the graphics and advertisements for the bookstore. Then, you're going to start writing and drawing the graphic novels that you've always loved, and then I'm going to start selling them once we figure out how to get them published."

She almost dropped the iPad. "Are you serious?"

"I'd never joke about your dreams."

"You saw?"

"Saw and felt." I sighed and put my hand on her shoulder.

She sniffled and nodded, but still had enough in her to give me a little smile of gratitude. That alone was worth what I had paid for the stinking tablet. If I hadn't already turned her father to ash, I would have animated his corpse, hung it in my garage, and taken up boxing.

∞ ∞ ∞

My grandmother finally answered the door after the twelfth round of knocking. "Dorothea?"

"Hey, Nana. Where's the witch."

"Which one?"

"The wicked one of the West."

"Entertaining some guests…in her room."

"Ewww." I stopped and stared at her in horror, hoping to the Lady that she was joking.

Yuki made a gagging noise behind me.

"Would you care for a cup of tea? Glass of wine?"

"Wine."

"Dear?" She peeked around me to look at Yuki.

54

"I'll have a glass of wine, please. Ma'am."

"Oh, shush. Call me Nana."

Yuki blushed and hid behind me. Nana scared her. And me. And the neighborhood, county, and tri-state area, so she wasn't alone.

"How long is she going to be entertaining?"

"For as long as they can keep her occupied, I would imagine." She led us through the modest house and into the kitchen. "Sit," she said and pointed to the kitchenette table in the alcove. "I'm assuming this is about the coven."

"You knew?"

She nodded and waved her fingers at one of the bottles of wine on the counter. Wiggling its way out of the top of the bottle, the cork ripped through the tinfoil and plopped merrily on the counter while Nana pulled three glasses from the cupboard. "The question is, how did you find out?"

"Stopped by Tir Na Nog for a drink."

She blinked in surprise. "That's a long way to go for a drink."

"Needed to get away for a bit. I ran into Nestor and some of the other coven. They're a hot fucking mess, Nana."

"Nobody stepped up?" She set a glass in front of each us and sat across from us.

Yuki was watching us like we were a tennis match.

"No."

She shrugged. "Someone will. The goddess will see to it."

"You're good with this? That was *your* coven, too."

She smiled and gave another noncommittal shrug. "And everyone I cared about has either moved on or moved here. Like it or not, Granddaughter, this is our home now. That includes your mother."

"She's really staying?"

"Called here by the goddess herself. She didn't have a choice."

"And did the goddess make you open your home for the woman you despise most in this world?"

Her smile turned into a frown. "Tone, Child. Your mother and I might not get along, but she is still my daughter."

"And she's still my mother. I love her, but I'd rather hug a moving Peterbuilt on the highway than let her move in with me."

Nana cackled. "It was easier to have her here with me."

I narrowed my eyes at her. "To do what?"

She sighed and stood, beckoning for us to follow her. Yuki shot me a nervous glance and followed Nana into the living room. I downed my wine and set my empty glass on the table before joining them.

Nana was standing in front of the far wall and waiting for me, watching me enter the room before facing the wall. "*Oscailte,*" she canted softly, and the wall shimmered and melted, splitting apart and revealing a workroom within.

Nana and Mother were more into potions than I was. The huge cauldron in the center of the room was proof enough of that. I didn't own a single one. Not even a quart sized one. "Double, double, toil and trouble," I said with a giggle and stepped inside. And whistled...

The workbench was natural wood that looked like it had grown from the earth itself, twisting and winding up to form a flat surface along the wall. The floor of the workshop was hard packed earth. Faerie lights illuminated everything from overhead as the ceiling spiraled up into nothingness. One thing was for certain... We weren't in Kansas anymore. "How come I don't have one of these?"

"I believe you skipped out on your magic lesson to snog your boyfriend from Ireland on the day we covered enchanted workspaces."

"He wasn't from Ireland; he was from Virginia. He *moved* to Ireland."

"He should have stayed a virgin. You would have learned a lot more." She chuckled at her own joke. I blushed six shades of crimson.

"So, what have you been working on?"

"That." She pointed a finger at the furthest wall. Nailed to the wall were sheets of parchment all overlapped until it looked a solid sheet, diagrammed with Tartarus and the adjacent planes. Seeing it on paper gave me a bit more understanding of what Dar had been trying to explain.

"Oh. I already know all that. Cania was inhabited by Mephistopheles who got offed by the angels so they're the only ones who can enter Tartarus, essentially making it an escape proof prison."

"Very good. If you're thinking in positive and negative planes of existence. That doesn't take into account the lateral planes."

"Lateral planes?"

"Did you pay attention to *nothing* I said in your studies?"

"Musta been sick that day."

"Snogging. You were such a horn dog once you found out the miraculous uses of the penis."

Yuki snickered behind us.

"You were saying?"

"About the penises or the planes?" Nana cocked an eyebrow.

"Planes."

"Well, travel to the planes is like taking a subway from one to another." She moved to the beautifully drawn circular diagram and touched the disk representing the mortal realm. It flared for an instant, gold light looking like embers as the brown ink blossomed to life and the disk pulled away from the others and started spinning.

"That's fucking cool," Yuki said in awe.

"So, what are lateral planes?"

"Just as there is the mortal realm, there are others on the same plane."

"The multiverse?" I had seen the Marvel movies.

Nana shook her head in disappointment. "That, I'm sorry to say, is bullshit. But there are three for each. Think of all of these as the *primary* planes of existence. They are

57

neutral." She waved her hand and the disk split into three, all overlapping each other. "Then there are the positive primary planes and the negative primary planes. They make up the lateral."

"That's the two kinds? So, Mephistopheles might be alive in one of them?"

She shook her head. "No. If you die in one, you die in all. They're that interconnected."

"So, how does that help us then?"

"It doesn't. I said there were two different kinds. I was explaining the first in hopes that you might actually retain some knowledge for a change."

"Yes. Two. Positive and negative."

"No, those are one kind. Laterals of the first."

"What's the second?"

"What do you think connects everything?" She motioned at the whole board.

"Subways?"

Her face fell in utter annoyance.

"Love?"

She smacked me in the back of the head.

"Just tell me!"

She motioned toward the board with both arms outstretched. A globe encircled *all* of the planes, glittering like stars.

"Space?"

"In a way, you are correct, Child."

I made a pumping motion with my arm. "Score."

"But if you think it's the space that a rocket can get you to, you are sorely mistaken."

"Drugs?"

"Nope."

"She is referring to Ethereum." My mother answered solemnly from the doorway behind us.

"So good of you to join us, Moth–"

Her hair was disheveled, her silk robe askew, and her usually pristine lipstick smeared across half her face. Seven guys were milling in the living room by the front door in various stages of undress, all of them putting on their shoes with dazed looks on their faces.

"Seven?" I hadn't meant to say the word aloud, but I hiss-whispered in disbelief. I was surprised she could walk from the bedroom to the workroom. But then again, the seven guys might have carried her. "They all on the same team?"

"Yes, actually. Thank the lady for softball!"

"Aren't there nine people on a team?" I vaguely recalled nine being the number, but I wasn't sure.

"Two of them were married and didn't feel like playing..." Mother wiggled her eyebrows.

Nana cackled and Yuki reverted to gagging noises. I was just in shock. Shaking my head, I turned back to Nana. "So, what's Ethereum? Like the digital currency?"

"No, Granddaughter. Ethereum is the space, energy, force, whatever, that connects all the planes. Theoretically, you could travel from the mortal realm to any of the other planes by cutting across Ethereum."

Something wasn't adding up. "If that is true, and travel to the planes is limited to the adjacent planes, how do the angels get to our realm, how did Dar get to our realm, and how did a portal to hell open up in the middle of town?"

"Magic."

"Ex-squeeze me?"

"She means conduits, dear." Mother strode into the room adjusting her robe.

"Conduits? Like subways?"

"Kind of. But, more like inside you."

She pulled out a stool from under the work bench and sat. "You think the blood inside you is human?"

"No? I'm a witch."

"And what do you think makes a witch a witch?" She crossed her arms and stared at me.

"Magic?"

"Precisely. And how do you think we got the power to use said magic?"

"Stole it? Bought it at Walmart? Gift from the gods?"

"Some is stolen, some was a gift from the gods, but some of it came from our ancestors. Humans that bred with demons, elves, dragons, you name it. Most non-magical humans have *some* fey or demon blood running through their veins, but it is so diluted they can't touch, see, or harness that power. Some of us have more than others and it keeps us young and it gives us magic. A few have too much, and you get the fey blooded, who are hunted for the liquid gold that flows through their veins."

"Do I want to know our family tree?"

"Your mother did the horizontal mambo with a god, and you're going to act shocked now?" Nana laughed.

"What about you, Nana? You never mentioned Mother's father. Was he human?"

Nana got a dreamy look on her face. "That was a time long ago. I have forgotten who sired her."

Nana was a fucking liar. That was a story I wanted to hear, and I would get it out of her sooner or later. The Blackwells were *powerful*. It had to have come from somewhere. It made me wonder about Nana's parents… She had never mentioned them either.

"So, what do family trees have to do with conduits and planes?"

"If you have the right blood in your veins, you can travel to those planes."

"So, when I summoned Dar, that means we have demon ancestors?"

"You can look at your mother and seriously ask that question?"

I looked at my mother. "Never mind. I believe you."

"Just as your Grandmother can open a portal to the Jurassic plane, dear."

"Again, with the dinosaur jokes, Madeline?"

"If the foo shits, *Mother*."

I sighed and rubbed the bridge of my nose. "So, how does all of this help us to get to Tartarus?" I wanted the Cliff's Notes version.

"By sailing the seas of Ethereum, straight into the bowels of Hell."

"Do we have a boat?"

"It's not the vessel you should be worried about, it's the *captain*." Nana sighed.

"Color me confused?"

"The only people who can safely traverse Ethereum are the gods."

"Okay? So, that rules this little current plan of attack out, right?"

"Did you forget that you are a god, Child?" Nana narrowed her eyes.

"No. But I've been trying to. So? What? I can go to Tartarus?"

"Not without a guide. You would be lost in Ethereum for eternity."

"So, who did you have in mind?"

Nana looked at Mother. Mother stared back. "Belenus."

"Who?" I asked out of shock, I knew who Belenus was. The god who hated my father and done everything she could to destroy him. The god I had fought in Underhill. The god of Light and the overworld. His ex-wife.

Chapter 6

"You want to take my car?"

Chief was holding open the passenger door of his police Jeep like it was a limo. I'd ridden in it several times, and between all of the communications equipment, laptops, shotgun, and other law enforcement themed paraphernalia, I had never gotten out of said vehicle without bruised knees or shins. Sure, I was a witch and healed shortly thereafter, but a bruise was a bruise. "Nah. We get better parking in the cop car."

"Okay," I acquiesced. "But you're rubbing my poor knees and shins later."

"Oh? You're already planning on being on them for extended periods of time?" He grinned as I got in.

"Well, I was. But if you're not going to show an iota of consideration…"

"How about I kiss your poor shins and your abused knees. Give you a gentle backrub, and then hold you tight for the rest of the night? Would that be considerate?"

"It's a start." I returned his grin and let him shut the door. "Where are you taking me to eat?" I asked once he got inside the car and started the engine. "And you better not say the diner."

"Nope. Some place new."

"New? There isn't any place new in Cedar Falls."

"Didn't say we were staying in town, now did I?"

He backed out of the driveway and headed for the highway. "We going to Amersville? My second trip today. I should write that down in my record book."

"You were there earlier?"

"Yeah. Yuki and I made a run to Wally World."

"I'm sorry."

"Meh. It wasn't that busy, really."

"It's a Christmas miracle."

"Christmas is over. Now we can concentrate on the three months of shit weather."

"New Year's will be fun. Our first."

"Yuki wants to have a party."

"Are you?"

"I might. Can't promise I'll stay up 'til midnight, though. That shit is for youngins."

"Oh, please. When was the last time you went to bed before midnight?"

I shrugged. My sleep schedule had been all sorts of fucked up as of late. There had been times when I stayed up for two days straight and got off with a light nap. Then there were days I didn't want to get out of bed. Especially when I wasn't alone.

Traffic going into Amersville was twice as bad as the traffic leaving. We drove past the Walmart and the mall and headed to the south side. I'd driven through it once or twice, but never noticed it was a little posher than the north side. More chain restaurants became prevalent and I figured we'd end up at the TGI Fridays, but Chief pulled into someplace called Brewskies.

"A sports bar?"

"Kind of. It's like a mixture of sports bar, raw bar, steakhouse, and brewery."

"Okay then." I chuckled, opening my door and sliding out of the Cherokee, careful not to let my dress ride up too high. Didn't need to be flashing the parking lot the skimpy black panties that matched my dress and had been Chief's request.

"Honestly, next to the seafood place, they have the best food in town. Their wings are to die for."

"Was just picturing something a little more romantic."

"Yeah. That isn't what this is about." He chuckled and opened the door for me, ushering me inside. "Hi. Reservation for Bill?"

"Not about romance? I think you're missing the point of a *date,* Chief." Something was afoot and I couldn't put my finger on it.

"Right this way," the hostess smiled at him, grabbed two menus, and led us to our booth. In the back. In a *very* unbusy area. In fact, the only other people close to our seats were Jimmy and Dennis in the booth adjacent to ours. I'd been set up.

"Really?" I blinked at him in disbelief.

"What? Oh, hey guys. I didn't know you'd be here…"

"Fucker. I'm surprised you told me to wear panties." I wasn't mad. Not in the least. I mean, how could I have been? It was Jimmy and Dennis. "I thought you guys were fishing?"

"We were. Until we got the call from Bill and told us where we should have dinner." Dennis looked confused; Jimmy looked hungry. And not for chicken wings.

"Um, excuse me Miss Blackwell. This is *our* date. You're supposed to ignore the hired help." Chief chuckled and slid into the booth, motioning for me to sit beside him, facing the boys.

"Oh. My apologies, oh great one." I bowed and scooted in next to him.

Chief put his hand on my thigh while he perused the menu with the other hand, slowly sliding his calloused palm over my sensitive skin.

Jimmy and Dennis were looking over their menu, giving me little glances and smiles.

"Hi! I'm Devin. I'll be taking care of you folks tonight. Can I start you out with some beverages?"

"Bud draft?" Chief answered first.

"Sure thing. And for you, ma'am?"

I almost ordered a glass of wine. But I had a feeling I was going to need something stronger. "Whiskey sour." It wasn't like I got to enjoy my last one, anyway.

65

"Since when?"

"My youth. Long story."

"Learned something new about you."

"Learned something new about you, too," I answered.

"What's that?"

"You bought another new aftershave."

He chuckled and went back to the menu. "Do you like it?"

"Best one yet."

"Tell you what. Next one, you pick out."

"Deal." I grinned.

He kept sliding his hand up and down my leg, stopping short of going under my loose dress. It wasn't just his aftershave that I smelled... It was his fear. Since the moment Dennis and Jimmy came into view, the whole situation felt *awkward.* Forced. I had an inkling why.

I leaned against him. "You don't have to do this you know."

"What?"

Turning my head, I kissed his cheek. "First, tell me why you set this all up." I already knew the answer, but I don't think he realized the truth of it.

"Because the last time–" He shut up when the waiter brought our drinks. Another server, in a skirt shorter than my dress, walked up to Jimmy and Dennis's table. I growled instinctively.

"Here's your drinks, folks. Need a few minutes?"

"Please," Chief answered for us while I watched the blonde bimbo engage in a little bit of flirt and serve.

Devin glanced at me nervously and left us alone.

"Did you just growl?" Chief's question had been the slightest of whispers.

"Maybe."

He chuckled. "So, as I was saying, I planned all this because that night...was the hottest thing I'd ever seen."

"So, you though to recreate it with the shoe on the other foot?"

He chuckled nervously. "Yeah."

"Not going to work, Chief," I answered adamantly.

"You don't want to?" I could hear his heart cracking.

"It doesn't matter if I want to or not. You don't want to."

"Huh?"

I sighed and took a long pull off my whiskey sour. It was heavy on the whiskey and light on the pucker. I coughed instead of squinting. Turning in the booth, I faced Chief. "Jimmy is Jimmy. You are you."

"What does that mean? You don't think I'm as fun as Jimmy?"

I put my hand on *his* leg to show my sincerity. "It's not who is more fun, or who is better looking. Hell, it's not even about who has the bigger dick." I wiggled my eyebrows at him. "I love all of you for *different* reasons. But this doesn't have anything to do with me, and everything with the two of you."

"I'm confused."

"You're a man. It's your nature." I patted his leg. "Jimmy likes to show me off. *You* like to watch. He's an exhibitionist. You're a Voyeur. Watching him have his way with me is what turned you on so fucking much. Why would you ever think the reverse would work out?"

He opened and closed his mouth several times while he thought about it. Then he gave me an apologetic look. "You're right."

"You did all this to show me a good time, didn't you?"

He nodded.

That earned him a kiss on the nose. "We could have eaten KFC on the couch, and I would have had a good time with *you*. You're kind of a pain in my ass most of the time, but even when we fight, even when I'm angry, one thing I love is talking to you. That's *our* thing. Conversation and extremely hot sex." I shot him what I *hoped* was a genuine smile.

When he did his little head tilt and smile thing, I knew he finally understood. "Sorry."

67

"For what? Trying to make me happy? Thanks for understanding that you don't have be somebody you're not to do it."

"Promise?"

"Promise."

"You're not going to get bored with me?"

I laughed, leaned closer, and kissed him like I meant it. "Can't. You piss me off too much for me to get bored."

"Gee. Thanks." He rolled his eyes and drank some of his beer.

"And you make me smile too much to get bored. Make me happy. Make me feel loved. And squishy. I love you, Bill."

"Uh oh. I'm in trouble." He threw his arm around me and I shifted in the seat, leaning into the crook of his arm.

"Because I called you Bill?"

"No. Because you're perfect." He kissed the side of my face.

"Awww. Suck up." I chuckled at him.

"No. That part comes later." He whispered in my ear and a shiver ran down my back. "So, what do we do with *those* two?" He nodded at the other table.

I turned and looked. They were very focused on their beers, trying their damnedest to not drop eaves. "Well? You kids wanna sit at the big people table?"

They let out the breath they'd been holding, smiled, and grabbed their drinks.

Jimmy let out the breath he'd been holding and looked at Chief. "Oh, thank the Lady. I mean Lambresco's was one thing, but this place is *packed*. No way I would have started anything in here. You and I are going to have a *long* talk tomorrow about when and where."

I laughed at Jimmy's relief.

"Nah. Stuff like that is better left to the perverted delinquents," Chief answered with a chuckle.

"Damn straight."

∞ ∞ ∞

"You sure you want to spend the night?" Chief had his hand on the key, ready to unlock the front door of his house.

"I'd love to. But only if you want me to. The memories in this house are yours, not mine. We can sleep at my house if you'd rather. I don't want to intrude."

He let go of the keys and wrapped me in his arms. "You're not intruding. Ever. I want you always. Not just in certain places."

"Then let's go in. It's fucking *cold*."

"Should have worn more clothes... Jeez. What were you thinking?" He laughed and unlocked the door. Not fast enough. I swatted his ass.

He laughed again and pushed the door open, letting me go inside.

"Beer?"

"Please."

He flipped on the lights and headed for the kitchen. I smiled at the cuteness of the place. I understood why he hadn't changed anything, Rebecca was *everywhere*. For the first time, seeing her didn't hurt so much.

The house wasn't much warmer than outside.

"You cold?"

"Yeah. It's freezing in here."

Chief shrugged and handed me my beer before turning and fiddling with the thermostat. The heat came on, blowing warm air from the duct above me. "Movie?"

"Sure." I smiled at him as he took my beer back, set both of them on the small table by the door, and got me out of my jacket. Mostly. Just before I was completely free, he grabbed it and pulled me close to him, his lips meeting mine.

"What was that for?"

"No reason except I couldn't resist."

The lights around us flickered, and the lamp on the table buzzed and the bulb blew. I couldn't help it. I yelped.

"Huh. That was weird." He reached over to the switch by the door and turned the rest of the lights on in the living room. They blinked to life and held steady.

"When was the last time you changed that bulb?"

"Couple of months ago. I knew I should have gotten the LED ones. They last forever. Sit." He pushed me gently toward the couch and grabbed our beers, handing me mine as he plopped down on the couch beside me and grabbed the remote.

The DVD player and TV both flickered to life and when he hit play, the movie started. "You planned this all out, didn't you?"

He grinned.

"Better not be porn."

He hit the stop button. "Do you think I would do that to you?"

"Before dinner, I would have said no. Now, I'm not so sure…"

He hit play again, and the Disney theme played loudly, filling the room. "Loser." He grinned and took a sip of his beer.

"If it's Frozen, I'm leaving. And telling all your friends."

Lucky for him, it was Maleficent.

"Oooh. I haven't seen this yet. I told Mother she should audition but she was holding out for the old hag role if they remake Snow White."

He chuckled. "Oh, shut up. You know your mom is hot."

"Should I change my name to Stacy?"

"I said she was hot, not that she had it going on."

"Should I be worried?"

"Uh. I'm the one that should be worried. I keep waiting to wake up on a platter with an apple in my mouth as she cackles maniacally and sets the oven temperature to three-fifty."

"Four-twenty-five. Otherwise the outside is crispy, but the middle is too rare."

"You're scaring me." He smiled, leaned over, and kissed me.

The rest of the lights blew.

"Okay, what the fuck is going on?" He stood up, walked over to the window, and threw open the lace drapes to look up and down the road. "I don't see any power trucks."

"Check the rest of the house?"

He walked across the room and leaned into the kitchen, flicking the lights on. "This one works. Check the others?"

I got up and moved to the hallway. "This one works!" I looked toward the kitchen, but he had headed toward the garage. Turning back, I moved to the end of the hall to the bedroom. Leaning in, I flipped the switch and screamed.

She stood there, billowing and angry as she frowned from the corner of the bedroom beside a dressmaking form next to the window. If I hadn't seen a hundred pictures of her in the living room, I probably would have been confused and angry instead of shitting kittens. It wasn't every day that you ran into your boyfriend ex. It wasn't every day you ran into her ghost, either. At least she was whole and normal looking. I don't think I could have handled burnt briquette Becca.

Chief's footfalls echoed down the hallway as he skidded to a stop behind me and gasped. "Rebecca?"

"Maybe we should go to my place…"

Chapter 7

One thing was for certain, after the night I'd had, I needed some fucking pie. And some coffee. I was fucking freezing and it had *nothing* to do with the weather. Chief had the heat pouring into the Jeep full blast. I don't think he was all warm and squishy on the inside, either. In fact, he hadn't said a word since we ran for the Jeep.

"Want some coffee and pie? We can talk."

He turned his head and let his eyes shift from the road to my face. Forcing a little smile, he gave me a slight nod.

"You okay?"

"We'll see after the pie and coffee."

He pulled into the parking lot between the station and the diner and we walked across the street. "Chief of police, jay walkin' like some sort of criminal." I chuckled and grabbed his hand.

"No jokes. Not right now, please."

Pursing my lips, I gave him a sad smile and nodded.

The woosh of warm air and the smells of the warmer food pushed some of the icky 'I just saw the ghost of my lover's dead wife' feelings out of the way. Tabby, Marge's niece who worked the night shift, waved from behind the counter and made coffee motions. Chief and I both nodded emphatically. Tabby narrowed her eyes and nodded.

Chief sat on the other side of the booth instead of taking the spot next to me. Not being a petty woman, I let it slide without comment. This was hard on me. It had to be like teaching Josie Calculus for him.

"All these years…" He shook his head and set it in his hands, resting his elbows on the table.

"She was right beside you and you didn't know?"

He pulled his face from his hands and shot me a rather unpleasant look. "No. All these years I thought she had moved to the next life or was roaming the celestial planes. Anything but being stuck in this world as a ghost." He nearly sobbed as he worked his way through the sentence.

"We don't know that she was. For all I know, it could just be my powers manifesting her spiritual imprint on the house. I don't know how all this ghost shit works." I reached over and took his hand. "One thing is, I do know I'm sorry if my being there gave her form."

"Can we lay her to rest?"

Yeah. If I punch her in the gut, turn her into a zombie, and let her melt into the ground. "I don't know, but I'll try."

Tabby stepped up to the table and set two mugs and two pieces of rhubarb pie in front of us. She had broken out the good shit for the occasion. I gave her a grateful look. "You looked like you all just saw a ghost. Figured you needed it. There's a bitta Marge Magic in that coffee, too. So, drink it slow."

We were both staring at her in shock.

"Marge Magic. That means whiskey." She blushed.

"We know. How'd you know we'd seen a ghost?" Chief gulped.

"It's an expression? Wait! You actually *saw* a ghost?" She plopped down into the booth next to him, turning her head back and forth waiting for someone to spill the story.

Chief pleaded to me with his eyes.

"Tab? Give us a minute. I'll tell you all about it later. I promise."

She opened her mouth to protest, saw the look on Chief's face, and understanding outweighed curiosity. "Oh. Yep. No worries. Holler if you need more pie."

"Trust me when I say we will." I nodded to drive the point home.

She smiled, rubbed Chief's shoulder, and headed back toward the counter. I forked a bit of my pie into my mouth, let the flavor seep into my buds, and washed it down with a little bit of whiskey splashed with coffee for flavor. It was no small wonder why Tabby was a waitress and not a bartender.

Chief took a bit of pie, too. Then, the worried expression etched itself back on his face. "We've got to do something."

"Well, I've gone to Nana and Mother for the ghost issue before. They weren't much help. If you want to go back, I can try."

"No. Not tonight. I don't think I can deal with it right this moment. Mind if I stay at your place?"

"If you don't mind the crowd, you can stay as long as you want or need." I smiled at the thought.

"Well, if I get to be a bother, let me know. I can bunk with the Jimmy."

"The Jimmy?"

Chief smiled for the first time since we'd run out of his house in a panic. "Slip of the tongue, but fitting."

"He is definitely the Jimmy. Just like you're the Chief." I forked the bit of pie into my mouth and grinned at him. Until I felt the storm behind me. No rain, no clouds, no thunder, just a heap of 'oh shit' brewing outside. Dropping the fork, I turned in the booth to see the storm front move inside the door of the diner. Three vamps were standing inside the door looking for someone while the remainder of the kiss waited outside. A moment later, their eyes met mine and relief and fear washed over them like a wet blanket. Apparently, I was the someone they were looking for.

"Lady Blackwell." The three of them paused to place their hands over their hearts and bow. "You are needed."

My first thought was of Yuki. In a panic, I stood. Chief did, too, and was rewarded with a brief but firm hiss from the three of them. "It's okay. Let me see what's going on." I put my hand over his arm, hopefully in a calming manner. *Yuki?* I didn't shout, I just wanted to make sure she was okay, even though I would have been the first one to know if she wasn't.

I can feel it. I'm on my way. Master? Don't do anything until I get there.

Nodding at the three vampires, I motioned toward the door.

"Everything okay, Dot?" Tabby called from across the diner.

Sighing, I nodded. It wasn't busy, but I had hoped to escape without being noticed by any of the other customers at all. Never knew which one was working for the paper and which ones weren't. "Yep. Just some friends of mine."

"Our apologies, Lady Blackwell," one of the vamps mumbled as he held the door open for me.

"Not your fault. I'll give you my cell phone number for emergencies," I answered as he shut the door behind me. "So? What's up?" I wanted to get to the root of the situation as quickly as possible while I was still in Chief's line of sight. He might have let me go, but that didn't mean he was happy about it.

"Sorry to bother you." The most powerful feeling one in my head bowed again. "We need your judgement."

"Oh. Well, I don't know if I can give you any advice that would be helpful…" I stopped talking when the ones closest started snickering. "What?"

"We are not seeking…advice. One of ours has committed a digression. We leave him to you to be judged."

"Oh. Oh! Wait a minute. I'm hardly–"

"The lord of our clan?"

Yuki. Hurry.

Almost… "Here," she finished as she suddenly appeared before a blast of wind nearly bowled me over.

"Princess Yukina," they said reverently and bowed to her. I smiled. It kind of made me feel like her mother. Or big sister. I found the latter thought more comforting.

She stared at them for a moment, tilted her head, and frowned. I don't know what she was sensing that I wasn't, but she didn't like it. "What?"

"Can't you feel it?"

My vamp powers weren't…engaged. I couldn't feel, sense, or smell shit. But as I was staring at them, it made more than a few of them more than uncomfortable. It was just enough for that tiny sliver of fear to make my mouth start watering. Then, I felt it. One of them had killed a human.

"Fuck." The paranormal population of Cedar Falls had enough trouble brewing without the vampires turning the residents into Big Gulps. "Why? You guys don't have to pay for blood anymore. Why the fuck would one of you kill a human?"

The fear wafting from the little group was enough to bring out my fangs and an evil sounding hiss at the end of my rant. They dropped to the ground and writhed, afraid for *their* lives. Yuki put a calming hand on my back.

"Maybe we should question the accused, Master."

"Get up," I told them, trying for a calm soothing voice.

Chief stepped outside. "Everything okay?"

"No. But come with me. This involves you, too."

"You would alert the human authorities?" Alpha vamp sneered, but was looking at Chief, not me.

Yuki tried, but failed, to stop me from grabbing a fistful of his leather jacket and dragging his face to within an inch of mine. "Somebody has to let the human's family know they won't be going home again. Ever. He is also my *mine*. You will show him respect."

"Yes, Lady Blackwell!" He was all piss and vinegar, the fear coming from him was twice as strong as any of the others. The smell might actually have been piss, though. I could only imagine what my face looked like.

"Dot?"

"Come on. We'll take your Jeep. Where are we going?" I asked the group instead of their self-proclaimed leader.

"The mall," one of them answered meekly.

"The mall is closed. That's trespassing," Chief said firmly.

It was going to be a long night.

∞ ∞ ∞

Vampires made it look easy. I, however, usually tripped going down the stairs. There's no way in hell I was going to drop into the center of the food court and trust in my vampiric abilities. They were sketchy at best. Instead, I pulled Nana's broom from the thong around my neck and whispered, "*Ag fás*." It cracked in my hand as I hoisted it over my head, and it exploded into full size.

"Okay. That was pretty fucking cool," Chief said in awe.

Show-off, Yuki muttered in my head as I dropped through the open skylight and floated to the floor.

"Hey, Dot? How am I supposed to get down," Chief called from the roof. Then he screamed.

Yuki landed next to me with Chief in a princess carry. Rolling her eyes, she set him on his feet.

"Thanks." He straightened his clothes, coughed, and tried to act cool.

Hiding my mouth behind my hand, I tried to contain the snicker that was threatening to escape.

He pulled out a flashlight from his pocket and flicked it on, finding himself standing in a semi-circle of hissing vampires, shielding their eyes from the bright beam. "Sorry! Sorry." He flipped it off and stuck it back in his pocket.

"What were you doing in the mall?" I pulled the leader, Damian as I found out he was called, back away from the others as the rest of them headed toward the western section of the only indoor mall in Cedar Falls. I'd been there once, found exactly zero stores that piqued my interest, and left. The mall in Amersville was twice the size and didn't have half the mall empty from failed businesses. If I *really* wanted to go to the mall, I went to Syracuse.

"There's no security or cameras in the entire place. With the open roof access, we can come and go as we please. Just a place for us all to hang out," he answered embarrassedly.

I nodded. "And do you bring humans to the mall often?"

He blushed furiously. "Sometimes."

"Why?" I already knew the answer.

"Snack packs."

A growl tore itself from my lips. Yuki calmed me again with a hand on my back. "Why? It's not like you need the blood anymore!"

The vamps and chief ahead of us, picked up their pace, putting some distance between us.

Damien lowered his head. "I'm sorry, Lady Blackwell. Old habits."

"Habits?" I wanted, *needed*, to punch something. "Humans are not habits. They're people."

"Master," Yuki said calmingly.

Damien held up his hands defensively. "We don't kill them!" He realized what he said and blushed. "Usually. This time… Franco didn't stop and… We couldn't pull him off her."

"No more humans. Got it?"

"Yes, Lady Blackwell." He bowed and I could feel the truth from him.

We started walking again. The other group had stopped by the fountain and was staring. I guessed that it was the scene of the crime.

"Did the humans know what you were?"

"Yes. It's why they agreed to feed. Our bite, as you know, is quite pleasurable. Some of them swear it is better than sex. We have several that we fe–*used* to feed from."

"The bagged blood not good enough?" I snarled in anger.

"We couldn't always *afford* to eat…" He trailed off nervously.

My fears had come to pass. By charging the vampires, they had resorted to feeding off humans. Exactly what I'd been afraid of, happened. Every day, I wanted to kill Abernathy more. More than I already had. Reanimating his body sounded better and better. "Well, you can now. Don't let this happen again, Damien."

"Yes, Lady Blackwell."

"Oh, for fuck's sake. Call me Dot."

Yuki coughed behind me.

"Master or Lady. Something other than dropping the B-word every time you address me."

"Yes, Master." He blushed and dodged ahead to the group surrounding the fountain.

"Do not become friends with them or show them any familiarity," Yuki whispered next to me.

"Why?"

"They become harder to control."

I nodded, not really agreeing with her, but letting it go. Now was not the time to get into a debate. I wanted to lead the vampires like I wanted to have a barium enema and a CT scan.

As we approached, the group split, and I gasped in horror. The bloody vampire sitting beside the fountain between two burly bouncer-looking vamps stared up at me defiantly, not caring an iota about the girl floating face down in the fountain with half her neck chewed off. I wanted to bash the smirk off his face with the broom still in my hand.

"Franco?"

He ignored me, earning a cuff in the back of his head from one of his guards.

"Yes."

I stepped around the throng of spectators and stopped when I was standing in front of him. Sniffing the air, there wasn't a hint of fear coming from him, which was unusual for someone as fucked as he was. He didn't care. Shaking my head, I left him there and moved back to the others, staring at the floating body in the bloody water, her blonde hair stained red.

I reached for her, just to flip her over, but the power within me had better ideas. Black flames burst from my hand and enveloped her, unimpeded by the water. She convulsed a moment and then stood in the shallow water, staring at me blankly. I'd unintentionally animated her, and almost gagged when the blood from her gaping neck wound started pumping again, landing in the water with a little splash.

"You poor thing. I am sorry," I said to her forlornly.

Her head wobbled a little as she bowed it in greeting, unable to speak. He hadn't refused to stop feeding, he had tried to chew through her neck. He'd *wanted* to kill her. If the damage had been localized to one spot, I might have thought the other vamps did it pulling him off her. The only question left was why he wanted to kill her.

Leaving her standing there, I walked back to Franco. After seeing his murder victim brough back from death, in a matter of sorts, the fear coming from him was almost tangible. I could see it floating from him in black threads of dread. "How did you do that?"

I squatted down in front of him, balancing myself with the handle of the broom beside me. "That isn't the question you should be worried about right now, Franco. The question is...*why*," I paused to point at the Nearly Headless Nancy, "you did *that.*"

"I don't know. I couldn't stop."

He was lying. I could feel it in his very bones. He knew damn well why he'd done it, but somebody or something scared him more than I did. If I wanted answers, I needed to change that.

Holding out my hand, I purposely called the black fire to my fingers, holding it in front of him. With my other hand, I lifted the broom, shook it, and tapped the butt of the scythe on the tile before him, shattering the twelve-by-twelve piece of ceramic with a crunch and a puff of dust. "I am going to ask you one more time, Franco. Why did you kill that poor girl?"

His eyes widened and the strands of fear floating from him coalesced into a cascade of mindless panic. "Wha– what are you?"

"Lady Death," one of the other vampires answered and knelt beside me. The others followed suit.

Franco started scrambling away from me, but the mountainous vampires held him still between them as I edged closer.

"Tell me, Franco. Why."

"Because Lord Abernathy told me to!"

"Wrong answer, Franco. He's dead."

"Not that one! His brother!"

There was a collective gasp. Not just from the vampires, but from Yuki and me, too. Turning, I looked at Yuki. She knew I was worried about her cousin George. This was his father we were talking about.

Franco screamed in frustration and started frothing in panic-induced fear. Not only was he facing death, he had just outed the traitor. His life was forfeit even if I let him go. I wasn't going to, not after what he had done, but either way, he was fucked.

Chief moved beside me and squatted down, giving me a sad look. "I'm the chief of police, Dot."

"I know."

"While I want to say I can't let you kill him, my jail probably wouldn't hold him, and we'd be screwed if anybody found out what he was."

"I think that was Abernathy's goal. To out the vampires in Cedar Falls."

"Why?"

"If they get outed, the world's eyes fall on our little town. I'll probably be outed as their leader next. I fall, he gets everything back nice and neat."

"That's pretty slick. Harder on his kind going forward, but not a half-bad plan."

"Glad you approve of his dastardliness."

He shrugged and nodded to the girl. "We can't let anybody find her, either."

"I'm surprised you're being so pragmatic about this."

He nodded and rubbed his chin and jaw with his hand. "The way I look at it, this is kind of like coven business. I would never have sent either one of the Connors to prison for murdering witches. I'll leave this in your more than capable hands." He put his hand on my shoulder, squeezing it gently. My boy scout was growing up. I was so proud.

Turning to the vampire shaking in his proverbial boots, I frowned. "Franco." I paused to sigh. "You are hereby condemned to death for your crimes and a lesson to the other vampires of this clan. No human shall be hurt ever again by one of ours. Does everyone understand?"

The vampires nodded while Franco screamed.

Standing, I eyed the scythe in my hand. "So shall it be." I lifted the butt of the handle off the floor and brought it back down, a little softer than before. A resounding *clang* resonated through the mall, but the tile didn't shatter.

I wasn't dumb enough to try to kill a vampire with a giant scythe while two innocents were holding him between them. Plus, the punishment wouldn't have fit the crime. Instead, I walked over to the zombie in the fountain. "Have your revenge, child. Feast upon the flesh of your killer. Tear him apart."

There was a flare of black fire in her eyes that made me shudder and step back as she scrambled out of the water and strode slowly toward the pleading, shaking vampire. Once she was upon him, the two guards let him go. All of us watched thoughtfully as she did as she was told, ripping off limbs, tearing through the soft flesh of his belly and neck, and finally tearing his still screaming head from the stump of his torso. As soon as it was free, he turned to ash.

She stood and flashed the barest of smiles at me, and the light faded from her eyes. Whatever spark of intelligence that was her, was gone. She was just an animated corpse once again.

"Rest," I whispered and doused her in black flame.

The tile floor beneath her rippled and popped as the concrete parted. The dirt below rose to swallow her into the earth. When she was gone, everything melded back into place without so much as a broken tile to show for it.

"That was fucking sick," one of the younger vamps whispered.

"He tore out her throat, she tore him a new one," I answered by way of explanation.

"No, Lady Blackwell. I don't mean sick as in disgusting. I meant that was the coolest thing I've ever seen."

"Pray that you never see it again," Damien whispered solemnly.

Chapter 8

It was another sleepless night. Finally, around five in the morning, I lightly dozed off. By six, I was awake again, Chief sleeping on his back beside me, snoring loudly. I reached behind me to smack him in the side, missed, and his impressive cock sprang back and forth like one of those doorstop thingies that go *waga-waga-waga* when you whack them.

Rolling over, I stared in rapt fascination as it stopped and throbbed. "Jeezus."

Chuckling softly to myself, I reached over and encircled it with my fist, letting my fingers slide up and down its silky smoothness.

Chief's snoring stopped as he opened his eyes and blinked before looking down at my hand slowly jerking him awake. His smile was heart, and other place, warming. "Morning."

"Wood." I grinned.

"You seem to like the model. Would you care to take it for a test drive, Miss?"

"Do you have the keys?"

"I do believe the engine is running."

"I don't know. Looks like it might be a little too big for me to handle."

"I'm sure a pretty little thing like you can get the most out of it."

"Is it automatic?"

"Manual. Be careful shifting gears, it has a tendency to leak oil."

I started laughing.

"What? I thought I was on fleek with my innuendo."

"Just had a tail pipe joke pop into my head. Don't mind me," I said between fits of laughter.

"Oh, please. Stay away from my exhaust."

"No worries there. The fumes are horrible. That a diesel?"

"Now, I'm going to make a Cummings joke." He smiled and rolled me over on top of him, trapping his throbbing rod between us. Crossing my arms over his chest, I rested my chin on my wrists and smiled at him.

"This is nice."

"Waking up next to someone?"

He knew exactly what I was thinking. I nodded.

"Yeah. Sleeping alone sucks."

"Could do without the snoring, but yes. It is nice."

"Don't be silly, Dot. You don't snore *that* loudly."

I leaned over and bit him on the chest. "Care to take that back," I said with his flesh between my teeth.

He laughed, put his hands under my arms, and pulled me up a little further on his chest. Close enough for him to kiss me. "Sorry about the chainsaws," he said apologetically as he pulled away.

"You weren't *that* loud. Kind of like thunder. Chief Rumblechest."

"You fart."

"Do not."

"And you drool a little."

"Only when you're sleeping naked," I answered.

"And you're awfully hot."

"Says the ceramic heater in my bed." It was no joke. Even in the summertime, I slept under the comforter most nights. I had a nagging suspicion that Chief was powered by a thermonuclear reactor. When he was in the bed, the temperatures sweltered.

"I didn't mean temperature. I mean I can't keep my eyes off of you."

"You seemed to do okay. You were asleep as soon as we got into bed. Nor did you dream."

"Huh. I didn't. No night terrors, either. The only time that happens is when I drink."

"You should drink more."

"I'd rather deal with night terrors."

He was right. Alcoholism was no joke. While it wouldn't kill a witch, our livers were too tough for that, it could wreck the fucking hell out of your life.

"Last night…just sleeping next to you… Thank you. I needed that."

Smiling, I lay my head on his chest.

"Well, aren't you two just the cutest…"

I looked over my shoulder at Jimmy standing in my bedroom doorway. A door I had sworn I'd closed when we went to bed last night.

"Morning, Jimmy. Everything okay?"

"Yeah. I was just checking on you two. Drove by Chief's house on the way to the hardware store and you weren't there."

"Yeah. Our night went to shit last night. We didn't get home here until three."

"Sorry. We good after that shit show of a dinner, though?" He laughed nervously.

Chief spoke up. "Yeah. That was my bad. Sorry about that."

"No worries, Bill. Just didn't want you to think I was mad at you."

"Where's Dennis?"

"He had a shift today."

"Ahh. Coffee?" I asked and got off Chief.

"I'm not interrupting?" He motioned to a very naked Chief, lying on his back and not bothering to cover his nakedness.

"I have more pressing concerns at the moment. Guys have morning wood. Women have to pee," I answered and headed into the bathroom, closing the door behind me.

When I got out of the bathroom, the boys were already in the kitchen, brewing up some magic in the Keurig.

Jimmy handed me a cup as I passed by him and ran my hand over his jean covered butt. Chief had slipped on some boxers and was waiting patiently for his turn. I was woefully underdressed. "Be right back. Gonna put on a shirt."

"Not on our account, I hope." Jimmy grinned and stuffed another pod in the machine.

"No." I lifted myself up on my tippy toes, seeing who, if anyone, was sleeping on the couch. I could hardly wait for the new year when Josie and Candace officially took possession of their new house next door. We were going to have so much more room. I was practically salivating in anticipation. I was going to have a guest room. They were going to have two. Josie had already offered the space for when, and if, I needed it.

"Don't know where Jaeren is, but Ellis is taking a shower before the girls get up," Jimmy answered, knowing who I was looking for.

"Gotcha. Be right back," I said and set my coffee on the counter before dipping into the bedroom and slipping into a T-shirt *one* of the guys had left. Didn't know, didn't care. It was mine now.

"Hey, that's my shirt! I was wondering where I left it." Chief pointed at my chest with his empty mug.

"Was. Was your shirt. Finders keepers."

"Thief."

"It's a shirt. I'll buy you a new one."

"I meant my heart." He smiled and put his mug in the machine when Jimmy pulled my mug out and handed it to me.

"Forget sloppy seconds, you get sloppy thirds." Jimmy chuckled and poured some milk in his coffee.

"Not the first time."

I stared in open-mouthed shock. He hadn't meant, or said, it maliciously, but Chief was acting…different than usual. His banter with Jimmy was proof of that. As was his lack of shyness in the bedroom when I got up. I *liked* it, but I was also a little concerned. Even dinner last night had been *far* out of the realm of his normal character. "What do you mean by that?" I cocked an eyebrow and shifted my weight to one foot, putting the hand not holding a coffee cup on my hip and giving Chief a questioning look.

Chief grinned and blushed while his coffee brewed.

"Tomorrow, you're getting sloppy fifths. If anything at all." I stuck my tongue out at him.

"I was kidding! Just keeping the conversation going."

"Jerk," I said, but with a laugh. I was definitely going to have to keep an eye on Chief. I wanted him to be happy, not pretending to be.

Jimmy sat at the table, and when I went to join him, he patted his leg. Cocking an eyebrow at *him*, I sat down in his lap knowing full well I should trust him about as far as I could chuck him.

"Good girl," he whispered in my ear and kissed my neck. I squirmed in his lap. He knew my most sensitive of sensitive spots. Well, the second most sensitive, but he knew the other one, too. Slipping an arm around me to steady me, he pulled away from my neck and whispered, "I love you."

"Love you, too. Don't trust you to behave, but I love you."

"Who's not behaving?" Chief sat at the end of the table next to us.

"I'll give you one guess."

"So, what happened last night?" Jimmy poked my side.

I looked at Chief, nodding for him to answer. Or not. It was up to him and not my problem to share.

"We went to my house, as planned."

Jimmy tensed under me, knowing something had gone wrong. Unfortunately, he had no clue as to how *badly* things had actually gone wrong. "Too many memories?"

"She wasn't a memory. She was a ghost."

"What?"

"Dot and I were watching a movie. We kissed. The lights blew. When we were trying to figure out what the hell happened, Becca's ghost appeared."

"You're shitting me," Jimmy said without thinking. Leaning to the side to see me for confirmation.

I nodded.

"Was she pissed?"

"She didn't look pissed, but I don't think the lightbulbs were an accident."

"That's not right. Can't you lay her to rest or something?"

Everybody expected too much from me. Granted, I had way more power than I had when I rolled up into town, but I didn't have a *fucking* clue on how to use it. It's not like becoming a godling comes with a goddess damned manual. I shrugged, hiding my frustration. "I don't know. Yet. I'll figure it out, but…"

"It might take some time," Chief answered for me.

"You're taking this quite well," Jimmy said to Chief.

"Not in the slightest. But I know Dot will do everything she can. And she has enough on *her* plate right now."

"Aren't you worried about going home?"

Chief blushed.

"You're not going home."

"No. Dot's letting me stay, and I was thinking about getting a hotel a few nights a week."

"Why?" It was my turn to ask.

"Not going to monopolize your time? Not fair to everybody else."

"Uh, Chief… Your deceased wife is a ghost. We'll be fine," Jimmy answered like Chief had stubbed his brain on a brick.

"Just don't wanna be a nuisance."

I'd had enough. "Spill it."

"Spill what?" He looked at me nervously, taking a sip of his coffee.

"Whatever the fuck is going on with you, Bill." I used his real name. He was in trouble. "The shit last night at dinner. The self-depreciating comments. All of it. What is going on with you?"

90

"Just trying to make you happy."

"You do make me happy. And insane. And angry. That's what I love about you. Now? You're being an acquiescent floob. I don't like *that*."

"Floob?"

"I made it up. But you're being one. Why?"

I leaned forward in Jimmy's lap, waiting for an answer. He pinched my butt to tell me to tread lightly. He should have pinched me sooner. I'd pushed Chief a little too hard. He slammed his mug down on the counter. "Because I don't want to fucking lose you. Okay? Happy?"

"That you're finally talking to me and not being a floob? Yes. Fucking ecstatic. Now tell me the fuck why you think you're going to lose me?"

"Because of Becca."

"Huh?" I blinked and set my coffee down.

"Last night wasn't the first time I've seen her. I've been seeing her all over the fucking place. I thought I was losing my goddess damned mind, Dot."

"You knew she was a ghost?" I stared at him in shock. "Is that why you invited me over last night?" Anger flooded my veins like ice. It had been hard enough to deal with *that*. If he set me up to see her...

"What? No! I didn't think she was real! I thought I was going insane. I thought guilt was turning me into a deranged lunatic. I thought that loving you was causing my brain to short circuit, and you know what? I welcomed that insanity rather than lose *you*."

It was official. I was an asshole. "Oh, Chief." I reached over and put my hand on his leg. "I'm sorry. You must have been going..."

"Crazy?"

"Yeah. That. Just not for real. I meant crazy with going crazy. I'll just shut up now. But you're not losing me, you dork."

"For a moment, last night, when *you* saw her. I was almost relieved. Then I realized the ten-million other problems that revelation meant."

"No offence, but I thought you were taking all of that a little too well."

"And it made me realize something else."

"What?"

He paused to gather his thoughts, drinking his coffee and staring out the sliding glass door behind us. "That I have been a jerk. Not a selfish one, but still a jerk. I used your other relationships like a blanket I could hide under. When things got bad between us, you had someone else to turn to. That made me happy that even when I was less than what you needed, you had someone to take care of you."

"You're an idiot," Jimmy chimed in.

"What?"

"When you and Dot fought, we all felt it. She was moody, irrational. More so than usual." He pinched me again, but this time it was to let me know he was kidding. I hoped. "We didn't line up to console her, you dumb fucking twat. We had to console her. Hold her when she cried. Wipe her tears. It wasn't fun and games and loving. It was getting her through you being an asshole."

Chagrinned, thy name is Chief. I could see the horrified look in his eyes as Jimmy's revelation lit the tiny candle in his head. "I'm sorry." Only, he didn't say it to me. He said it to Jimmy. I've never been prouder of him than I was in that moment.

"Your problem, Bill, is that you see us all as individuals."

"We aren't?"

"We are. In everything that isn't Dot."

"I'm confused."

"We aren't her *boyfriends*. We are her boyfriend. Her love. Her mate, her partner, her family. All of us. We're in this together and all of us need to start acting like it. Especially you. I don't mean to be the bad guy, or the voice of reason, because... Well, because that just isn't fucking me. I'm the fun one. The risk taker. The kinky bastard who likes showing her off. *That* is me. You're the stable one.

92

The rock. The voice of reason in this relationship. Dennis is the sweetness. Jason is the drive. Shea is the shyness, Dar is... Dar is Dar. He's blue and horny and Dot loves him. We all do. So, shit or get off the fucking pot."

"You think I should leave?"

"No. I'm saying get your shit together. Because Dot loves you and Dot needs you, and some of us do, too."

He sat for a moment, silently sipping his coffee and staring off into nothing. *Finally*, he nodded, set his cup down, and stood up. He was going to bolt. I could feel it. We'd gone too far.

Just when I was going to jump up and stop him, he dropped to his knees and wrapped his arms around the both of us, silently sobbing into my lap. I started stroking his hair, running my fingers through its softness and let him get it out. Jimmy put his hand on his shoulder and was silently rubbing circles, letting him know it was okay, and would always be okay. *We* would be okay.

How long we stayed like that, I didn't have a clue. Ellis came out of the shower, saw our moment, and retreated into the darkness of the bathroom. Candace came out to pee and pushed him in their room once she realized what was going on. Yuki had felt the whole thing and sent me a bit of love down our link and Dar must have felt the same. He and Shea stepped from the shadows and knelt beside Chief, joining in the tender moment and offering their support and love.

It was quite the moment, and even though I was smiling, the tears were flowing down my face. The wetness on the back of my shirt told me I wasn't the only one.

Finally, Chief lifted his head and stared at me with red-rimmed eyes and offered me an apologetic smile. I returned it, letting the back of my fingers brush the stubble on his cheek as he choked out one last sob.

"Nothing like a bit of group therapy to get you through the shit storms. Thanks, guys."

Chapter 9

The best part about getting up early is going back to bed. Emotional outbreaks were draining. I felt fine until Chief let everything out, thanked everybody profusely, and used work as an excuse to hightail it the hell out of there. I debated making him stay, but I know if it had happened to me, I'd want some time alone, too. So, with a smile and a kiss, I let him escape with a promise to have lunch with me at the diner. *Then*, I got a couple hours more sleep after Jimmy, Dar, and Shea left.

But I didn't sleep alone. In an unusual moment, Yuki came into my room, lifted my arm, and crawled into the bed in front of me. With a small chuckle, I wrapped my arm around her and gave her the snuggles that I needed.

"Snuggle whore," she whispered, and I felt the life drain from her as she fell asleep, too.

She was better than a teddy bear but wasn't one of those long term snugglers. She was gone by the time I woke up again. In fact, the entire house was empty when I went to go make another cup of coffee. Even Ellis was nowhere to be found.

"Well, okay then," I said crankily and hit the brew button.

The machine sputtered, and I grabbed the mug to go sit at the table and check my messages, but suddenly, there was somebody already sitting in my seat. Somebody I didn't recognize. Somebody I'd known my entire life. He smiled as I took a step closer, my hand shaking badly enough that coffee sloshed on my hand. It burned, but the pain wasn't any worse than the tear running the length of my heart. "Father?"

He smiled and faded but came back with a nod. "I can't stay long."

"How are you here?" I dropped the mug on the floor, splashing coffee across the tile and up the cupboard.

"You're getting stronger." He smiled as if that was the answer.

"So, what? I can just bring you back?"

He shook his head slowly. "You are projecting me, nothing more. Much like your lover's wife. You need to get a grip on the power flowing through you."

"I would if you would tell me how? I'm just fucking winging it here, *Dad*."

"Language, Daughter."

"Sorry." I bowed my head in shame and sat next to him, trying vainly to touch him, but my hand passed through his leg.

"I am nothing more than a waking dream. Here in spirit, but my body is far, so far, away."

"Just hang in there. I'm coming to get you!"

"No. You're not."

"Bet?"

"I was in your grandmother's workspace. Their plan is foolish. There is more to crossing Ethereum than just having a guide. Do you truly think Belenus will help you? It is because of her that I am where I am. She would just as soon as add you to her prison than release me. Do not be foolish. You are too smart for that."

"No. Not really. If I have to whip her ass to get her to free you, then I'm going to start taking kung fu lessons."

"She has been a god since the dawn of time. While your power grows, she would…wipe the floor with your face, as they say. Do not do this, Daughter. I beg of you. I led a full life and have no regrets."

"But your people need you."

"They have you."

"I need you."

"You have me. I am always with you, Dorothea. Do not forget that. Time, space, and the planes separate us, but I am always right here."

The tears were already dripping hotly down my cheeks. When he reached out and I felt his fingers touch my face, the waterfalls started. "I don't want your power. I was happy being me. Just plain old Dot."

"You were never plain, and just like your mother, you will never be old. Use the power I have given you to change the world. Too long has the mortal realm been separated from the fae and magic. Technology is making them cold, selfish, and ignorant. Find ones you trust, share your power, and make the world as it *should* be."

"Magic?"

"Better."

He faded away and I knew I would never see him again.

∞ ∞ ∞

Chief was already sitting in my booth talking to Marge when I opened the diner door at one minute after noon. It took one look for him to know I wasn't having the best of mornings, either.

"You okay, Darlin'?" Marge did that mom thing where she grabbed my head and checked my temperature with her lips. "Not runnin' a fever at least. Can't be too careful with all those nasty bugs goin' around."

"Thanks, Marge. Just been a long morning." I sat and she took off running.

"You're either going to end up with chicken soup or a Marge Totty."

"Do I want to know?"

"Here you go, Darlin'." She set a coffee in front of me. I could smell the whiskey in the vapors. The slice of lemon I could have done without.

"Thank you." I managed a smile.

She was watching me, eyes flickering to the coffee cup in front of me.

I took a sip, made some appropriate *Mmmm Mmmm* noises and set the mug back down.

"You drink that all up, Sweetie. I'll be back to take your order in a minute!" She wandered off to pick up an order in the window.

"What the fuck did I just drink?"

"Coffee, lemon, cinnamon, turmeric, and something else that she won't divulge. However, I have never failed a drug test at the department, so I don't think it's illegal."

"Pretty sure its fucking illegal to serve tar to customers."

"Should have just told her you weren't sick." He chuckled and clinked his mug against mine before leaning back in his seat and putting his arm up on the back of the booth.

"You look more relaxed."

He nodded and smiled. "I feel better, too." His face darkened. "I'm really sorry about this morning."

"Don't be. Everybody is entitled to a few breakdowns now and then. Considering that was your first and you're dating me, you are doing exceptional."

"So, what's going on with you?" He dropped the subject of him and switched to me.

"Just tired. I got a bit more sleep but had a ghostly visitor when I woke up."

He paled and scooted forward in the seat, wrapping both hands around his mug. "Becca? Did you lay her to rest?"

I shook my head. "My father."

"What?"

"Sitting at my table. Dropped by to say hi."

"That's amazing? You don't have to rescue him anymore?"

"He was a phantom. Not really real. He's still in Tartarus."

"What did he say?"

"Abandon all hope. Live my life. There was no way to rescue him, blah, blah, blah."

"You gonna listen?"

"Would you?"

He sighed and took a sip, thinking about it. "I don't know. Maybe."

"You just want me safe, too."

"Yep. I'm a bastard like that."

"You guys decide on something other than a damn cheeseburger?" Marge slipped up while we were talking and pulled out her order pad, shooting Chief a disgusted look.

"Cheeseburger," he said with a smile.

I swear she growled before looking at me.

"Tell Herb to surprise me."

"Oh, no." She rolled her eyes. "He's had twenty friggin' recipes he's had in his head, *waiting* for you to say those damn words. I'll alert the fire department." She huffed and wandered back to the window. "Herb! Fatty patty for Chief, and a Cauldron Special for Dot."

"It is *time*," he said and lifted his head, grinning at me through the window.

He hit the play button on the ancient boombox in the window and turned his hat around. The heavy beat of *Eye of the Tiger* filled the diner.

"Should we run?" Chief turned his head slowly and looked at me worriedly.

I couldn't stop myself. Hysterical laughter burst out of my chest and I sat there in the seat, wiping my eyes for a good three minutes before getting it under control. Every worry, doubt, and crappy feeling that had been weighing me down vanished with the gigglefits. Laughter truly was the best medicine.

Chief had sat back to watch the show, joining me in a few of my more raucous cackles. Sometime during my display, Nana and Mother had entered the diner, grimaced at my hysterics, and sat at a booth along the back wall, pretending not to know me. That just set me off more.

"You gonna live?"

"Yes. Just give me a minute." I rubbed my eyes with one hand and held up the other.

Where are you? Yuki's thought stifled my laughter.

Lunch with Chief. Diner. I sent to her. *Everything okay?*

The chime answered that question and she slipped into the booth beside me. "Thought you'd still be sleeping. I cleaned up your mess." She shot me an angry glare.

"Oh, shit. I forgot about the coffee."

"You feeling okay?" She put her hand on my forehead.

"Yes!" I pulled away from her cold hand. "Sheesh. Everybody is my mother."

"That would make the world a better place, Dear," Mother whispered from across the diner. I had forgotten about her bat ears. Which was hard to do, since in entirety, she was an old bat.

Ignoring her, I looked back at Yuki. "I got up and everybody was gone."

"Candsie went to work. Jaeren had elfly duties to attend to and went back to faerie last night. And Dar took Ellis to the bookstore. Said they were short on stock help."

"Candsie?"

"Candace and Josie. Candsie sounds better than Jondace."

"You shipped them?"

"They shipped themselves." She started giggling.

"Ellis? They're going to put him to work at the bookstore? In public?"

"Apparently, he's some kind of master wizard or some shit. He looked human when he walked out the door."

"Huh. Learn something new every day."

"He even did Dar. He doesn't have to wear that stupid hippie looking headband anymore."

"He did Dar?" I wiggled my eyebrows as the vision danced in my head.

Yuki rolled her eyes.

"So, what were you up to?"

100

"I got...hungry," Yuki answered embarrassedly.

"Oh, shit. Why didn't you wake me up?"

"Because your blood is like doing shots of Everclear. No offense. Shea volunteered."

"I bet he tastes like Cinnabon."

"Nope. Chocolate."

"Are you two done?" Chief was several shades of green.

"What?" We asked in unison.

"I'm about to eat. The thought of drinking blood..."

"Now you know how I feel watching you scarf down cheeseburgers." Yuki stuck her tongue out at him.

"You're just jealous," he answered and stuck his tongue out back at her.

"A little. Yeah." Yuki pouted.

"Sorry, Kid."

Yuki was lying. That wasn't all she had been up to. I felt it during their little banter session. "How's George?"

She blinked at me in surprise before her eyes narrowed. "You can smell him on me."

"Ew. He's your cousin!" Chief had missed the point.

"And gay, dumbass." Yuki snarled. "I went to the house to talk to him. To talk to *them*."

"Who's them?" He let the dumbass comment go.

"The other vampires. Amir and whoever was left at the house besides George." I didn't take my eyes off her. Wanting to gauge her reaction.

"Don't worry. Amir is still yours. As is George, which is the real reason I went over there. I mean, we are talking about his father, but he's too afraid to go against you."

"Smart boy," Chief answered.

"No. An honest one. He's pissed at his dad for trying to take over. He thinks Dot will *really* take care of the fatally anemic population of Cedar Falls. Not use them to turn a profit."

I felt the low rumble from her. She was angry at all of them. Her father, her uncle, and her mother.

June Abernathy had struck me as sweet and timid. Her husband was an asshole. Yuki was somewhere in between, inheriting the best of both parents. I didn't see June as an enemy, but I saw her as powerless against her husband's brother. Only time would tell, though.

"Here we go!" Marge set down a Coke and a burger in front of Chief, and a coffee in front of Yuki. She sighed before she hoisted the plate off the tray and set it in front of me with a Coke to wash it down.

I stared down at the plate. There was a tiny black iron cauldron filled with guacamole over a bed of French fries splashed with hot sauce. The effect was meant to make it look like it was sitting over burning wood, and he actually pulled it off. I could see Herb bent over the counter arranging each fry just right, too. The rest of the plate was taken up by a sandwich. I lifted the fluffy brioche top and inspected the contents. "What's in it?"

"Your guess is as good as mine."

I poked at the neatly stacked meat. He had medium sliced fresh roasted turkey breast and put it on the bottom. That was covered with a layer of finely cut cucumber. On top of that, he had stacked frizzled onion straws and then, I dipped my finger to taste it, drizzled sage aioli over everything. Smacking my lips, I picked it up and took a bite. "Holy shit," I managed to stammer around the mouth full of food.

"That bad?" Marge shot me an apologetic look.

"No! It's fucking delicious. Tell him I said thank you!"

"Oh!" She bowed low and made a sweeping gesture with her hand. "I present to you, the Witchwich. Forgot that part." She rolled her eyes and turned toward the kitchen. Herb was practically hanging out of the window. "She likes it!"

The relief in the diner was real. Everybody seemed to start breathing again.

"Betcha the menu's gonna have a new sticker tomorrow." Yuki giggled.

102

Chapter 10

D*ing dong.*

I took my finger from the modern looking doorbell and waited, uneasily. Since Dar and Shea had started seeing each other outside of our relationship, it had always been my intention to make Shea's apartment their own little sanctum and not intrude.

However, after lunch at the diner, I'd stopped by the bookstore. The two of them had taken my comment about crashing at their place at face value and had arranged dinner and planned on me spending the night. Chief had winked at me and told me to go. He didn't mind spending the night in my room without me, thanking me for letting him crash there. I even offered to ask Yuki to cuddle with him. He'd been less than pleased, even though I'd been joking. Yuki smacked me in the back of the head when he wasn't looking. I thought their whole damn rivalry thing was kind of cute. And fun to exploit for my own entertainment.

"You could have just shadow walked into the apartment," Shea said as he pulled the door open with his hands encased in oven mitts.

"That would be rude." I kissed him on the forehead as I walked inside the earthy apartment. Truth be told, I loved spending time there. His wood furnishings and taste in décor ranged from Middle Earth to elven assassin.

"Dinner is almost ready. Wine?"

"As long as it doesn't knock me on my ass."

"No promises, Lady." He let out a string of musical laughter and headed back to the kitchen. He was wearing a leather apron and had his hair tied back with a black ribbon. Even without the leather pants he was hot. Watching his ass in said leather pants, he was drool worthy. I had failed to get him in the habit of wearing jeans or sweatpants. While he would have looked *magnificent* in gray sweatpants, you wouldn't have been able to see every ripple of every muscle in his ass and legs as he walked.

"Where's Dar?" I was making conversation.

"In the shower. He just got home from work."

"You should have told me to come later."

"By the time he gets out of the shower, dinner should be done, Lady." He pulled off the oven mitts and pulled an ancient bottle of wine off the wine rack that looked like it had been grown from grape vines. Deftly cutting the wax from the top with the dagger he kept somewhere on him when he wasn't wearing the heavy cloak he fought in, he tucked it away and held his palm to the bottom of the bottle, whispering something too softly for me to hear. I watched in fascination as the cork wiggled itself out of the bottle and fell deftly into his hand.

"Telling you. You should get a job as a sommelier."

"And spend time away from my beloved books? I think not, Lady." He smiled at me and started pouring the amber liquid into three crystal glasses on the counter.

"What's this one?"

"Elven fire wine."

"Sounds spicy."

"Not at all." He grabbed two of the glasses, handed me one, and then lightly touched the rim of his glass to mine before taking a sip.

I brought the glass to my lips and inhaled. It smelled like summer. I could practically hear the waves of the lake as they gently lapped the shore. Laughter filled my ears as I took a sip. It went down smooth, settled in my belly, and then began to warm me from the inside out. "They should call it summer instead of fire."

104

"It is in reference to the warming effect. Elven travelers often brought this on cold voyages. I thought it fitting considering the weather and the meal."

"What are we having?'

"Seared venison loin astride roasted root vegetables and fondant potatoes with a port reduction."

"Deer, veggies, and taters?"

"Yes." He stared at me blankly.

"Well, if it's as good as it sounds, I'm sure I'll love it." I chuckled and pulled him in for a hug, careful not to spill our wine.

He pressed his face against my chest. "I have missed you."

"Missed you too, my Shea."

He looked up at me with one of those innocent smiles that made my heart melt and lady bits get squishy. Leaning in, I kissed him.

"I see the two of you are skipping to dessert."

Turning around, I grinned at the half-naked blue demon in the doorway to the bedroom. My squishy bits drooled. He was wearing nothing but a white towel and the contrast between it and his azure skin was mesmerizing. As was the bulge in the front of the towel.

"Let me throw on some pants," he said and blew me a seductive kiss.

"Not on my account, I hope." I wiggled my eyebrows at him.

He returned before I got my staring situation under control, wearing the gray sweatpants I'd been picturing on Shea. "Dar, we have a guest. You should wear something more appropriate. At least put on a shirt."

Dar frowned. *What say* you, *Master? Would you like me to wear more, or divest Shea of some of his…*

Divest away!

Dar laughed and walked over to Shea, untying the thong on the apron and taking it and his peasant shirt off. Shea rolled his eyes in protest.

"Master's orders," Dar whispered in his ear loudly enough for me to hear.

Shea looked at me shyly, his protests turning to a smile. "As our guest wishes."

Dar took the third glass of wine and motioned for the table, pulling out the seat on the end for me. "Thank you, sir."

When I sat, he reached down and grabbed the hem of my shirt, lifting it over my head after I set my glass down. "What are you doing?"

"If you wish us to be shirtless during dinner, we cannot allow our guest to stand out." He kissed my shoulder as I instinctually covered my breasts with an arm.

The only problem was, next to them, I felt inadequate.

One look from Dar as he sat next to me, quelled my inhibitions. I couldn't have pried his eyes from me with a two-by-four. "How was work?"

"Busy as usual."

"How did Ellis do?"

"Ask him yourself."

"That good?" I felt bad for him. To be thrust into working a mundane job with no experience must have been quite the culture shock.

"No, I mean ask him yourself. He should be here any moment."

Shea chuckled and set his and another glass of wine on the table. He had purposely not told me and only put out three glasses, the little shit. One thing was for certain, I was putting my shirt back on. I reached for the garment, but Dar stopped me with a hand.

"Do not tell me you do not desire him, Master. I've been around when you were together."

I narrowed my eyes at him. "So?"

He leaned a little closer. "I could smell your desire." He rubbed my leg for emphasis.

"So? He's hot. If I bedded every guy I found hot...I'd have a bed full of guys," I finished lamely. If I were being honest with myself, I had. Except for Jaeren and Ellis. At

106

least the guys weren't pushing Jaeren on me. I would have loved to know what their obsession was with Ellis, though.

"What gives?"

"Pardon?" Dar blinked in confusion.

"Ellis. You're not the only one pushing me at him. What is it?"

Dar sighed and looked at Shea who set a roasting pan on the glass topped table. "You tell her."

"Tell me what?" I was losing patience.

"Your power calls to him."

"My what?"

"He is a dark elf. Your power calls to him. Every one of us can see it but you."

"No. I can feel it. But I can also ignore it." I took another sip of wine, almost angrily, and let the burn add to the fire in my belly. "Besides, I already have a dark elf." I rubbed Shea's butt, which had a miraculous calming effect, I might add.

"I am only half. And I am your link to the shadows. Yuki is your link to the vampires. Dar is your link to the demons. You need Ellis as much as he needs you," Shea answered as if it were the most normal thing in the world. "He will be your link to the *unseleighe sidhe*."

"I'm not sleeping with Yuki!" There was no way in hell that would ever happen. I liked guys and she liked…anime.

"But you love her."

"Yes, but…"

"The link does not need to be sexual in nature. Love is enough," Dar said and lifted the lid from the pan, earning himself a swat on the hand from Shea.

"Wait!"

"But it smells so *good*."

It did. All thoughts of Yuki and Ellis flew out the fucking window as soon as Dar lifted the silver lid and a puff of steam filled the air around us. My mouth started watering even *more*. As if Shea and Dar weren't enough to make a person drool.

"He is ready," Shea said and walked to the corner of the room, disappearing into the shadows and returning a moment later with Ellis in tow.

"Greetings, everyone." He smiled at Dar and practically *beamed* at me.

I couldn't help from noticing his bulging pectoral muscles unencumbered by any sort of clothing. He was dressed identically to Shea. Leather pants and naked from the waist up. I forgot about the food in front of me. The meal that had just walked through the shadows looked *way* tastier.

"See?" Dar chuckled beside me.

"Fuck off." I mouthed the words out of the corner of my mouth, refusing to turn my head away from Ellis. Realizing I was staring, I shook my head and shot Dar a dirty look. "What about Jimmy, and Dennis, Chief and Jason?"

"What about them?"

"Uh…hello? Haven't even discussed this with them."

"I have."

"Have what?"

"Discussed the addition."

"You did?"

"I did."

"Don't you think you should have consulted me first?"

"To what avail? You would have balked and procrastinated. I made sure all of them were okay with it before I invited him to dinner. Now he is here. You are here. You can make a decision without worrying about what anybody else thinks. The ball is…in your court?"

"You're a mother fucking pimp." I pouted and crossed my arms.

"No. That would infer that you, my master, is a whore."

"No. I'm the john. He's the whore." I pointed at Ellis.

Ellis looked confused. "I'm a whore?"

"Metaphorically."

108

"Oh, good. For I have not lain with a woman. I did not see how that would be possible." Shea handed him a glass of wine as he sat.

"Shut the fuck up. You're a virgin?" I blinked at him. Several times. Maybe even a hundred.

"You saw the lack of females in my land? I have had many lovers, but none that were not male."

I looked at Dar.

He looked at me. And so help me, fucking goddess, he grinned.

"I suppose I could be a man whore," Ellis added thoughtfully, taking a sip of his wine and coughing.

"Are we going to eat?" I rubbed the bridge of my nose and focused on anything but the half-naked dark elf on the other side of the table. It was probably safer that way.

"Let me get the meat," Shea said and walked back into kitchen.

"You already did," I mumbled to myself.

Dar nearly choked on his wine as Ellis smiled at everyone confusedly. It was going to be a very long night.

You should have talked to me first, Dar.

I am not forcing you to sleep with him, Master. I have simply removed any inhibitions that might have stopped you from choosing for yourself. Bed him or do not. The choice is yours.

Eat the steak I have laid out in front of you, or don't. I thought snidely at him. *But here is a napkin and some utensils in case you're hungry.*

I'm glad you understand.

"Wait! I am a steak, not a whore?"

"You could hear us?" I stared at Ellis.

"Clearly," he answered, a blush on his dark cheeks.

"As could I, Lady," Shea answered from the kitchen.

Me, too. Yuki's thought interjected itself into the conversation.

"Dinner is served," Shea said and lifted the cover off the pan, sliding the sliced rare meat atop the delicious looking potatoes surrounded by carrots and other veggies I didn't recognize.

The meat gave a little hiss as the cold mixed with the hot. The juices on the venison began to run as they touched the warmth beneath it, bathing the other offerings with flavor. Over that, he took a tiny metal boat and poured a thick red liquid over everything. It looked like blood but smelled like wine. My stomach growled, or maybe it was just me.

"Fuck, that smells good."

"Thank you, Lady."

"Dar, would you serve?" Shea ran his hand over Dar's shoulder.

"Yes, Dear." He chuckled and stood. "Ladies first," he said and forked a couple of slices of meat onto my plate and then filled the rest with potatoes and vegetables.

I tried to wait patiently as he served the rest of them, but I couldn't help but dip my finger in the sauce and slowly bring it to my tongue. It exploded with flavor. "Woah."

"You like the reduction?" Shea sipped his wine, watching me intently.

"If there's any left, I might be pouring it over you later."

He laughed. "I shall make some more. Unless you find one of the desserts preferable."

"Dessert?"

"Grand Marnier Chocolate Souffle."

"I'm moving in."

"We would love that," Shea said sweetly, beaming at me over the table.

Once Dar filled his plate, he nodded and I practically swiped the fork and curved knife off the napkin by my plate, cutting a sliver of meat off and letting it melt in my mouth.

"Is it good? Try it with a bit of fondant potato."

"Good doesn't even begin to describe this succulent meal," I managed to stammer as I tried a bit of each of the items, not bothering to wait as I praised it. It was literally the best food I had ever eaten.

Shea couldn't wipe the smile off his face as he picked at his food. Dar kept shooting glances at me and grinning. Ellis... Ellis was staring at me adoringly the whole meal. Even after the plates were cleared.

"Dessert?"

"Wait a bit," I answered Shea, rubbing my tummy.

"Coffee?"

"Now I'm never leaving."

"Your plan worked, Dar." Shea nodded at him.

"She was rather easy to trap. No sport at all. Shall we move to the living room?" Dar offered me his hand.

"You might need a crane," I groaned. I hadn't gorged myself, but the food itself wasn't light fare. I was more than full.

Dar chuckled and scooped me out of the chair, careful not to bang my knees against the glass top. He smiled at me and let his eyes travel over my flesh as he walked us to the couch and sat down on the corner. I cuddled into his chest as he lightly stroked my back.

"I have missed you, my master." He lifted my chin with his blue fingers and gently kissed me as I stretched out over him. I expected Shea to sit next to me, but Ellis took the spot, lifting my legs and placing them in his lap. He offered me a smile.

A smile I returned. Then he started gently rubbing my legs through my pants and worked his way down to my feet. It was official. I'd died and gone to heaven.

"Does that feel good, Lady?"

"Very."

He continued his massage as Shea slipped into the room and shut off the kitchen light. "Movie?"

"Which one?"

"Dar has yet to see the Lord of the Rings. I was waiting until you joined us."

"Oh, hell yeah. Legolas for the win."

"What is a Lego lass?"

"Legolas. An elf. He's hot."

"You prefer the fairer of our races?"

"Nope. But Orlando Bloom is hot."

"Is that a type of flower?"

"Watch the movie, Ellis."

"Yes, Lady."

Chapter 11

My head was on Dar's lap, my legs were in Ellis's, and Shea was in my arms as I hugged him like a stuffed animal until the movie finished and the credits started rolling.

"That was astounding," Ellis said almost reverently.

"I agree," Dar seconded.

Shea was quiet. I'd been nibbling on his neck and licking his tender flesh for the past thirty minutes. I doubted he was capable of speech. The blue glow from his tattoos wherever my flesh touched his had been mesmerizing, but what was underneath those tattoos became more interesting.

"I love you," I whispered.

"As I love you," he answered, turning his head and smiling.

"And I love both of you," Dar said with a chuckle, letting his hand slide down my side.

Ellis remained quiet, but he hadn't stopped massaging me through the entire movie. I know he had pledged his very existence to me, but that right there, was at least the *beginnings* of love. His hands had to be cramping. "Aren't you tired?" I finally asked him.

"Of touching you? I doubt that day would ever come."

The rumble of Dar's laughter made my head shake.

You win. I sent the thought hopefully to just Dar.

Since he was the only one who smiled, I thought I might have succeeded. "Shea?"

"Yes, Lady."

"How about dessert?"

"I shall get it." He got up from in front of me and stretched, arms raised toward the ceiling.

"You already have it," I answered him, rubbing the bulge in his leather pants to know what I was talking about.

"What about the souffle?"

"Would you rather have chocolate or me?"

The little shit actually pretended to think about it for a moment, comically rubbing his chin. Sighing, I reached under my head and rubbed Dar instead. Shea gasped in horror before laughing.

Dar hardened under my hand. The sweatpants made it easy to fish him out and take him into my mouth as I rolled over on my stomach. The hands that had been moving over my legs all evening worked the backs of them, kneading my flesh.

"She is so beautiful; how do you stand it?" Ellis asked Shea and Dar.

"Sometimes, we can't. Her beauty and love are enough to drive us all mad," Dar answered breathily as I sucked him slowly, enjoying the feeling of him against my tongue.

I pulled him from my mouth with a little, wet *pop*.

"He's lying. I just drive them nuts." I winked up at Dar and kissed the tip of him, letting my tongue dance through his opening. I was rewarded with a little gush of fluid. Reaching up, I rubbed it over his head and then stroked the length of him as I engulfed him once again.

"We should get her out of those constrictive clothes," Shea said solemnly to Ellis. He stopped rubbing for a moment and then two pairs of hands began to tug them down my legs.

"We should move this to the bedroom. How big is your bed?"

Dar's chuckle should have been warning enough.

They stood me up, encircling behind me and shedding their clothes as we headed toward the closed bedroom door. Shea ducked ahead and opened it, flipping the switch.

It wasn't a bed. It was a playground. One tiny nightstand beside it, the bed took up the room except or the dresser closest to the door.

"Holy shit," I said in awe.

"California King," Dar whispered.

"Planning on hosting parties in that thing?"

He looked at the three of us staring at him.

"Apparently so," he answered and pulled me to him, kissing me as he lifted me from the floor, lowering us to the bed and nestling me beside him. He began stroking my flesh with his fingers as Ellis took the spot on the other side of me and began following Dar's lead, matching him movement for movement.

I moaned as I arched my back, their featherlight caresses sending shivers over my skin as Shea crawled between my legs and kissed me gently on my thigh.

Dar leaned down and kissed my lips as Ellis kissed the hardened nipple beside him. Uninhibited, I reached down and grabbed both of them, their hard flesh throbbing in my grip.

I breathed into that kiss as Shea's lips grazed my flesh, spreading my wetness all over me before he gently ran a circle around my clit with the tip of my tongue.

I pulled away from Dar's lips, groaning, "No teasing."

He sucked it gently between his lips and let his tongue bat against me. My hips bucked, I hissed, and called out his name as he slipped two fingers inside me.

"Fuuuck," I thrashed between Dar and Ellis.

Shea pushed my legs down beside me and I felt something soft slither around my ankles. Lifting my head, I gasped as silk cords wrapped themselves around me and pulled my legs apart even farther. "What is that?"

"Bindings," Shea answered as he lifted his mouth from my flesh. Kissing me again softly after that.

"For what?"

"To keep you from thrashing," Dar answered as two more snaked their way between Ellis, me, and him. They gripped my wrists and lifted them up slowly, giving me time to let go of their flesh in my hands. They rolled out of the way for the moment as my hands matched my legs, spreading me out toward the four corners of the bed.

I wasn't afraid. If anything, being bound only made me that much wetter as two of them knelt by my head and Shea continued his ministrations below.

"May I taste?" Ellis looked down at Shea.

"Absolutely. We should share this dessert." He moved over.

Ellis got off the bed and walked around, lying down in the space beside the shadow walker between my legs. Together, they kissed my thighs and worked their way up to my apex, their tongues dancing against my wet lips.

"Holy fuck."

"You like that." Dar leaned down and kissed me.

All I could do was nod as pleasure filled me from the bottom up. "Give me your cock."

"You wish to taste it again?"

"Yes. I need you in my mouth."

"As you command." He moved closer and lifted one leg over me, straddling my chest. I stared down at the beauty of him, nestled between my breasts.

"Are you going to titty fuck me?"

"No," he answered and gripped himself at the base, letting the head of his cock graze against my achingly hard nipples.

"Ooooh," I groaned and tried to lift myself off the bed to drive him against me harder, but I was held fast by the bindings. He nestled the tip of one nipple in that sensitive divot just under the ridge of his head and stroked that supple flesh against me. I couldn't move. I wanted him in my mouth. I begged him with my eyes.

He understood and moved forward, dragging the head of him over my bottom lip as I lashed out with my tongue, slapping against the tip.

"How badly do you want my cock right now, Lady?"

"I don't want it. I *need* it."

116

He let his hips move, giving me the head. Wrapping my lips around it, I suckled him with every ounce of love, want, and need coursing through my veins.

He let out the breath he'd been holding as I worked him with my lips and tongue, bathing him, teasing him, torturing him, wanting nothing more than for him to splash me with my reward.

"You're going to make me come, Lady."

"That's the plan," I mumbled around him.

He reached down and started stroking himself as the feeling of the two of them lapping me started to take its toll. I wasn't going to last much longer than Dar. He pulled his cock away and rubbed it against my cheek. Closing my eyes, I nuzzled him against my face, cooing at the sensations flooding my body.

"Open your lips, Lady," he said with a groan.

"Do it." I opened my mouth as he held his cock over me, lashing out with my tongue against the tip.

He angled himself down as the first blast coated the roof of my mouth. That pushed me over the edge, and I managed to buck my hips once or twice until the bindings tightened further, permitting no movement as I came and was came on. I felt dirty, I felt wicked, I felt loved, and I loved every fucking moment of it.

Dar finished and rolled off me, putting his back against the headboard beside me. I managed to lift my head and look down my sweat soaked body at the two of them still feasting on my flesh. They were kissing each other as much as me, creating a three-way junction with their lips and mine. They were unrelenting as they feasted and stroked each other between them.

A second orgasm washed over me, and still they didn't stop.

I was panting and almost crying when Dar finally spoke up. "Enough, gentlemen. I do not think she can take much more and retain her sanity."

"My apologies, Lady." Shea planted a gentle kiss against my lips.

117

"I was alone and starving. It was hard to resist such a beautiful bounty," Ellis added and did the same.

"Fuck me," I groaned and let my head fall back against the pillow. Grateful for the respite.

They shuffled between my legs, and then I felt something nudge its way inside me. I gasped as Ellis kissed my breasts and then drove himself the remainder of the way.

"Oh fuck!" I started spasming around him.

"Did you not say?"

"I believe she meant it as an expression of delight," Dar said with a chuckle.

Ellis started to pull himself out.

"Stop! Don't move. Just give me a minute."

"I cannot believe how good you feel, Lady," he whispered in awe and pleasure.

"Yep. You feel pretty fucking good, too. Stop throbbing inside me. I need a moment."

"I cannot," he groaned and I felt him spasming. He wasn't coming, yet. But he was close. Damn close.

"You gonna pump me full of your cum, Ellis?"

He yelled and his hips curled as he drove himself further in, grunting in pleasure as he unloaded his pent-up lust. I chuckled as he came, resting his head on my chest and grinning madly. If I had a hand free, I would have stroked his hair and whispered sweet things into his pointed ear.

"I am truly sorry, my Lady. That was too much and exquisite in feeling."

"Not your fault, Ellis. It was your first time." I winked at him. "You'll do better in a few minutes."

"Again?"

"And again, after that, if you can." I grinned at him.

He had the same look on his face as Jaeren when I gave him the box of crayons. I wanted my hands free to hold him. Looking at Shea, he nodded and whispered something to the ropes. They immediately let go of me and slithered back under the bed.

118

"You're putting some of those on my bed," I told him and wrapped Ellis in my arms, finally stroking his silky white hair.

"They can be finicky and require much testing before casual use…"

"Shucky darns. Guess we'll have to be crash test dummies then." I laughed at his ecstatic expression.

"Elleslyn, may I?" Shea tapped him on the shoulder.

"My apologies for not removing myself from this place of honor sooner." He untangled himself from my embrace and lifted his body off of mine, reached down, and slowly pulled himself from me. When he stood, Shea immediately went to his knees before him and pulled his cock into his mouth, groaning at the taste of our combined flavors.

"If he gets to lick the spoon, I get to lick the bowl," Dar said with a chuckle and leaned over me, letting his tongue dive inside me and moaning against my flesh.

Reaching up, I cupped his balls and gave them a little squeeze. His cock throbbed and slapped up against his belly. Guy parts were amazing, and I chuckled as I fondled him as he dined. When he lifted his head, Shea offered Dar a taste of his cock before he pulled away and dipped it in me. I watched the whole show and I felt myself spasm in delight.

"Shea. Would you like my ass?" I made the offer.

He grinned as he stopped see-sawing inside me. "Truly?"

"Truly, truly."

He pulled out and I rolled over on my stomach. He dipped his fingers inside my wetness and used it to tease my ass, slowly working the tips inside. I moaned as he played and then I felt him press the tip of his cock against me. I winced as I spread, but he knew better than to thrust the rest of himself inside me. Instead, he leaned over and kissed the back of my neck lovingly. Slowly, he worked himself inside me between my groans and moans of pleasure. "Fuck," I stammered once he was fully inside.

"Do not grip me so tightly, Lady."

"I don't have a choice!"

He chuckled. "I shall not move. Try and relax." He lowered his chest and pressed against my back, kissing my shoulder softly while the familiar blue glow surrounded us. He deftly rolled us over onto his back, exposing me and managing to keep himself inside me. It must have been their plan once Shea was comfortably inside me.

I spread my legs for stability, and Dar slipped between them. With nothing but love in his eyes, he lined himself up against my other entrance before pushing the length of him inside me.

I felt so full I could have screamed, and I did. Feeling the two of them as the slightest movements shifted them against each other with only the slightest walls of me between them became the focus of my everything. Then they started fucking me.

Shea's movements were slower, more deliberate, intending not to hurt me in any way as Dar started bucking his hips. It was too much. It was overwhelming. I wanted more.

As if on cue, Ellis offered me his cock.

Dar smiled as I reached up and pulled him closer and took him in my mouth. *Then*, I was full. A lover's cock in each of my available openings, the four of us made love.

Dar groaned, eyeing Ellis's cock hungrily. I pulled it from my mouth and turned it to the side, offering to share with a smile. Around that hard shaft we kissed, our tongues dancing over and under it as they touched. Ellis's hips began moving of their own accord as he pulled back until the tip was trapped in our kiss.

Shea was the first to come. I felt him spasming in my tightness as he started moving in and out faster as his cum turned me into a sodden mess. That was enough to bring Dar to the brink as he exploded inside me, filling me and dripping out over Shea.

"*Do'vorth h'maal belen da, vokuth dormal di'edra,*" he mumbled as he filled me with his seed. *I invoke the fourth rite as is our right.* The words filled my mind and my ears as my brain translated his words.

"*Melan prtu viie p'al vodru b'lek,*" I answered. *This is the choice we have made.*

"*P'daal gotru s'med boraan, molak da'bor ju.*" *From this day forward, we are one*, he answered.

Just as Ellis erupted between our lips.

Hot salty wetness splashed my tongue and infinite pain shot from my body, exploded through my mind, and then lashing out toward the universe. There wasn't a clock in the fucking room, but the *tick tock* came from somewhere as time slowed and everyone stopped moving. Everyone but me. Shea flared beneath me as a blue miasma from his tattoos enveloped me, wrapping me in light, and lifting me from the bed beneath me.

I gasped as they were pulled from me as I floated in the middle of the room. A tiny mewl escaped me. Naked and afraid, I had no idea what was going on as a thousand shadows burst from me and encircled me in a swirling mass of blackness.

My back arched as spines erupted from between my vertebrae, piercing my skin and filling the room with my cries of agony. My fingers locked as claws burst from the tips, wicked and curved. My gums bled as agony enveloped my mouth as fangs ripped through, lengthening, and threatening to cleave my bottom lip. All of that almost equaled the agony of having wings shred my skin as muscles and bones reknit themselves as they started flapping behind me, alleviating some of the strain on the magic keeping me aloft.

The shadows burst apart soundlessly and then stretched in every direction. Three of them aimed low, piercing Dar, Ellis and Shea through their chests and lifting them up beside me. Closing my eyes and praying to anyone and everyone that I wasn't hurting them, the remaining shadows burst through the walls of the bedroom.

In my head, I saw the first one find Yuki. She tried to run, but it caught her in a moment, much faster than her vampiric speed. She was skewered, lifted, and closed her eyes.

Chief was driving and managed to pull off the road and slam it into park as he was dragged from the Jeep.

Jason sat at his desk and every light in the bookstore sizzled as the filaments snapped and the LEDs fried.

Jimmy was picking up his phone, smiling as he dialed my number.

Dennis was asleep in his bunk at the firehouse.

All of them shut down as they were hoisted into the air silently. I was flung back into myself and something snapped inside me, clicking into place. The smokey tendrils of shadows flared as the tattoos etched on Shea's flesh began to bleed blue and copy themselves in lines of text through the shadows.

Looking down at my wrists, I saw the tattoos encircle my pale white flesh. Fearing the same was happening to the others, I sent my consciousness back down the lines as the runes appeared on each of their wrists, matching mine in design and color. When the last one filled in, they flared to life and disappeared, fading under their skin.

There was an echo from the clap of thunder that exploded around us as the shadows melted and lowered us to the bed. Everyone passed out but me as I writhed in agony while my flesh knitted itself back to normal. After it finished, I joined them in oblivion.

Chapter 12

I didn't wake up until the next day, Shea lightly tapping my cheek with the tips of his fingers.

I winced as Yuki's *Master* echoed in my mind for the trillionth time. It felt like I had a hangover on steroids. *What?* I groaned and opened my eyes to see a very relieved looking shadow walker hovering over me.

What the fuck did you do? I could feel Yuki's pain through her voice.

Don't fucking ask me. Ask blue boy. Without looking, I pointed at the sleeping demon beneath me, even though she couldn't see him.

Don't ask me, either. I'm dead.

You're not dead, you're talking, you dumb fucking dog. Yuki was a little pissed.

If I'm not dead, would one of you be so kind as to kill me?

There were muffled other voices in our conversation, but I couldn't make out any of their words. *Somebody turn off the voices.*

You hear them, too? Yuki sounded spooked.

"We can hear you. All of you. That might be the others trying to respond." Dar groaned.

I lifted my head from Dar's chest and instantly regretted doing it. The light from the window was blinding. Waving my hand, the shadows created willowy drapes blocking most of it.

"How did you do that?" Shea asked in awe.

"Bright light." I covered my face in my hands and rolled over, burying my face in the pillow.

I am starting to feel better. Ellis' voice in mind-speech was unmistakable. Lifting my head again in surprise, I blinked at him.

You can hear me?

Yes.

We all can, came a cacophony of voices.

Hold up. Yuki?

Yes?

Dar?

Yes.

Ellis?

Aye.

Shea?

Lady?

Chief? Chief? Jimmy? Dennis? Jason?

Muffled rumblings, but no speech. They could hear me, just not respond. "Well, I guess that answers that. How come Shea and Ellis can answer me now?"

"Dark elves," Dar answered. "Spheres. Can we go back to dead now?" He groaned and rolled over, sobbing silently.

Shea appeared with a tray of glasses filled with water and a bottle of pills. He was also dressed.

"What's that?"

"Advil."

"You have Advil?" Witches didn't get headaches. I didn't have any at my house.

"No, but the drug store on the corner does."

Nodding, the scene played out in my head. As soon as he saw the state we were in, he shadow-walked to the pharmacy, stole the biggest bottle of pain reliever he could find, and came back. Greedily, I popped four of them in my mouth and washed it down with a bit of water. Being the considerate little assassin he was, he shadow walked all over town, dispensing medication to everybody who had been caught up in the metaphysical backlash. He knew where they were just by feeling around for them in his head. The same way I had seen what had transpired the night before.

"Does anybody need anything?" An annoyingly chipper sounding Ellis asked as he lifted himself from the bed, found his pants, and got into them.

"A shower." I was…gross.

Dar lifted his hand and pointed at the bathroom door beside the bed.

I shook my head. "I'm going home."

"Come, my lady. I will carry you," Ellis answered reverently.

That sounded about as appealing as listening to Skrillex.

Calling the shadows, I felt their coolness as they slipped under me. Once they had gathered enough, they swallowed me up and spit me out in my own bed at my own house. I'm sure anybody in the room would have seen me rising from the comforter like some ghostly apparition. It was a cool, handy new talent, and one I would explore further once my head stopped throbbing and my ass was squeaky clean. Figuratively and literally. *No more metaphysical sex. Ever.*

I'm home, I let everybody know and slammed a mental barrier up, praying it would keep out the voices. It seemed to work as I was bathed in silence.

"You okay?" Yuki practically fell into the room.

"I will be as soon as the planet stops spinning and I have a shower."

I heard her clothes hitting the floor as she stripped and then took my hand, hoisting me up off the mattress. She got her shoulder under my arm and practically dragged me into the bathroom, turning the water on as she waited and kept me from falling to the floor.

"That was some party."

"I'm too old for that shit."

"Come on, Nana. Let's get you clean." She giggled, lifted me up, stepped over the edge of the shower, and stuck me back first under the spray of water. "Let me know when you can stand. I'll wash your hair and stuff. You're washing your own butt, by the way."

I giggled and wrapped my arms around her shoulders to hang on, resting my cheek against her shoulder. "Sorry for all that."

"It was Dar?"

"Not entirely. He pulled that binding shit again, and it exploded. Goddess knows why." I had a feeling, but I wasn't sure, and I had no intention of talking out of my ass. "Water feels good."

"You smell different."

"Bad?"

She sniffed the crook of my neck. "Stronger."

"Bad?"

"No. Not at all."

"You smell yummy," I said dreamily and nibbled her neck.

"You're hungry, aren't you."

"I could eat. A steak sounds yummy."

"I meant blood," she answered warily.

As soon as she said the word, my eyes snapped open and my mouth started watering.

"I'll take that as a yes." She chuckled, feeling me tense in her arms. "Go ahead. Gently. And just a little bit. Find somebody who doesn't need blood to live to feed off, though."

I nodded, bit her neck, and was rewarded with a splash of blood that tasted a thousand times better than Shea's reduction sauce.

"Tone it down," she gasped, and I focused on the taste instead of the happy feelings welling up from my very sore parts.

"Woah."

"What?" I asked after pulling my mouth from her flesh.

"You shut it off."

"What?"

"The feeding frenzy. You know. The bow chicky wow wow that comes with it."

126

"Is that good?"

"I'm more comfortable with pain compared to that. If I'm being honest with you." She pulled back and blushed at me.

I kissed her forehead and leaned back into the spray, a little more stable on my feet. "I got this now. Thanks for the snack. I feel almost...human again. Pardon the expression."

"You've got a bit more color in your cheeks, too. I'll wait on your bed. Holler if you need me."

"You'll be the first to know."

She slipped out of the shower and I could see her toweling the excess water off her skin as she walked out of the bathroom, leaving me alone with my guilt, shock, and fear. Still uncertain as to what *exactly* happened in Shea's apartment, I knew only one detail. I didn't want to know. My back still cringed at the feeling of the wings that had torn through my flesh. Of all the things that had happened, that freaked me out the most. *Dar didn't have wings, why the hell did I suddenly sprout a set of flappers?*

Catching myself starting to doze under the spray of the shower, I shook my head and soaped up before I collapsed in a melted puddle of Dot.

By the time I got out of the shower, Yuki was fast asleep in my bed. I covered her in the comforter and threw on a pair of jogging shorts and a T-shirt.

I made myself a cup of coffee and sat in silence on the couch avoiding the world outside. And inside.

∞ ∞ ∞

"You look like shit."

"Morning, Jay," I said and stuck my tongue out at him. He was behind the register and unable to retaliate in any way, shape, or form.

"Is the reason you look like crap the reason that half my employees didn't show up for work this morning and I feel like I woke up with three hangovers after spontaneously orgasming while floating in my office?" He cocked an eyebrow at me.

"Maybe."

"Could you give a guy some warning next time?" He was playing, but I still felt guilty.

"I will, next time I'm conscious."

"Oh, shit." He looked at the two noobs still running the one register together. "You guys have the desk. I'll be back shortly. If you get into a jam, just scream really loudly."

"Yes, Sir," They answered in unison, both shooting me shy glances. They weren't vamps, but I could still feel the fear coming from them. It made me wonder what horror stories Jason had been telling them about me behind my back.

"Come on," Jason said as he walked around the counter and put his hand on my back. "I'll buy you a cup of coffee."

The store was busy, but not *packed*. It was after noon but not quite evening when things would pick back up. Even the coffee shop was a little slower than usual. The line was only five people deep, which saved me an *extended* period of Josie's nervous glances. At least Candace had her back to us while she was slinging espressos. She probably would have taken one look at me, abandoned her post, and run over to me to give me a hug. She did turn around when Josie asked if I'd been run over by a train.

"Sort of." I blushed.

She sputtered at my response. "Not your first train wreck, how come you look like death?"

True to my musings, Candace wandered around the back of the counter and wrapped my stomach in a hug before wordlessly going back to the espresso maker.

"Beats the hell out of me."

"It looks like it already did." She leaned over the counter and pulled at the bags under my eyes.

She eyed the line behind me. "Tell me later."

"I will." I nodded for emphasis.

"What'll it be for you today?"

"I'll have a cup of caffeine, please."

"Make it two," Jason said with a chuckle and pulled out his wallet.

"Put that away," Josie told him and nodded at Candace.

We moved to the waiting counter so the lady behind us could order and watched Candace as she grabbed two paper cups off the stack, flipped them into the air, and slammed them down on the counter. She set the espresso machine to brew four shots, poured coffee into the cups, filling them halfway full, waited a moment for the espresso, and then dumped two of them into the coffee. Greedily, I held out my hands, but she gave me a dirty look as if I was interrupting her performance. She flipped a bottle of vanilla syrup over one handed like a bartender, splashing a swirl into the brew before flipping it back into the stainless-steel rack. Then she committed the ultimate sin, she poured milk into a frothing pitcher and jammed it onto the steam spout, twisting the spigot and filling the air with an angry hiss.

I opened my mouth to protest and debated jumping the counter to stop her madness, but she held up her hand in a preemptive measure. Once the milk was heated, she stuck the end of an electric frother inside and whipped the ever-loving shit out of it. My lip quivered as she brought the pitcher over the cups. "Please, no," I whispered.

She grinned and stuck a long spoon into the milk and extracted a puffy cloud of foam and dolloped it on top of the coffee. *Please be done.* She couldn't hear me, I knew, but I hoped my inner pleading reached her ears somehow.

She wasn't. She slammed a shaker of sparkling powder against her wrist, shaking it over the froth.

Now?

She took a squeeze bottle and nested a jewel of caramel on top.

I just want some fucking coffee!

She used her thumb to trace an intricate pattern on her forehead with one hand and held the other over both cups and muttered something in her native language. I could

129

have sworn her hand glowed pink and then the froth glistened iridescently like unicorn barf.

She looked up, smiled, and nodded, passing both cups over the glass partition. "Enjoy," she whispered.

"Can I get a lid?" Jason hesitated before taking the coffee.

He withered under Candace's disgusted glare.

"Never mind. This is quite beautiful. What is it?"

"It's not on the menu. I call it a Witch's Tit."

"That explains the caramel nipple." I stared blankly at the cup in my hand, unsure if I could handle all the floofiness. There was no way to drink it without snorting milk mush.

I'd made up my mind. The whole damn thing was going in the trash. The diner had real coffee. I lifted my head to shoot Candace a fake grateful smile, but she was leaning over the counter, watching me expectantly, shifting her gaze between the cup in my hand and my face as she waited for me to take that ever-important first sip. It was the doe eyes that did me in. She could have handed me a cup of molten lead and I probably would have drank it if she looked at me like that. It was impossible to say no. Josie was in trouble for the rest of her life.

Hand quivering, I brought the cup to my lip and parted the sea of foam with the tip of my tongue, hoping to actually get some coffee in the first sip. If it still tasted good, maybe I could flick the shit off the top and still salvage my drink.

Never judge a book, or a coffee, by its cover. As soon as my tongue tasted the floating confection, I was *hooked*. The shaker must have had crack in it. Candace smelled like sunshine; the fucking coffee in my hand *tasted* like sunshine. I could feel its warmth on my tongue as sweetness shined down from the heavens on the earthier flavors beneath.

For the first time in my life, I licked my coffee like a goddess damned ice cream cone. Candace giggled at my indiscretion. I was an addict and I probably looked strung out as caramel dangled from my lip down my chin.

"Holy shit."

"Good?"

I moaned in response and tried to guzzle the overly hot beverage, burning my lip, tongue, and throat, but not caring in the slightest.

"I'd like to change my order," said the woman beside us. "I want one of those!"

Jason nudged me to get going with his hip. "Come on. There's something I want to show you."

"What?'

"That would be telling you. I want to *show* you."

"Okay, Mr. Surprises." I huffed and let him lead the way back to the store and into the office. He took a sip of his coffee and set it down on the edge of the desk. "Holy shit."

"I know right?" I almost set mine down, too, but that would have made it hard to keep drinking.

"That's really good," he said and pulled a printed sheet of paper off a stack of others. "This is what I wanted to show you."

"What is it?" I took it with my free hand and looked at the extraordinarily large numbers.

"Profit and loss. The first column is how much in sales we've brought in. The second is what we spent, not counting the initial investment and stocking costs. The third column... That is your profit."

My eyes widened and I whistled in surprise. It was almost ridiculous. I'd almost made enough in the first few weeks to pay off the renovations to the building. In a month or two, the initial stock would be paid for. His calculations included rent and all the other operating expenses. By the end of spring, we might actually be pulling a profit. It was astounding and...unnatural. The store was always busy, but just looking at the numbers almost each and every person that came into the store walked out with a hefty purchase. "Woah."

"Exactly. The place is doing amazing."

Not wanting to jinx it, I smiled and stroked the wall, whispering, "Thank you," to the building around us. Something akin to pride and love flowed into my outstretched fingers.

Then I did the same to Jason's chest. "Thank you, too. This place wouldn't be an *eighth* of what it is without you. You are amazing, you are perfect, and I'm keeping you *forever*."

He blushed furiously and suddenly became very interested in the froth on his cup of coffee, unable to meet my eyes.

"All right, I'm outta here." Grabbing my coffee, I planted a quick kiss on the still smiling Jason's lips and headed for the door.

"Have fun."

"I doubt it," I answered with a chuckle.

Chapter 13

"I do not see why you insist on meeting in this less than sanitary establishment when we both have perfectly good, *clean*, houses. We could have even met at your office inside that biblio-nightmare across the street." Mother looked around the diner disgustedly and waved her hand in the direction of the bookstore.

"You don't like the bookstore, Mother?"

"Your mother doesn't like *anything*, Child. What did you want to discuss?" Nana slid into the booth and smiled at me across the table.

"That is untrue, Mothersaurus. I do love a nice hard–"

"Block of cheese," I finished for her and shot her a dirty look as Marge ambled up behind her. "Sit, Mother."

She *humphed* and did as I asked, sitting next to Nana.

"Mornin', Ladies. Tea, Cathleen?"

"Please, Margaret."

"Coffee, Dot?"

"Coke, actually. I had a coffee at the store." I instantly regretted my words. Marge shot me a look like I'd slept with Herb. The utter look of betrayal was more of a guilt trip than I *ever* got from my own mother. "On second thought, give me a coffee. I had one of those floofy things they try to pass off as real coffee. I still need a jolt."

She beamed. "Never understood people's fascination for overpriced coffee flavored cocoa drinks. Silly, if you ask me."

I had never understood it, either. Until I tried the Unicorn Jizz. Witch's Tit. Whatever. It was sparkly and nummy, and I would definitely order again. "You and me both." I agreed to make peace.

"And for you, Your Highness?" She shot my mother an evil glare.

"Whatever weeds you plucked from the parking lot and try to pass off as tea, Dear."

"My pleasure," Marge answered, sneered, and headed for the kitchen.

"What the fuck happened between you two?" I blinked in disbelief. They'd never been chummy, but that was a far cry from open hostility.

"I may have mentioned that someone forgot to remove the saddle before grinding the poor animal into Salisbury steak."

"You what?"

Nana started chuckling.

Mother looked at me like I was an idiot. I mean, that's how she usually looked at me, but even more so than usual. "I told her that the Salisbury steak tasted like horse."

"That's not all," Nana said with a bray of laughter.

I put my face in my hand and rubbed my eyebrows vigorously. "What did you do, Mother?"

She sighed. "I may have mentioned that it was a coincidence that her husband was a coroner…and that's where he and Midge met…"

"What?"

Nana was crying and waving her hand in front of her face.

"You know. The *morgue*, Daughter?" Mother picked up a menu and started perusing the specials.

"A table for two she called it!" Nana had given up trying to hold it in.

I looked over at the window to the kitchen. Marge was yelling something at Herb in a hushed but angry tirade, pointing in our direction.

"Mother? Why is it that you just can't be human for once in your life?"

"Because I'm a witch, Dear," she answered without looking at me from over her menu.

"Do I even want to know what happened?" I'd given up on Mother and asked Nana.

"She accidentally spilled a hot open-faced turkey platter in your mother's lap!"

Marge headed back in our direction, and for the first time I noticed her limp. "Mother? What did *you* do?"

"Nothing."

"Mother?"

Without a word, Marge set our drinks down on the edge of the table, muttered something about being right back, and headed for the back of the restaurant. Hopefully, not to arm herself.

"What did you do?" I hissed the question.

"Gave her a penis."

"Why is she fucking *limping*, Mother?"

"It was a big penis dear. I can't imagine trying to walk with that thing tucked wherever she hid the damn thing. If Herb is limping, I guess we'd know the answer to *that* question."

Nana spilled her tea.

I stared in horrified shock.

My mother wiggled her eyebrows at me over the menu.

"Fuck me."

"That's what *he* said!"

Somewhat composed, Marge came out of the back and pulled out her ordering book as she tilted her head at Nana.

"I'll have the pork cutlet with mashed potatoes, please."

She nodded, wrote it down and looked at me. "Dot?"

Reaching out, I touched her arm and whispered, "*Mar a bhí tú.*" I watched as Marge visibly shuddered and I tried very *hard* not to think about what was going on under her teal skirt. "I'll have a burger, please."

"*Thank you,*" she mouthed the words, giving me a look of utter gratitude, and shot my mother a disgusted look. "What do you want, *Hag*deline?"

"I'll have the Salisbury horse steak."

"I thought you didn't like it?"

"The bits and reins were rather distracting, but on a whole, the meal was almost edible, Barge."

"Huh. Thought you would be used to having a bit in your mouth."

"Only when I'm being ridden, Dear." Mother smiled saucily and handed Marge the menu.

"Oh. Then you must not be used to wearing one." Marge smiled back and took our order to the kitchen.

All in all, I was quite proud of Marge. If I were keeping score, I might have even said the match went to her. If I could just get my mother from altering her reproductive organs in the future, that would *definitely* be a win.

"Mother. Knock it the fuck off. She's good people."

"But she's still people, Darling."

And there it was.

The mood at the table shifted as I frowned at my mother. Nana could feel the storm coming and became very interested in the happenings outside the diner window.

"Don't you ever fucking say that again, *Mother*."

"Watch your tone, Daughter." She wasn't even trying to look sorry as she stared me down over the table.

"I will not watch my fucking tone," I hissed back at her. "You're as bad as *they* are."

"Who?"

"The humans that hate us. The ones that used to round us up with pitchforks and torches. The ones that spray paint our garages and want to gather us up in the center square and burn us because we're different."

"I don't want to burn anybody, Dear."

"The hell you don't." I lowered my head closer to the table as if that would help keep my whispers from being overheard. "Those two people right there," I paused and pointed at the window to the kitchen, "have done more *good* for the people of this town than I could ever *hope* to do. So, if you're going to be a racist asshole, go the fuck home, Mother. Go back to Ashville, fix your broken fucking coven, and stay out of my life."

Power slid down her arms as the anger flared in her eyes. I swear there was a low rumble of thunder that spread through the diner. "I said, watch your tone, *Daughter.*"

"And I should have been a little clearer. Fuck off, *Mother.*"

It had been a long time coming. Truth be told, I was afraid. Afraid of both my mother and my grandmother. Their power was immeasurable. Against a couple platoons of marines, I would have bet all my money on the two of them without a second thought. For the first time in my life, my anger outweighed my better judgement.

The lights above us dimmed as the shadows pulled from beneath every table and corner in the diner. The windows darkened as the sky blackened. Somebody in a booth on the far end of the diner screamed as they looked out the window at the overhead sun. Their fear only fueled my fire.

"Knock it off, the both of you." Nana slapped us both in the head. When the shadows abated and the sky cleared, only then did she shoot us a reproving look. "Daughter, Dorothea is right. I think it is time for you to leave."

"What?"

"You heard me. Go. Goddess knows what her purpose was bidding you to stay, but the benefits could not possibly outweigh your moronic outlook on life. I did *not* raise you to look down your nose at mortals. Your power, and your position, have gone to your head. How they got through that thick skull of yours, I shall never know. But go." She pointed at the door.

"Are you serious?"

Nana nodded.

Mother looked back at me and found only a smoldering glare. The slap Nana had placed upside my head hadn't shocked me into forgiveness, it had only stopped me from doing something monumentally stupid. For that, I was grateful.

137

Without a word, my mother got up and burst through the diner door without so much as a single word.

You could feel the tension drain from the diner when she was gone. "Well. That went well." Nana shot me a reproving look.

"What?"

"I may have sided with you, Granddaughter, but that does not put you in the right."

"Are you kidding me, Nana? She was being a stodgy elitist douche."

"She was. That is why I agreed with you. However, you lack the experience to wage a war with your mother in a town full of innocent people." She motioned to the people behind us.

"Huh?"

"In all our disputes over hundreds of years, how many people do you think were injured in our squabbles?" She cocked an eyebrow at me.

"Uh…none?"

"Precisely. And do you think *you* could accomplish the same?" The disappointment in her look and voice was real. "Especially with all these newfound powers that you can't control? You blotted out the sun, Granddaughter."

"Just for a moment."

Nana just shook her head.

"Everything okay?" Marge asked gingerly as she brought out our food, minus one plate. "Should I keep the other one hot in case she comes back?"

"Everything's fine. Just scolded my daughter for her prank," Nana lied smoothly.

"Remind me never to get scolded by you." She leaned over to me and whispered, "Thank you." And then she kissed me on my head. It didn't go unnoticed by Nana, either. She smiled as Marge stood up. "So, keep the chop steak?"

"No. Give it to another customer," I told her.

"Can't do that. I'll chuck it," she answered.

"Health code?"

"Yeah. They get pissy when they find spit in people's food. Refills?"

Nana and I stared at our plates, shaking our heads.

"Oh, don't worry. I *like* you two." She cackled and wandered off.

"That woman scares me," Nana said deadpan.

"You and me both."

∞ ∞ ∞

"So, what did you wish to talk about, Dorothea?" Nana took my arm as we exited the diner and looked at me out of the corner of her eye. After the incident with Mother, I had gotten sulky. I wasn't feeling guilty, but I regretted starting a fight. It had put me in an untalkative mood, and we'd never gotten around to discussing why I had asked them to lunch in the first place.

One of the diner patrons walked out of the diner and practically shouldered me out of the way. "Fucking witches," he muttered under his breath.

I gripped Nana's outstretched hand and lowered it. He wasn't worth it, and after the show we put on in the diner, we didn't need to stand out any more than we already had.

"I was just going to give him a pig tail."

"Save it for the crowds bearing pitchforks."

Nana sighed but nodded. "Fine. So, what is it?"

"Come on. Let's take a walk."

Arm in arm, I lead her to the park in Central Square and finally parked us on a worn green park bench facing city hall. Staring at the stone architecture and broken clock, I gathered my thoughts.

"You saw him."

"Who?" I asked out of reflex.

"Your father. I can see it on your face."

"You're pretty smart for an old bat."

"Dumb bats don't live long. How?"

"He showed up in my kitchen."

"What did he say?"

139

"That I was a moron for even thinking about coming to rescue him. Then he forbade it and said goodbye. It felt, I don't know. Final?"

"And you sought our counsel on the feasibility of your plan?"

"Do you think I should go through with it?"

"If I thought you had a bat's ass chance in Hades of convincing Belenus to get you there, I would. But she put him there, Granddaughter. I thought maybe we could find another guide to cross you through the Ethereum, but there isn't a god or goddess that would or could."

"She's right, Sister."

Nana and I both froze. My grandmother might not have recognized Candace's voice, but she could feel the power of the goddess behind us. And we both stared as she walked around the park bench and settled down between us. Nana looked at me in wild shock over Candace's head.

We sat for a moment as she lifted her head to the sun, smiled. And sniffed the cold air around us. We'd hit a warm patch, and had a snow melt, but it was still winter in Upstate New York. What she was smelling, I didn't have a clue. The snot was frozen inside my head and I wouldn't have been able to smell a burger under my nose.

"There are times that I do miss walking this world." The goddess smiled up at me.

Without thinking about it, I returned her smile with a gentle pat on the leg. Power flowed through the touch and almost shocked me, numbing the tips of my already frozen fingers. *She*, however, was sitting on the park bench without so much as a jacket.

"So…uh…what brings you to the mortal realm?"

"It is not every day that a new god is born. I thought I would come pay my respects."

"Huh?"

"Did you think you could come into your power and think that the whole universe wouldn't feel it, Sister? Your tryst with *all* of your spheres broke your seventh seal, the one imparting godhood."

"Uh...that was just some freaky shit with my father's spheres and some...uh...intercourse gone wrong."

"That wasn't your father's power, Dorothea. It was *yours*."

"Excuse me?" I blinked down at her doe-like eyes, confusion warring with fear.

"What are gods, Dorothea?"

"She skipped that day in class," Nana quipped.

I shot her a dirty look over Candace's head. "It was just yesterday that I found out where little witches came from. I haven't got a clue where gods come from, Lady." I bowed my head in a little respect.

"The elder gods aren't born. They're made. Forces of nature, creatures and people of immense power, even weapons have become gods. The only thing they need is people worshiping them."

"Like movie stars?" I blinked in confusion.

"No. Humans, for the most part, stopped worshipping and believing in gods a long time ago. They worship their gold, their coins, and ideals that give them the belief they are better than their neighbor. They don't want to believe in *gods*. They want to believe they are *right*."

"They want to fear and believe in their righteousness," I added sadly. All too familiar with the issue.

"Exactly."

"Well, nobody worships me. I can't be a god."

Both the goddess and my grandmother laughed.

"What?"

"Child, you collect people who believe in you and love you with all the power of their people behind them."

"Huh?"

"Think of a god as a pentagram." She drew one in the air in front of us with her fingers. Glowing golden trails followed her fingers until the encircled five-pointed star hovered and stayed. People passing by did a doubletake and hurried away. I fought the urge to rub the bridge of my nose. "The four points below are the spheres. The apex is the god. The quintessence. That is you."

A sinking feeling welled up inside me. "And my four spheres are the dark elves, the demons, the shadows, and the vampires."

"Yes. Just like your father."

"How do you know it wasn't just *his* powers reacting with my lovers?"

"Because his powers are gone."

"Gone?"

"No longer inside you."

"Where'd they go?"

"I do not know. If I had to wager a guess, they went *exactly* where you wanted them to go."

"Back to him?"

She looked at me like I was stupid. I knew, because I got that look a lot. "No. You would've had to have given them to him personally to do that. What was your plan?"

"To put them into the gem."

"Exactly."

There was a glowing red ruby in the jewelry box on my dresser that I *really* needed to put in a safety deposit box. In Fort Knox. Staring at her in amazement, I started hyperventilating. "Why?"

"Why what, Sister?"

"Why does this shit keep happening to me?" Leaning forward, I put my head between my knees and sucked in lung burning gulps of frigid air.

The goddess placed Candace's hand on my back, and I was immediately filled with warmth and love as she stroked me comfortingly. "The universe gets what the universe needs."

"Needs, not wants?"

"Times have changed. People and races have changed. They need a hero. A savior. Someone to guide."

"Isn't that you?"

"My spheres do not reach the darker races. You are *their* goddess."

"I seem to be saying this a lot lately, but I'm just a Dot."

142

Nana *humphed*. "You are a Blackwell, Child."

Instead of taking offense, the goddess nodded and smiled at Nana. "Tis true. She has the blood of more than one god running through her mortal veins."

"What?"

Nana's face darkened.

"What does she mean by that, Nana?"

"Another tale for another time. Let us worry about your future."

The goddess must have agreed with her. She stood and turned to face us. "I cannot help you any more than I already have, Sister. Just know that not all of us agreed with the decision to incarcerate your father for his supposed crimes against the natural order. He is not the only one to have loved a mortal and born or sired offspring. His only crime was his atrocious timing. I have been working long and hard to see that you would have everything you needed to set things right. You have it all right now, you just don't see it."

"What? What do I have?"

"Everything you need to free your father."

"What is it I needed?"

"A way to get to him. A map to find him. And the key to free him."

There was a brief flare of golden light and Candace, the real Candace, blinked at us confusedly. "Dot?"

"Hey, Candy."

"Did you want a coffee?" She looked around the central square.

"Yeah. I think we could all use one."

Chapter 14

"Bill didn't want to go?" Jimmy sounded disappointed. Knowing Jimmy, he probably was.

"He said we should have fun. He had an event he needed to work."

Jimmy shot me a dubious look from the driver's seat of his truck and put it in reverse. Then he did that 'put his arm across the seats so he could look out the back window while he reversed' move. I didn't know what it was about the simple act that turned me on, but it did. It seemed so manly. But when I added in the factor that he had a backup camera in the dash, it seemed kind of stupid, too.

"What event?"

"I don't know. He said something about a protest outside city hall. He wanted to be there in case things got out of hand?"

I shrugged my shoulders.

"What the hell do the people of this town have to protest?"

"Beats the hell out of me. Could be witches for all I know." I laughed at my own joke, and then realized it might not have been.

Jimmy stared at me while I stared at him. "What time?"

"Eight."

"We'll grab some dinner and then check it out. We can catch the later show," he answered levelly.

"Good idea." I sighed and stared out the window, my appetite halved from the worry. "What reason would they have to stage a protest? I mean even *if* it was about witches, who the hell would go stand outside in the middle of winter to hold up as sign that says, 'Down with the witches.'"

"Dumb people."

"We're doomed."

Jimmy chuckled half-heartedly.

"What's for dinner?"

"Well, I was thinking pizza and beer."

"That sounds kinda fucking perfect." I grinned at him. "Antonios?"

"Is there any other place to get pizza in this town?"

"There's the Hut."

"That's not pizza."

"True story."

He turned toward the hospital and hung a left on Elm, parking us across the street from the entrance. "I don't know why I don't order from here more. It's literally two minutes away." I sniffed the air outside the truck as I vacated the vehicle.

"This is Cedar Falls. Everything is two minutes away."

"Fair enough."

Jimmy pulled out his phone. "Dennis just got off. He's meeting us here."

"Sweet."

We walked across the street and Jimmy stepped ahead of me to pull open the brass handled wood door.

"Thank you, Sir."

"Ooh. You called me sir. I like that."

I leaned toward him and took his earlobe in between my teeth, giving it a little squeeze and a lick. "Would you like it better if I called you, Master?"

He shivered in response.

"Keep dreaming." I kissed his cheek and stepped inside.

Antonio's was more of a takeout place, but they did have a small seating area to the right of the kitchen and counter. Jimmy pointed at the tables and nodded to whom I assumed was Antonio.

"Sure thing, Jimbo."

146

"Jimbo?" I chuckled as he pulled out a chair and offered it to me.

"High School. Don't ask."

I giggled and had every intention of asking. "Split a pie and a pitcher?"

"Now you speaka my language." He grinned and sat.

"Pepperoni or sausage?'

"Meatza?"

"Depends on what the hell that is," I answered fearfully.

"Pepperoni, sausage, bacon, and meatball."

"Fuck yeah."

"This is why I love you. One of the three million reasons."

I just grinned.

The only waitress, a fifty something brunette who looked like she could have been Antonio's mother, took our order and brought us a pitcher of beer and three glasses.

"How'd she know?" I nodded at the glass next to Jimmy.

"Because I don't think I've ever been here without Dennis," he answered thoughtfully.

"Not even on a date?"

He chuckled and poured us each a glass. "Couldn't go on a date without my wingman."

"You have issues."

"I know." He grinned and handed me my beer.

Two guys at the table two away from ours kept looking in our direction. One was openly staring, and the other was glancing occasionally over his shoulder. Jimmy was facing me and couldn't see them. I was trying to ignore them, but they were wearing identical T-shirts with the same owl logo on the front and chest.

"What's the matter?" Jimmy asked and took a sip of his beer.

"Nothing yet. Ever see a T-shirt with an owl on it?"

"Nope. Wait. I saw a tootsie pop one once."

"Different owl," I muttered quietly, not wanting them to hear our conversation.

Jimmy, not one to beat around the bush, turned around and caught both of them staring. "We got a problem, guys?"

As if by magic, they both focused on their pizza.

Jimmy turned back around and smiled. "Problem solved."

"Real smooth." I chuckled.

"Let me know if they start staring again."

"How'd you know they were staring?"

"Only one thing in this world would bother you."

"Being the center of attention," I answered for him, with a little sigh and nodding in agreement.

He smiled in response and then waved at the door.

I almost yelped when a set of lips touched my cheek. "Sorry, Dot."

"Just startled me." He had. The guys in the OWL shirt's kind of put me on edge. I'd jumped when Dennis kissed me, even though I had known he was there. Not a good sign. I took a sip of beer and tried to relax.

"What's up?" Dennis could feel the tension in the air.

"Nothing Dot couldn't handle, handcuffed and blindfolded." Jimmy poured Dennis a glass and slid it over to him.

"So, what movie are we seeing?"

"New Star Wars."

Dennis groaned. I couldn't help myself; he was just to nerdy cute. I leaned over and kissed him.

"Well, if they would make another fucking Star Trek, we would go see *that*. Quit your whining, Trekkie."

"Tell you what," I said and rubbed his leg. Next week, you and I will have a Star Trek marathon. All the movies we can watch. Just you and me."

"Will you talk dirty to me in Klingon?"

"I'll have to get a dictionary, but yes."

"Deal." He grinned.

Outnumbered, the two guys with the staring problem decided it was time to leave. Thankfully. "Fucking witch," one of them mumbled as he walked past me, bumping the back of my chair with his hip.

"You're sorry," I muttered and added a gratuitous, "Asshole."

I waited for them to round on us, and when they didn't, I looked up at their retreating backs. Closer, I could make out the words under the owl motif.

"Fuck."

"What?" Jimmy asked, ready to go after them.

"I think we'll be seeing them tonight. Did you read their shirt?"

"No? Just saw the owl."

"OWL is an acronym. Oswego Witch Lynchers."

"Oh, this is gonna be *fun*," Jimmy said with an eyeroll.

"What the hell did I miss?" Dennis looked from Jimmy to me.

∞ ∞ ∞

"Maybe the Meatza wasn't such a good idea," I said and burped a cacophony of sausage, pepperoni, bacon, and meatball flavored air as I stepped down from the truck and slammed the creaking door shut.

"It's the gift that keeps on giving." Dennis grinned as he got out of the back.

"Look at the bright side. You don't live with Dennis," Jimmy said as he stepped up onto the curb by the bookstore. "Meatza farts peel paint."

"You sure you want to park all the way over here?" I nodded at the store.

"One, parking in center square sucks. Two, I don't want those assholes anywhere near my truck." He rubbed the side of his battered baby.

"Yeah. Goddess forbid, they knock some of the rust off." Dennis rolled his eyes.

"That's what is holding this magnificent work of art together."

"Come on. Let's check out the owl party so we can go enjoy the movie," I told the both of them and waved at Shea through the front window of the bookstore before leading the way to central square.

I yelped again when Shea stepped out of the shadows beside the bookstore. "I would not advise you going this way, Master," he said solemnly, with a little bow.

"If it's about the protest rally, I already know."

He lifted his head. "And you would still go there?"

"Yep. Tis better to know thyne enemy and all that. Don't worry. I won't hurt them." I leaned over and gave him a little kiss.

"That was never my concern," he said dreamily as I pulled away.

"What was? You don't think they would hurt me? You know that would never happen."

He shook his head. "No. Not that either. I'm worried about someone doing them harm and you using your magic to protect them."

"That would be a good thing, right? They'd see how awesome we are and forget about the whole little protest thingy."

"No. They would see it as you bringing their nightmares to life. They will see how powerful you are and fear us even more."

That was Shea. The wise sage. Thinking things through from twenty different directions while I had trouble picking out which underwear I wanted. Sighing, I nodded. "That may be true. But if there are people who might be injured, I cannot sit by and let it happen."

"Which is exactly why you shouldn't go down there. Call it a foreboding. Call it a premonition. Call it whatever you wish, but please. Go have some pie instead." He paused and looked over my shoulder at Jimmy and Dennis. "Or sex. You like that almost as much as pie."

I nodded. Pretty emphatically. I may have even looked over at the diner for a moment and thought about pie. Then the realization of what might, and what might not happen made up my mind. Either way, I had to know. Sighing, I put my hand on Shea's shoulder. "You know I have to go. I will do my best not to be seen, but I have to."

He sighed and bowed, moving out of my way. "I am going with you."

What the fuck is going on? Yuki was drawing on her iPad, in her bed at the house. I could feel her tension and anxiety.

Nothing.

Bullshit. She appeared at my side with a gust of wind a moment later. "Please tell me you're not about to do something abysmally stupid."

"You know I can't make that promise. Ever."

Ellis and Dar stepped out of the store. I could feel Chief standing in the square, hands on his hips as he turned toward my direction. Jason sat down at the desk in the office, rubbing the bridge of his nose.

None of them said a word, not one of them tried to stop me. They were all there for me. Except Yuki. She was a little white ball of snarling canine fury. "Gah!" She raised her hands to the sky and then slapped her thighs in frustration.

"Come on, Squishy. It'll be fun."

"I said gah, not glaaah." She made zombie motions with her hands, wiggling her forearms back and forth.

We headed for the central square.

As soon as we made it, I started laughing. The others chuckled and shifted nervously. In the park, the one that had been an open pit into the deepest reaches of Hell hardly a month before, stood about thirty people in dingy jeans and freshly printed OWL T-shirts. A few of them were toting effigies of witches in nooses, a couple of them were holding unlit tiki torches, and the rest were holding up poster boards with badly written racial slurs towards the magically gifted community. No one else was paying any attention to them. Not even Chief, who was striding purposely towards us trying to hide his smile.

"Impressive turnout." I snickered when he was close enough.

"Yeah. Don't know why you thought you needed to be here. I wouldn't even let them light the torches. Fire Marshal said it was a fire hazard."

"Well, I feel like an idiot." I was almost disappointed. I thought we were facing a major problem. In a town of a couple thousand, if thirty of those hated me, I'd call that a good day. I had more people than that in Ashville who hated me, and *everybody* knew about witches. I blamed my mother for that ratio, though.

"Thought you were going to a movie?"

"And miss all this excitement?" I motioned toward the crowd with my hands.

"Coffee?"

"Love some." I turned around. "Everybody get back to work. Party's over."

The tension in the group lifted. The nervous chuckles turned into full-fledged laughter of relief. Not that I could blame them. It was one thing to expect to be hated and feared, and another to realize that maybe you were imagining the whole thing. "Try and stay out of trouble, Master," Shea said with a grin and pulled Dar and Ellis into the shadows of the building entrance we were skirting.

"I'm going back to bed." Yuki *humphed* and disappeared with a mini tornado of leaves.

"Can we get out of the cold now?" Jimmy had his hands stuffed in the pockets of his jeans and implored me with his eyes.

"You bet. I'm buying." It was only fair. He bought dinner.

He and Dennis started walking toward the diner, gratefully. Chief had just put his hand on the small of my back to move me along when a scream tore through the square. The crowd of thirty protesters had scattered. Where they had been standing, one of them was lying on the ground, hands clutching his throat as red stained the brown grass before him.

Another was pinned against a tree, vainly batting against the head of the vampire that held him there while he fed from the gaping wound he'd torn open. Four more were herding the scattering protestors toward the large alleyway beside city hall.

Lord Abernathy Jr. had made another move.

"Fuck," I grumbled and ignored Shea's warning. Striding toward the commotion, I yanked the broom charm from my neck and held a broom a moment later. One shake of my arm and a silent command later, I held the scythe.

The vampires were having a ball. There wasn't an iota of fear from them. But the scared shitless humans assaulted my olfactory senses and brought out the vampire in me. I snarled in rage. Then, and only then, did the vampires sense me. Slowly they turned. The one that was feeding dropped the human and sighed when he saw my approach. A moment later, Yuki was back at my side as we bore down on them.

Normally, when she moved, I couldn't follow her movements. She was that fast. Time slowed as my other senses took over illuminating the square in silver light. Each of her footfalls echoed in my ears as she broke off and headed toward the corralling vampires, breaking them up with well-placed kicks and punches. The humans didn't stop to watch the show, not that their eyes could have followed what was happening.

One moment I was launching myself at the feeder, and the next I was beside him, unsure if it was my vampiric powers that had gotten me there, or if I had simply stepped through the shadows. Either way, a moment later, his head thudded against the nearly frozen ground as he disappeared in a burst of ash.

We're killing them? Yuki wasn't delighted, but she wasn't sad either.

At this point, we have to.

I felt her mental nudge of agreement. Kicks and punches turned into bone crunching, wet squelches as she used the only weapons she had to separate their heads from their bodies. Her hands.

Shea stepped out of the shadows and separated another head with his keen, wicked looking dagger. Dar and Ellis ran back into the square. Dar immediately joined the battle while Ellis, surprisingly enough, aided the wounded, and hopefully not dead, humans. His hands were aglow with purplish fire.

Some of the vampires in the local branch of the clan were formidable. Not one of the ones in the square were anywhere close to being remotely powerful. Abernathy had managed to cultivate the weakest of the bunch. But his intention had never been about winning, it had been about exposure. In *that*, he had succeeded.

"Fuck." I stood atop the steps of city hall and surveyed the damage. Of the vampires, there was nothing left but dust. The one human sat at the base of the tree covered in blood. Another was being held up by his brethren. The one lying on the ground didn't make it. Ellis' stare and sad shake of his head told me that much. Absolutely *pissed*, I banished the scythe and hung the broom charm back on the leather thong around my neck. Shoving my hands back in my pockets, I headed toward Chief to figure out if there was any way to salvage the situation.

I made it halfway toward him when one of the OWLs pulled a gun and shot me in the head.

Chapter 15

"Will you shut off whatever the fuck is beeping. My head is fucking killing me." The nurse's shoes screeched against the linoleum tiled floor. Then her voice matched the sound of her shoes still echoing in my cranium as she took off running without shutting off the goddess damned beeping machine.

Holding up my hand, I smothered it with shadows until it was muffled enough that the pain subsided, and my eye stopped twitching in time. Muffled meeps I could stand. Ear piercing beeps, not so much.

Two sets of racing footsteps returned a moment later.

Without opening my eyes, I knew it was Dr. Shapiro. I recognized his scent the moment he walked through my door. "I guess I shouldn't be surprised you're awake. Let alone alive."

"Hey, Doc."

"Can you...uh...release my machine? I want to check your vitals."

"Can you put it on mute?"

"Yes."

I waved my hand, releasing it from its shadow cocoon. It beeped twice before he found the right button and made my fucking day. "Thank you."

"You're welcome."

"So, what's the prognosis?"

"Your vitals are stable, EEG normal, and you seem fine."

"Why do I feel a but coming on?"

"You need surgery to get the bullet out of your brain."

"It's still in there?"

"The guy shot you with a thirty-two ACP. I can't believe it made it through your thick skull to begin with." He sighed.

I opened my eyes and instantly regretted the decision. The blinding white lights of the overhead fluorescents were twenty times worse than the incessant beeping. My eyes twitched and started watering. Closing them as quickly as I could, I felt for the wound in my skull. That wasn't there.

"Don't bother. You healed right up."

"With a bullet in my brain."

"Yep."

"Lucky me."

"Come on. We're going to take you down for some more X-rays. I want another look before we put you on the operating table."

"X-rays? Not an MRI?"

"Steel jacket. Probably not the best idea to put you in a machine with giant spinning magnets. You'll scramble what you got left."

"That's pleasant."

"Oh, I'm sorry. Did you want me to sugar coat the fact that you have a fucking bullet lodged in your brain?"

"Maybe." I grinned without looking at him.

"Just do me a favor. Promise me that if you survive this, you'll stop putting yourself in situations where you end up in my hospital?"

"I didn't plan on being here to begin with. Not every day you get shot by the dickhead you were trying to save."

"I heard."

"You did?" I opened my eyes again. Involuntary reflex. The lights didn't seem half as bright and the pain was almost gone.

"Yeah. You came in with an entourage. They were calm but chatty. Almost like they knew you weren't in any danger?"

"Yeah. Short of incinerating me, I'm a pretty tough cookie."

"Nut."

"Nut?"

"Cookies are sweet. Nuts…"

"Are crazy?'

"Tough. Hard to crack."

"I don't know if I should be flattered or insulted." I sat up and turned on the bed, attempting to stand.

"What the hell are you doing?" He stepped forward and pushed me back down.

"You said I have to go for an X-ray?"

"Yeah. I've got some orderlies coming to wheel the bed down, dumbass." He *huffed* and shook his head, staring at me incredulously.

"Don't think you're supposed to call your patients dumb."

"I didn't. I called you a dumbass. It's a term of endearment."

"Awww. You like me." I grinned.

He chuckled and leaned over, pushing a few more buttons on the machine. I was kind of surprised. Usually doctors didn't have a fucking clue how the arcane machines worked and left them to their much smarter counterparts. Nurses. "I've never seen you do harm. Only good. That makes you sort of okay in my book."

"Gee. Thanks, Doc."

"Don't mention it."

"I'm surprised Materos let me in through the front door."

"You came in the back. ER entrance."

"Well, I'm surprised he didn't wheel my bed out the front door into traffic."

"Materos is…indisposed at the moment."

"How so?" He had officially piqued my interest.

"He's sitting in a jail cell."

"What? What for?"

"He was the one who shot you."

∞ ∞ ∞

157

"I don't fucking believe it." Shapiro was holding the X-ray up to the light, blinked twice and actually took the time to clip it into the wall reader. He flipped the switch and put his face about three inches from the giant picture of my skull.

"What?"

"It's gone!"

"My brain?" I chuckled at my own joke.

"I'm not sure if that was ever there to begin with. I meant the bullet."

"It just disappeared? You sure it didn't come out the other side?"

"See this darker area?" He used the tip of his first two fingers to swirl around a spot somewhere between my ears.

"Yes?"

"That's where it *was*. I saw your initial X-ray. I was thinking it was scarring, but now I'm not so sure."

"What do you mean?"

"I think the bullet disintegrated."

"Disintegrated?"

He sighed and turned to me. "Are you just going to repeat everything I say?"

"No."

He turned back to the X-ray. "See the pattern around what should be a wound? It's too dark to be scarring. I think it's metal."

"So, I have metal swirling around my brain?"

"It looks like it. The walls of your veins are pretty thick. The veins in your brain…they're a lot thinner. Probably because they're not surrounded by muscle. It's like the bullet's being absorbed into them. See how the darkening gets worse along this line?"

"Yes?"

"That's an interior cerebral vein. Now see how it turns here?" He slid his finger over a little more.

"Doc. Blah, blah, blah, science stuff."

"That's your inferior anastomotic vein. It's like it's getting sucked into it. I can't believe it. You are pretty fucking incredible. If there wasn't metallic dust in your head, I would send you down for an MRI anyway." He put his hand under his chin and refused to tear his eyes away from the film.

"When I'm dead, I'll donate my body. You can study me to your heart's content."

He turned to me and narrowed his eyes. "Can't study a body once it's been incinerated. Since that's the only way you'd end up in my morgue, I'm shit out of luck."

"You'd totally dissect me now if you could. Wouldn't you?" I was almost afraid. He had that mad scientist look in his eyes. When he turned to look at me, it was like I was a big juicy steak.

"Of course not. But, when you're all healed and the metal is out of your head, would you mind stopping by for a couple of tests and scans?"

I narrowed my eyes at him. "For your own personal curiosity or for a medical journal?"

He sighed. "I'd love to say my own personal curiosity, but the temptation to share what you are, and what you can do, with the world would be too great. Even if I ask again, say no."

I chuckled, slid off the hospital bed, and kissed him on his cheek. "That was for being honest. And not poking and prodding me while I was unconscious."

"Judging by my waiting room, I think you get enough poking and prodding." He chuckled and wiggled his eyebrows.

For the first time in a *very* long time, I blushed. "You have no idea."

"No, but I can imagine. Go on. Get out of here. You're taking up a valuable hospital bed."

"How much do I owe you.?"

"You were never a patient here. Can't charge you." He winked and left me standing there.

A nurse came in moment later with a set of hospital scrubs. "I managed to save your shoes, but they were about the only thing not soaked in blood," she said and set them on the bed beside me. She turned to leave, but stopped and faced me. "You're real, aren't you?"

"Last time I checked?"

"I mean witches. What those assholes were protesting in the square. You're really, really real, aren't you?"

I opened my mouth to deny it, but I stopped myself. A vague recollection of a nurse eating her lunch and running for her life stopped me. She was there. "Does that scare you?"

"Honey, I was in the square. I just saw shit that would scare a doctor's handwriting straight. You weren't the bad guy."

"No. Those were vampires," I answered slowly. "But not all of them are like that."

"It wasn't them that scared me, either. It was the crazy look in those assholes' eyes. Especially Dr. Materos. You had literally just saved his life when he pulled a gun on you and *shot* you. *Those* are the things that scare me." She shuddered but then flashed me a brief smile. "You keep true. And tell Candy that Roberta says hi. And we really miss her here."

"You haven't seen her since she left?"

"No?"

"She works at the coffee shop in the bookstore."

"I'll have to stop in there for lunch one day." Her eyes brightened a little, but Candace did that to everybody.

"Her fiancé is my–" I stopped myself from finishing *that* sentence. "Best friend. Tell 'em I sent ya."

"I will." She flashed another small smile and gave me a nod, leaving me to get dressed and get the hell out of there.

∞ ∞ ∞

"We missed the movie." Jimmy huffed, but I could tell he wasn't serious.

"I'm sure I can think of *some* way to make it up to you." I chuckled in the seat next to him.

"Not tonight. I'm taking you home and putting you into bed. A bullet in the brain counts as a 'Not tonight, Honey. I have a headache.'"

"That's just it. I don't. I feel fine. It's kind of scary."

"It is," Dennis added from the back seat. "But it's also fucking awesome. If you'd been a normal witch, you would have died tonight."

I could feel the sadness radiating from him like heat. He'd been scared. They all had. Until they saw the wound close and my continued breathing. It was the only reason Materos was sitting in a cell and not a grave. Even still, it had been close. Yuki, believe it or not, had been the voice of reason.

As soon as I had walked out of the hallway into the waiting room, Jimmy, Dennis, Shea, Dar, and Yuki had swooped me outside the hospital to tell me who had shot me. They'd been almost disappointed I'd already found out. After he pulled the trigger, Dar shifted into a hell hound, Jimmy hit him with a right hook, Shea had his dagger pulled and an arm around his neck as he was falling to the ground. Dennis was casting a petrification spell, while Chief was drawing his gun. But it was Yuki who dislodged my little assassin and put herself between Materos and everybody else, shaking her head sadly. All she had said was, "No."

And they listened.

I owed Yuki big time.

"So, what happened to the rest of the OWLs?" I looked over at Jimmy for an answer.

"As soon as Materos shot you, the rest of the OWLs scattered like vermin. They wanted nothing to do with Materos or the murder charges."

"That was smart and kind of cowardly."

Jimmy nodded. "Please don't do that again."

"Do what?"

161

"Get shot. Even though we saw the wound close and you not dying, we knew you were going to be okay, but still. That was one of the most horrific moments of my life."

I nodded and gave him a reassuring kiss. "I'll try. So, what is going to happen to Materos?"

Jimmy just shrugged.

While he deserved whatever he got, I still couldn't shake the nagging feeling that I was responsible for his actions. I needed to make it right if I was ever going to get rid of the guilt. It even came before a shower. Which was saying a lot since my hair was caked with blood. "Stop by the station a minute. I want to check on Chief."

"He wanted to be there when you got out, but he had to haul that dick down to the jail."

"I know. I'm not mad!" I laughed and held up my hands defensively. "I want to know what he's going to do to Materos."

"Charge him for attempted murder?"

"He can't. Then he'd have to explain me walking around. The new DA is a thousand times better than the last one, but still. No."

"Well, he can't let him go. The fucker shot you, Dot. He deserves…"

"To die? No. I'm going to talk to him. I'll figure something out."

"You're going to scare him?"

"He's already afraid. I think that's what's driving him insane. And making him go to such great lengths to make our lives miserable."

"Then there's nothing left."

"There's always other options, Jimmy. Pull over."

He sighed and parked by the bookstore. "Want us to go with you?"

"No." I softened my response with a smile and a kiss.

"I get one of those, too. Right?" Dennis' head appeared between he seats.

He was just too damn cute. "Of course. Even bigger than the one I gave Jimmy." I put my hand on his cheek and held him steady while I locked my lips to his.

"Hey! How come he gets a bigger kiss?"

"He didn't try and stop me from talking to Materos." I stuck my tongue out at him and slipped out of the truck.

I opened the station door and Marcus turned around from the copy machine and dropped the stack of paper in his hands. "Holy fuck."

"What'sa matter, Marcus?"

"What the hell are you doing out of the hospital?"

"A mere flesh wound. Bullet grazed me," I lied with a grin. "Chief in?"

"The back," he answered and hooked his thumb over his shoulder. Marcus could only stare at me with his mouth hanging open. As I reached for the knob, he finally found his words. "Glad you're okay."

"You and me both." I smiled and pulled the door open.

Chief was sitting at his desk, head in his hands, when I finally made it to his office. When he heard me, he looked up and sighed. "Thank the Lady."

"Missed you, too."

He got up, walked around the desk, and threw his arms around me, burying his face in my neck. The non-bloody side. "Thank the goddess for your vampiric healing…"

I let it go at that. "You keep thanking her like that and she might show up," I chided softly.

"Why are you here?" He pulled back and narrowed his eyes at me.

"Came to talk to Materos."

"No. No way in hell."

"I'm not going to hurt him, jackass."

"That's not what I'm afraid of. If you wanted him dead, Yuki wouldn't have stopped us," he answered thoughtfully.

"What?"

"Nothing. Just think she knew how you felt and was acting as you while you were…out."

"Probably. So, can I see him?"

163

He wanted to say no. I could feel it. I could see it on his face. But he didn't. "Fine. But not alone."

"Of course not." I motioned toward the holding area.

Chief grabbed his ginormous ring of keys off his desk and led the way. Unable to stop myself, I frowned at the all too familiar setting and my butt puckered at my memory of the last time I was in there. When he moved out of the way, the look on Materos' face was pure terror as he finally let his eyes focus on me.

"No. No no no no noooooooooo. You can't be!"

"Alive? Sorry to disappoint you. Though, you shouldn't be. I just saved you from a lifetime of orange jumpsuits and an eternally sore anus." I grinned at him through the bars. "Why'd you shoot me, Materos?"

"Because you are the spawn of *Satan!*"

I sighed and shook my head. He was loony tunes. You could see it in his eyes. Getting attacked by vampires and shooting me had been the last straw. He was gone and there was no reasoning with him whatsoever. "Let him out, Chief."

"What?"

"Look at him. He's literally insane." I motioned toward his cell.

"Well, I can't let him go! He shot you!"

"And what are you going to tell the DA? That he missed? You know this can't go to court."

Apparently Chief hadn't been thinking about it at all. I saw the little lightbulb go off in his head.

"Of course not. I uh…fuck. What the hell are we going to do?"

"This is your job. Not mine. I'm just the target dummy."

"That's not funny." He narrowed his eyes at me.

"Spaaaaaawn of Satan. Satin. Finish."

"Shut up," we both said to Materos.

"Boil me up. Put me in an oven. You know you're going to."

His ramblings gave me a flash of brilliance. "Have him committed."

"What?"

"Well, fucking look at him. He got hit with all the draw fours and he's still not playing with a full deck. Call a psychiatrist. Have him put in a mental hospital." I paused to look at him. "Hell. I'll even pay."

"Why?"

"I don't know. I mean between everything. Jimmy, his brother getting eaten by Squishy the Third, getting attacked by vampires... I feel kind of guilty."

"And sometimes bad shit happens to bad people. It's called Karma, Dot. And it's a bitch."

"But so am I." I grinned at him.

"I'll make you a deal. I'll make the call and have him remanded to a *state*-run facility. Either they can take the cost out of his savings or the state can pay. You're not footing the bill for this asshole."

"Fine. But it was a good idea, yeah?"

"Yeah." He actually smiled.

"What about the other body?"

"What other body?" He winked at me.

Chapter 16

"There. That's the *last fucking one.*" I straightened up slowly in the back of the delivery truck. Normally when we ordered stock, they shipped it freight on a delivery truck from the distribution center in Syracuse. Unfortunately, our last order had been so huge we'd gotten the whole front half of an eight-wheeler. It was no small fucking wonder why Jason had snickered and said, "Sure," when I asked if he needed any help.

He hadn't even let me use the old 'but I just got out of the hospital' routine, either.

Dar grunted as he took the last box of books and headed through the back door. I just slid them from the front of the truck to the back. He and Ellis had carried every single one inside First Moon Books. I probably shouldn't have complained.

I hopped down off the back of the truck and almost collided with the driver walking around the back at the same moment.

"Woah!" He gave a startled jump.

"Sorry. All done. She's yours again."

"You know, if you had a loading dock, they could have palleted and shrink wrapped all the boxes."

"And miss all this fun?" I laughed as he held out the bill of lading and a pen.

I signed in the received box and handed it back to him without even looking at the box quantity. He seemed honest enough. If anything was missing, Dar would let me know and I could bitch later. "Thanks…"

"Mickey."

"Thanks, Mickey. Can I buy you a coffee?"

He smiled and tipped his hat. "I'd love to, but I have to get back and loaded up again. Maybe next time."

"Suit yourself. Have a good one." I headed toward the back door, turned, and yanked it shut behind me as I stepped into the much warmer back room. Sighing in relief, I shucked my jacket and screeched.

Candace was standing there holding out a warm cup of coffee for me. "Sorry, Lady."

"No, you're not." I returned her grin, took the coffee, and ruffled her hair. "Thanks, Sweetie."

"Welcome."

"How come Josie let you out of the pit?"

"Lunch." She leaned against one of the metal shelves filled with cardboard boxes.

"Why aren't you eating?"

She shrugged.

"Everything okay?" I narrowed my eyes at her in suspicion.

"Now that we have some help, we can actually take breaks. But Josie doesn't think we should be away from the shop at the same time." So help me goddess, Candace pouted. My heart broke. I couldn't take the cute.

"And you're lonely?"

She nodded and huffed, the blast of air directed upward, blowing a few loose strands of her corn silk hair out of her eyes.

"You want to have lunch with me?" There was a moment of excitement, but then she eyed the chafing dishes full of Herb's finest with a bit of distaste. "Too much meat?"

She nodded.

"Want to go get a salad?"

"Can we?"

"Sure. Come on." I held out my hand and grabbed my jacket with the other.

She took my hand and we headed into the store, not stopping until we were out the front door. I eyed the diner.

The last place in the state you wanted to go for a salad. Marge would probably flog you if you tried to order one and bring you a burger instead. In fact, I was at a loss. A fact that didn't go unnoticed by Candace.

"Come with me." She snickered and pulled me toward the central square.

As far as I knew, there wasn't any restaurants there, but the few times I'd actually set foot in the area, I'd been fighting demons or vampires and not looking for food. "Where are we going?"

"It's called Charlotte's."

It sounded like a place that would serve salads. "Never noticed it before."

"Most people don't. It's quiet. I like it." She grinned up at me.

We rounded the corner but stayed on the sidewalk instead of heading toward City Hall. Charlotte's Bistro was at the end. It was no wonder I'd never noticed it. You couldn't even see it unless you were standing in front of it. Candy opened the door and the warm rush of baking bread wafted over you like a warm and fuzzy blanket. "Holy shit."

Candace just nodded.

"Welcome to Charlotte's! Oh! Hey, Candace," a twenty-something or other walked out from behind the counter and hugged her. "Who's this?" She looked up at me after she pulled away.

"This is Lady." For some reason, Candace took a step back so Charlotte could get a better look at me.

"I've heard a lot about you." She didn't frown, but it was pretty damn close.

"You must be Charlotte?"

Candace snickered. "No. This is her daughter, Charlie."

I blinked in confusion. "Really?"

"Really," Charlie answered and held out her hand.

The moment my fingers touched hers, her human seeming melted away. Her round eyes elongated into a very familiar almond shape, and her ears stretched and

169

tapered until they were almost even with the top of her head. Charlie was an elf. She noticed my surprise.

"Charlie is just short for Charlenthiel. Figured I should make it easy for the common folk."

"Doesn't exactly roll off the tongue." I didn't yank my hand away, but something inside me made me want to. Probably because Jaeren was such a prick.

"You have forsaken the light. Tis only natural," she answered as if she were reading my thoughts. Either that, or I was making an unpleasant face.

"I didn't forsake anything. The night is just more fun."

"And yet you walk in the company of the sun." She smiled down at Candace. Somebody had a little crush. I wondered how Josie felt about that... "Sit anywhere you'd like. The lunch rush is over." Since the small shop only had about ten tables, the lunch rush must have been spectacular, to say the least.

Charlie walked over to the counter and grabbed a couple of menus. Candace gave me an embarrassed, apologetic look and tugged my hand to the table closest to the door.

"What can I get you to drink?" Charlie put our menus down on the table and folded her hands in front of her.

"Water, please," Candace said almost too softly to hear.

"Do you have Coke?"

She frowned. "No. We have assorted teas and juices."

Luckily, our lunch date was about Candace and not me. "Tea?"

"Sweet, unsweet, peach, raspberry, dragon fruit, or boba?"

"Boba?"

"It's juice infused tapioca balls."

"I didn't know tapiocas had balls." I laughed at my joke. I was the only one. "Sweet. Please." I was definitely in the wrong restaurant. Marge would have at least chuckled.

"Be right back with your drinks." Charlie headed toward the back.

"I don't think she likes me very much…"

"You are the queen of the night and the master of the undead. Give her some time."

"She'll like me when she gets to know me?"

"Probably not. But she might learn to school her dislike."

"I can live with that." Picking up the menu, I frowned at the selections. Ninety-eight percent of it had kale in it. "What do you suggest?"

"They have a turkey burger."

"Does it have kale on it?"

"You can hold the kale."

"I'd prefer not to touch it." I found the turkey burger on the menu and frowned even more. I could only pronounce half of the toppings. "When in Rome."

"Do as the Romans?"

"Try not to get stabbed in the back."

Charlie returned and gave us our drinks. Candace ordered for us both, and Charlie didn't hesitate before heading back to the safety of the kitchen.

Sighing, I put my chin in my hand, leaned against the arm of the wicker-encrusted chair, and looked around. As much as I hated to admit it, the place was cute.

"You will like the food, Lady."

"As long as Charlie doesn't slip some elven poison in it, I'm sure it will be delicious." For the first time in my life, I fervently wished I had brought Jaeren with me. He was royalty. That might have put the snooty elf in her place. He might have been king of a different elfhame for all I knew, but still. Elves respected royalty. Even when they were pompous airbags.

"Light elves would never resort to poison, Lady."

"Too pure for that?"

"Magic is more efficient."

She wasn't making me feel any better. "I see why you like this place."

"Because?"

"It's light and airy. Cute. Just like you."

Candace blushed, almost putting her face behind her hands. I couldn't help but smile, and I relaxed a little. With the opening of the bookstore, she and Josie had been run ragged. I missed my little fey-blooded ball of sunshine.

"How are you and Josie doing? Getting excited about moving into your house?"

She nodded, very emphatically. I was almost worried about her head toppling off her neck.

"Getting sick of your old Aunt Dot already?"

She shook her head as equally as violent. But then she sighed and sipped her water. She seemed to be struggling to ask me something but finally blurted out, "Are you ever going to tell her?"

"Tell who?"

"Josie."

"Uhhh. Tell her what?"

She raised one of her perfectly manicured eyebrows at me. Maybe they were natural. It wasn't as if I'd ever seen Candace plucking them, but nothing could be that natural and perfect. It wouldn't have been fair to the rest of us. "The truth?"

"What truth?" An icy fist clamped around my heart.

Candace sighed, set her water down on the table in front of her, and leaned forward on her elbows. "I know."

"That…"

"She is your sibling."

"How did you find out?"

She smiled at me. "Since the moment I saw you in the same room as her. Your power is very similar, just in vastly different quantities."

"Why didn't you say anything?"

"Because neither of you knew. I could tell that much, too. But then when you found out, I could feel it. It wasn't my place to say anything in front of Josie, but now that I have you alone… When are you going to tell her?"

"When that knowledge won't be a danger."

"You're fooling yourself."

Candace was shy and demure. *Most* of the time. When she had her moments of...clarity, she was almost scary in her conviction and sincerity. "About what?"

"That you think Josie is the reason why you haven't told her."

I forgot to mention that she was pretty fucking insightful, too. "I don't know what you're talking about."

Candace trailed her finger through the condensation on her glass and then rubbed it between her thumb and forefinger, thinking. "You're afraid that she will be upset."

"Of what?"

"Exactly."

I blinked in confusion.

"Do you honestly think the joy of finding out you are her *sister* would outweigh the shock?"

I sighed. "It's not the shock of it that I'm worried about. Josie... She's been my best friend forever. Since the day we were born. Our *lives* were vastly different."

"How?"

"You've met her mother?"

Candace shuddered. "But I have also met yours. I see problems with both."

"You hit the nail on the head. But my mother was the high priestess of the coven. Magic came easy to me. I had a super-hot boyfriend. There were *many* times that Josie and I drifted apart."

"Because she was jealous."

I shrugged. "I don't know. Maybe."

"I wasn't asking."

"Oh."

"And you think if she finds out you are siblings, she will be angry because you are so vastly different?"

"Yes."

"You both have one very important thing in common."

"What?"

"You both can be very stupid." She finished just as Charlie set our food in front of us and picked up our half-

173

empty glasses for refills. She did snicker when she heard Candy call me stupid but left it at that.

I was shocked. Candace had called me stupid and I didn't think I'd ever been more proud of her.

She realized what she had said, blushed, and picked up her fork. She immediately started rummaging through the leaves and scooped out a candied almond. "Sorry, Lady."

"Don't you dare be. I am being stupid. My little Candace is growing up. Sniff."

She stuck her tongue out and put the candied nut in her mouth, groaning in pleasure.

"Good?"

She nodded and plucked another on out of her salad and put it on the plate next to my giblet burger. It looked about a thousand times more appetizing than the faux lunch on my plate, so I tried it and groaned a little, too.

"See?"

"Yeah, yeah. Salad good. Burger bad. Bad Dot."

She snickered.

"Kind of surprised, though."

"About what?"

"I never thought I'd see the day you put nuts in your mouth." I grinned at her, earning myself an eyeroll.

"So, are you going to tell her?"

"Fine. Yes."

"When?"

"At your wedding. How's that?"

A tear actually slid from the corner of her eye and she nodded even harder than before, smiling as she nimbly bit the leafy greens from her fork.

Charlie set our glasses on the table and blinked as a thundering boom echoed in time with the contact. She even picked them up and looked at the bottom of the glasses. "What was that?"

Candace pointed outside.

Charlie turned, gasped, and backed toward the register.

"Relax. I think they're here for me," I said and stood, frowning at the winged angel through the glass.

It stared back at me, not moving from the rippled grass where it landed at the edge of the park. From its back, it unsheathed a silver sword that erupted in yellow flame as it was exposed to the sunlight. Pointing the tip of the blade in my direction, its maw opened, exposing rows of razor-sharp teeth. Something told me it wasn't there for the turkey burger.

"What does an angel of light want with you?" Charlie's voice quivered in fear.

"Beat's the hell out of me. I haven't seen one in a month. Thought they gave up trying to drag me to Hell."

I could feel her 'I told you so' stare at Candace.

"Do not go out there, Lady."

"If I don't. It will come in." I headed for the door, practically dragging Candace with me as she tugged on my shirt, frantically trying to keep me inside.

"Please."

"Stay here, Candy." I looked at Charlie over my shoulder and nodded toward Candace. When the elf's arms were around her, I opened the door and stepped outside. Only when the door clicked behind me did I started walking toward the very un-angelic looking angel. How anyone who had ever seen one could mistake them for creatures of good, I would never know. They were the stuff of nightmares, with pretty wings. "What can I do for you?"

"You have shattered the natural order and are an obscenity."

"What the hell are you talking about? I'm not pregnant."

It tilted its head in confusion. They were bright on the outside just not in the head. "You have accumulated the powers of a god."

"I had the powers of a god. The god you dragged kicking and screaming into Tartarus. So?"

"It was decreed eons ago that there shall be no new gods."

"You know you guys should really advertise this stuff. How the hell was I supposed to know? Don't get a mortal preggers. Don't become a god. I swear, you guys make this shit up as you go along."

It closed the distance between us and brough the sword down in an arc that nearly sliced me in half. Under the bright, midday sun, I was practically powerless, but I was still a witch. My shadows couldn't help me. The only vampire at my disposal was Yuki. Ellis could function in daylight, but he probably didn't even know I was in danger. Dar, on the other hand, was already running from the store. I could feel him. Yuki wasn't far behind him. Either way, I'd most likely be dead before they got there. I barely managed to dodge the sword as it sliced into the concrete beside me.

I almost laughed. It had barely missed, but the blade was embedded in the ground. Just as I thought there was an opening, I launched a bolt of fire but nearly got cleaved in half as it swung its sword sideways, flinging chunks of concrete behind its blade.

Luckily, my vampiric speed kicked in and my body bent like a reed in the wind, the flaming trails close enough to my face that I wouldn't need to bleach anything for a few weeks. At my awkward angle, I didn't have a chance in hell of blocking the fist that bashed me in the midriff.

Every ounce of air in my lungs exploded as I gasped for breath and instinctively rolled away. Yuki shot over me like a cruise missile and blew the thing back long enough for me to catch my breath and un-collapse my lungs.

"Are you alright?"

"Yeah." I managed to wheeze as Dar helped me off the cold concrete.

"We need to get it away from the center of town." He lifted his head and frowned over my shoulder.

Turning, I saw why. Yuki wasn't holding her own. It was faster than she was, a far cry from the other angelic beings I'd fought in the past. "What the hell?"

"It is an arch angel," he answered.

"That's bad?"

"Very." He nodded without tearing his eyes from the battle behind us.

"Can we beat it?"

"I doubt it. Maybe."

A chair flew through the window of the bistro and Candace hopped down onto the concrete in front of us, Charlie screaming her name from inside. Candace gave me a once over, to make sure I was okay, and then turned to face the angel. I was getting ready to scoop her up and run away when she bent at the waist and unleashed a blood curdling scream at the arch angel.

Ignoring Yuki, it turned its head and the searing hatred in its eyes ebbed, just as my vampire sliced through its robes with sharpened nails, spilling silvery blood in a spray across the street. It frowned at the wound and kicked Yuki in the chest, launching her at the brick wall beside the bistro window. Concrete and bone crunched as she slid down the wall and landed in a heap on the sidewalk.

The angel turned to Candace, took a cautious step forward and stopped. Uncertainty held it in place for a moment until it finally spread its wings and launched itself into the sky.

Dar and I stared as Candy straightened herself, paused a moment before turning around and giving us a sad look before collapsing not far from Yuki.

"What the hell just happened?" I started walking toward them.

"If I didn't know better, I'd say it was…afraid?"

"No. It couldn't have been," I answered certainly. Candace was *many* things. Frightening wasn't one of them.

Chapter 17

"You know, I'm going to have to start sending the public works bills to you if you don't stop destroying the center of town." Sherry, Jimmy's cousin and Mayor of Cedar Falls, ran her foot over the hole from the angel's sword and grimaced at the Yuki sized dent in the concrete wall.

"Well, I'll come by tonight, when nobody is around, and fix it all up." I wiggled my fingers in the air.

"An angel. Came down from heaven. With a flaming fucking sword. And proceed to bat the three of you around like a cat with a mouse. You're going to tell me you're worried about you performing magical street repairs?" She eyed me incredulously.

"Good point." I slammed my hand on the ground and canted, "*A bheith mar a bhí tú.*" The concrete rippled and reformed, fully unscathed as the magic traveled up the wall of the bistro, filling in the cracks and healing the brick.

"Okay. That was *fucking* cool." Sherry stared in open amazement.

I turned and saw at least ten people milling around to watch the show. They shook their heads and carried on with their activities, pretending not to notice the magical road and building repairs. One little girl, about five or six, wasn't old enough to pretend not to stare and grinned at me from across the street, waving. I couldn't help but chuckle as I waved back.

"Looks like you have a fan." Sherry stifled a giggle behind her hand.

"Don't make fun. She's my first one."

"Well, if you're done and can keep out of trouble, I'm going to head home," Yuki said and straightened her back. She had definitely taken a wallop from the building and was still moving funny while her body healed itself.

"I think I can manage. Thanks for the save, Yuke."

"My pleasure." She rolled her eyes and started walking away, as best she could. Her massive limp impeded her exit.

"You good?"

"Yeah. I'll live."

"Dar, can you make sure she gets home okay?" I leaned in a little closer. "Make sure she's eaten, too... She seems to be healing a little slower than usual."

"Yes, Master." He bowed and hurried away, ducking under the arm Yuki was holding her back with.

"Is she going to be okay?" Sherry whispered her question, not knowing Yuki could still hear her.

"She'll be fine after a good meal," Yuki answered with a wave over her shoulder. I didn't elaborate.

"Well, if you'll excuse me, Sherry, I need to pay for my lunch." I patted her hand and opened the door to Charlotte's.

"I've been eating here for years. I've never seen you in there once. You trying to get away from your mayoral scolding?"

I chuckled. "No Blackwell backs away from a good fight with the mayor. Ask my mother." The truth was, I loved Sherry to death. The odds of her ending up with a horse's anus magicked to her forehead were less than zero.

"Well, it's too late for lunch and too early for dinner. But a nice hunk of French bread and some tea might be nice." Sherry ducked inside.

Candace was gone. Of course. Her lunch break was short, and she needed to get back to the store. At least, that's what I was sure she would have told me if she hadn't run right after the angel encounter. I had questions that she didn't want to answer. Odds were, Candace was going to be avoiding me until she thought I had forgotten. Little did she know, I was a master ambusher. And I knew where she lived *and* worked.

I looked at the table. She had taken a few bites of her salad before taking off. My turkey burger still sat on the plate, untouched. "Hey, Charlie. How much do I owe you for lunch?" I motioned toward the table. At least I had an excuse not to eat it.

"Don't worry about it. Want it to go? I can make you a fresh one."

"Uh. No thanks. Lost my appetite." I frowned at her, hoping she would buy my horrible acting skills.

She nodded and walked over to the table, clearing the plates. "You want anything, Sherry?"

"Bread and tea emergency rations please."

"Be out in a minute. Have a few loaves coming out of the oven. Butter?"

"Oh, God. Yes, please." Sherry groaned a little. My stomach warbled in envy.

I'd planned on stopping by the diner to get a burger, but the bread sounded sinfully delicious. "Actually, make that two and put it on my bill. Along with the food we *didn't* eat."

Charlie smiled in response and headed to the back with the dishes.

"So. How are things going with Derek?"

"Extremely well. We're having dinner tonight. Why don't you and Jimmy join us?"

Uhhh... "Where?" I found myself asking, horrified that I hadn't declined right off the bat. The last thing I wanted to see was Derek with another woman.

"Bunyan's."

"Ooh. Steak."

"Yep."

"What time?"

"Seven."

"Sounds fun. We'll be there." It was like I had absolutely no control over my mouth. Which on any given day would be normal for me, but this time was different. I'd been trying to say no from the minute I started speaking.

Sherry's eyes lit up in excitement.

Luckily, I could use Jimmy not being available as an excuse not to show up. I started to tell her I would check with her cousin and let her know when Charlie stepped out of the back with a picnic basket on each arm. As far as take out containers, that was a first. "Nice baskets."

"Thanks. Make them myself."

"Isn't it adorable? When you buy bread, she gives it to you in a basket. You're supposed to return them, but I kind of suck at it. I never remember. There's like five of them up in my office." Sherry blushed. "I promise, Charlie. I'll bring them down tomorrow."

"No worries," Charlie answered her with an amused chuckle.

"I'll have Candy bring mine with her tomorrow," I told her. "How much do I owe you?"

"I told you, it is on the house, Dorothea."

"And I don't do that." I fished my wallet out of my jacket and put a hundred on the counter, far from her reach. "See you all later," I waved over my shoulder and headed out the door before she could stop me. If there *was* one thing I remembered from all of my grandmother's lessons, it was never owe a fae a favor.

The thought of taking the bread back to the bookstore and eating in the office didn't sound half as appealing as sitting in the park across the street and doing it. Looking both ways, I cut across and staked my claim to the closest park bench.

Lifting the lid, the aroma of hot bread steamed beside me. My mouth started salivating as I pulled the wrapped loaf out and saw a paper container of butter beside a cup of tea. Happily, I pulled out my treasures, took a sip of the tea from the cup made of ninety-percent recycled materials and set it beside me before tearing off a piece of bread and dipping it in the whipped butter.

Heaven became a tangible place in my mouth. There were few things in the mortal realm better than hot, fresh bread and butter. I dipped my hand in the basket to grab a napkin and my fingers wrapped around a small wheel of cheese. It was officially the best day ever. Aside from the part of being almost killed by an angel. That part sucked a little.

"Can you fly?" The little voice behind me almost made me jump. I turned and saw the girl who had waved at me, staring at me incredulously. Her eyes as big as saucers.

"Sometimes."

"Why was the angel mad at you?"

I chewed what was in my mouth and swallowed. I could manage one word with a mouth full of food, but I didn't want to pepper her with chewed bread. "Well, that wasn't a *real* angel. It was a bad guy pretending to be one."

"Oh." She waddled around me and sat on the bench on the other side of my basket.

"Would you like some bread? It's fresh."

"Mommy says I shouldn't take things from strangers."

And mommies shouldn't let their children run around the park alone. I looked around for her, but she was talking to another woman by the statue in the middle of the park. "Well. My name is Dot. What's yours?"

"Caroline."

"Well, Caroline, we're not strangers now, are we?"

The little girl giggled and shook her head happily. I ripped off a hunk of bread and handed it to her. She greedily started munching on the corner, cute as a button. "You're a real witch?"

"Yep. Does that scare you?"

"You're not green. And you don't have any warts. So, you must be a *good* witch."

"Most of the time. But my mother..."

"She's green and has warts?" She blinked in astonishment.

"Yep. And a foul temper. She lives in a swamp and has long claws at the ends of her fingers."

183

"Why does she have a foul temper?"

"Somebody dropped a house on her sister!" I giggled.

The girl's mother waved goodbye at her friend and started heading toward us. I waited for the moment of panic when she realized I was talking to her child, but she smiled sadly, ignoring me right up until the moment she walked right past us. I looked down at Caroline and then turned in my seat. "Aren't you forgetting someone?" I pointed at the seat next to me when the woman turned around. She tilted her head.

"Who?"

"This girl isn't yours?" I started to panic.

"What girl?" She gave me a strange look and kept walking away.

Horrified, I looked down at Caroline who had a tear leaking from the corner of her eye. "Mommy can't see me," she said sadly and faded from view.

∞ ∞ ∞

"Next time you're going to use me as an excuse not to have dinner with your ex-boyfriend and my cousin, you should let me know beforehand," Jimmy said with a chuckle and opened the truck door.

"Well, how the hell was I supposed to know your cousin would have called you within five minutes. Hard to tell her that I can't make it because my date had other plans when he already agreed," I said as I climbed up into the truck and smoothed my dress beneath me to protect my backside from the cold pleather.

Jimmy shut the door and walked around the truck, getting in on the other side and starting it up. "Good point. I'm sure I can come up with an excuse if you really don't want to go…"

"No. It's fine. I can be a big girl for one night and suck it up. Plus, Sherry seemed really excited."

"She is. Even though she's the mayor, she doesn't have many friends or get out much," he said thoughtfully.

"Why? She's super sweet and super cute. She could have more guys than me if she wanted to."

"She's not a witch, Dot. But she's…quirky." He laughed and put the truck into gear, backing out of my driveway slowly.

"Quirky?"

"Intuitive. She can usually tell what people are thinking."

"And?"

"If you were a guy, would you want your date to know what you're thinking?"

"Pervs?"

"To say the least."

"Oye."

"But she can't seem to read witches. She could never tell what I was thinking, so I'm guessing Derek is a nice change."

"And the Irish accent doesn't hurt."

"Or his sad eyes," Jimmy added.

"Don't get any fucking ideas. No."

He chuckled.

"And you behave yourself tonight. No funny business."

"In front of my cousin? I don't think you have to worry."

"This is you we're talking about. Of course, I'm worried."

"Ewww. That's just gross. I don't even want to think about it." He made a few gagging noises to top it off. "It was a month before she could look me in the eye after the pencident."

"What the hell is a pencident?"

"You know."

"Enlighten me."

"The incident. With the *pen*."

"Oh. That pencident." I blushed.

"Just remember, payback's a bitch."

"Blah blah blah. Talking pretty big for a man without his wingman." Just to make sure, I checked the back seat. "Where's Dennis?"

"Pulling an extra shift. One of the guys was…sick."

"Sick?"

He sighed. "Scared shitless. Even the fire department has its share of racist assholes in OWL T-shirts…"

"Oh."

"Yeah. Kind of ironic that he asked his good buddy Dennis to take his shift."

I chuckled. "I'm surprised he said yes."

"He wanted the OT. He has grand designs on buying a Corvette."

"Dennis?" I was a little shocked by the revelation. I always saw him as a truck kind of guy. Not a sports car fanatic.

"It's been his dream since we were kids. He's getting close, too." Jimmy didn't sound too impressed.

"Whatever makes him happy."

"You mean besides you?" He grinned at me.

"I hope I do."

"Don't doubt it for a moment. You have that effect on all of us." He reached over and rubbed my leg reassuringly until we pulled into Bunyan's packed parking lot.

Luckily, Sherry and Derek had already gotten one of the larger booths, wide enough for six people, but perfect for the four of us. I slid in across from Sherry and Jimmy sat next to me, across from my ex-boyfriend. The only way it could have felt more awkward would have been if Chief had shown up and pulled up a chair.

"I'm so glad you guys made it! This might be my first double date since high school." She grinned and leaned against Derek.

"Wouldn't have missed it for the world," I lied through my teeth. "Hey, Derek."

"Dot." He gave me a small smile.

"You remember Jimmy?"

"The fireman. Yes." He reached across the table and shook Jimmy's hand.

"So, what's new and exciting?" I asked Sherry, not Derek. Wanting to get the conversation going and away from Derek.

"Since I saw you a few hours ago? Not much. Thanks for fixing the war zone."

"My pleasure."

"War zone?" Derek leaned forward a little, his curiosity piqued. Even Jimmy was staring at me. I probably should have told him, too.

"Yeah. Had a visitor this afternoon. The flaming sword wielding kind. Downtown took the brunt of the damage."

"Was everyone okay?" Jimmy asked concernedly.

"Well, it was close. Not every day you get your ass handed to you by an arch angel. I managed to dodge most of it, but Yuki learned what it felt like to go in like a wrecking ball."

"An arch angel?" Derek asked dubiously.

"Yeah. They don't like me very much."

"How did you kill it?" That was my Jimmy. Straight to the point and assuming I'd won.

"I didn't. Believe it or not, Candace came flying out of the Bistro we were having lunch at and scared it away." I cocked my eyebrow, still uncertain how she had managed to pull it off. She was about as scary as a Pomeranian in a tutu.

"Well, just try to keep the fighting to a minimum. We don't want a repeat of the other night, either," Sherry said absentmindedly as she perused the menu.

"The other night?" Derek asked. With every question, his eyebrows moved closer to his hairline.

"Vampire attack on an anti-witch coalition. Fun stuff. You should hang out more," Jimmy answered him with a chuckle.

"It would appear so." He took a long pull from his dark beer and didn't sound honest at all. For the first time since we *had* broken up, I felt as though he might be glad. Which was good.

"Lady Dorothea!" The bubbly, non-human, blonde waitress that I always seemed to find myself saddled with, the one whose name I could never remember, stopped at our table. "Good to see you again! The usual?"

"Please." I shrugged. I was kind of starving, and sixty-four ounces of steak sounded like it would fill me up quite nicely.

"Jimmy?" She blushed when she said his name.

"Not for me. Just the porterhouse, please."

"Beer?"

"You betcha." He flashed a smile at her. I gripped his knee and gave it a little squeeze.

She turned to Derek and Sherry and took their orders before flashing Jimmy a demure smile and heading for the kitchen. "She wants me," Jimmy said jokingly.

"Probably between two pieces of bread with a light coating of mayonnaise," I answered him warningly.

"Well, I'm safe. The only person's lips who are touching my exquisite flesh are yours, love." He grinned and kissed me.

"Keep flirting with her, and I'll carve some of your ass off for her sammich."

"Me? I never flirt."

His cousin scoffed.

"What?"

"You flirt. You just don't realize it. Nor do you pay attention when girls flirt with you, which makes you doubly dangerous."

"Right?" I nodded at her.

"Don't know what you're talking about," Jimmy answered defensively.

"I don' think he was flirtin'," Derek agreed.

"You shush. You're twice as bad with that honey-dipped accent," I said with a laugh. Sherry grinned and nodded.

"I don't think they appreciate the fine subtleties of the finer points of our personalities, Jimbo."

"We're totally unappreciated."

"Slaves to the women we love…"

"Love?" Sherry's eyes grew twice as wide as she turned to him and stared at him like a doe in headlights.

It was at that moment that Derek realized he fucked up.

Chuckling, I curled up into the crook of Jimmy's arm to watch the show. But not before whispering, "Just remember. You can't flirt if you're dead."

Chapter 18

"Well, that was fun," I said as I got back into Jimmy's truck, half meaning it. While it had been nice to hang out with Sherry, spending time with my ex had been more than a little awkward. No matter how hard I tried, I couldn't stop imagining the feel of his fingers, the taste of his kiss, or the sound of his voice as he whispered in my ear. I found myself staring off into nothingness more than once as we finished our meal.

"Which part?" Jimmy asked softly, shutting the door and walking around the truck to get in. It took me until he started the engine to realize he was expecting an answer.

"Hanging out with your cousin. I really like her."

"Good. She likes you, too. What about Derek?" He asked as he put the truck in reverse but didn't let go of the break.

"You want the truth?"

"I wouldn't have asked if I didn't."

"Even if the truth sucks?"

"You still have feelings for him," he stated flatly.

"Not so much as feelings for him, just the memories of the time we shared are rather…"

"Vivid?"

"Yes. Vivid. Vivid and happy."

"So, you don't want him?"

"Oh, hell no. He had his chance. Two of them in fact."

He leaned across the truck and planted a gentle kiss on my cheek. "Well, if you change your mind…"

"I won't."

He held up his hand. "The heart gets what the heart wants, Dot. Just do me a favor and try not to devastate my cousin. You saw her face when he mentioned the L word."

"I did. More importantly, I saw his face when he realized what he said. Tell you what, I'll make you a deal."

"What's that?"

"I promise not to hurt her, but if he hurts her, we can hurt him together." I grinned proudly.

"Such a deal." He winked and backed out of the spot and headed for Main.

"Want to go back to my place?"

"Maybe in a little bit. I have something else planned..."

"Fuck me." I sighed and slumped in the seat.

"Oh. I will. I *will*." He grinned mischievously.

"That's not the part I'm worried about."

"Oh? What is, pray tell."

"Who's going to be watching..."

"I would never do something so dastardly..." He feigned shock and put his hand over his heart.

"Both hands on the wheel, mister."

He kept driving, taking us closer and closer to the center of town. My heart stopped when he pulled in the parking lot of the bookstore. "Uh. Why are we here?"

"I figured you could use a coffee..."

"*Jimmy*, so help me goddess. If you cause a scene in *my* store, I'll flog you."

"You promise?" He sounded a little too hopeful for my tastes. "Come on. It will be fun!" He flashed his famous, patented, boyish smile and opened his door.

I counted to ten and then once again while I waited for him to open my door. If he was going to drag me into the store for a bit of fun, he could do it with me kicking and screaming.

But, truth be told, I could already feel myself dampening at the thought. Jimmy had that effect on me. Whenever he mentioned the word "plan", my bits started quivering in anticipation and drooling in excitement.

Basically, my vagina was a dog who heard the words, "Hey, girl. You wanna go for a ride?"

"My Lady," he said as he opened the door and offered me his hand. I slid down out of the seat and managed not to fall on my ass as my feet wobbled on the concrete before I caught my balance. Most days, I really hated his truck. The other few, I mostly despised it.

"Thank you, Sir James." I chuckled and moved out of the way for him to slam the door closed.

"Come on. Let's get some coffee."

The café was packed. But *somehow* Josie was expecting us and had two cups of coffee with lids prepped and off to the side of the register. She handed them to Jimmy over the glass partition without so much as a second glance. He took a sip of one and handed me the other.

"Busier than I was expecting."

"Foil your plans?"

"Nope. C'mon. Let's go say hi to Jay," he offered me his hand and led us through the entrance to the store and straight to the office. It was definitely a setup.

The closer we got, the quicker my breaths came. By the time he knocked on the door, I was practically hyperventilating. Nervously, I sipped my coffee as I walked into the dimly lit room.

Jay was sitting at the desk. The door closed behind me and the lock clicked, echoing in the small room. "What's going on?"

Jimmy flipped the switch and Jason smiled. "Hey, Dot."

Narrowing my eyes at him, I took another sip of coffee, letting the liquid heat flow down my throat and warm the chill I felt creeping up my spine.

"Is that coffee?" Jason tilted his head.

"Uh. Yeah?"

"Gosh. I sure could use a sip of that. I am so sleepy."

An actor he wasn't. He sounded like he was reciting lines from a fifth-grade rendition of Romeo and Juliet. But

193

he and Jimmy had gone through *all* that effort. "Would you care for a sip of my coffee?"

"I sure would. My back hurts, though, Dot. Do you think you could lean over the desk and hand it to me?"

I was trying *so hard* not to laugh. It was pathetic, yes. But it was also the cutest damn thing I had ever seen in my life. "Why sure, Jason. Let me lean over the desk and hand you this steaming cup of coffee." I pressed my legs against the desk and did just that, straining as I handed over the paper cup.

His fingers wrapped around it.

Jimmy canted, "*Ceangail*," behind me. His words melted the last bit of chill as the Scots Gaelic rolled off his tongue. It was one of the only spells I'd ever heard him cast. It was similar to the Irish I normally spoke, but the inflections and lilt were a tad bit different. Either way, I didn't care that the mahogany desk morphed, and two wooden circles reached out and bound my wrists to the surface, effectively trapping me. Jimmy's voice was still echoing in my ears and I shivered.

"What are you doing?" I mimicked Jason's superb acting with my plea of fear.

"We caught ourselves an evil witch, Jason. What do you think we should do with her?" Jimmy lightly slapped my butt.

"Gosh, Jimmy. I don't know. Aren't you supposed to stake witches?"

"No. That is vampires, Jason. But maybe we should try it and see if it works. Do you have any long hard pieces of wood we could use?"

The entire scene had turned into an 80's B movie of epic proportions. Even Jimmy had adopted horrible acting skills. I literally had to *fight* not to giggle. "No! Please, Mister Witchunters, don't impale me on your massive stakes!"

Looking over my shoulder, I saw Jimmy put his hands on his hips as he started cackling dramatically. "We will! And you will like it. And be impaled. Upon our wood. We shall drive the evil from you, vile witch!" He stepped forward and lifted my skirt. "I think I shall let the young one teach you the errors of your ways first!"

He walked around the desk and stood beside Jason, who looked confused, horny, and horrified all at once. "Are you sure this is okay?" He whispered the question to Jimmy as he stood.

"Trust me," Jimmy whispered back.

"Famous last words from you. You don't work for her."

Jason looked at me imploringly. I winked to let him know I was totally okay with the situation. He breathed a sigh of relief and walked around the desk.

Jimmy took the seat he had just vacated and scooted a little closer, smiling at me cockily. "She's wearing too many clothes, young Jason. Why don't you divest this saucy trollop of her accoutrements?"

"Trollop? I thought you were a witch hunter, not a pirate?"

"I am Sir Van of Helsing, pirate witch hunter lord. And ye, the accused, shall not speak!" He leaned close to my face and whispered, "*Sàmhchair*," his breath caressing my cheek before leaning back in the high-backed swivel chair.

The office became rather drafty as Jason lifted the hem of my dress off my waist and I heard the *snick, snick* of scissors.

I opened my mouth to protest, it was one of my favorite dresses after all, but no words escaped. Jimmy's spell had been one of silence and I silently growled in frustration.

Once the back had been bisected, he cut the straps from my shoulders and let the remnants flop to the desk around me. I was completely naked except for the little red pair of panties that were plastered to my flesh. It was quite obvious I liked being bound to furniture. Even if Jason cut the panties off me, they weren't going to fall off anytime soon. Unless I gushed them off.

"Is she wet?" Jimmy asked curiously from his seat.

Jason spread my legs and squatted. I could feel his breath against my thighs. "Holy shit. Yeah, she is."

"Told you."

"Yeah, yeah. You're the expert."

"I heard you can tell if a woman is a witch by taste. Why don't you give it a shot? See if she tastes magical."

"Oh, I'm sure she does. Should I remove her panties first, Captain Witch Hunter Pirate Lord, Sir?"

"No. Leave them on."

Jimmy's eyes never left mine all through their banter. He was watching my face, not the show behind me. I met his gaze and refused to look away. I may have blinked once or twice when Jason spread my ass cheeks and used his tongue to press the gusset of my panties into me. If there hadn't been a silence spell, I might have gasped, moaned, or possibly even said, "Oh, fuck."

"She's a silent one, young Jason. See if you can get her to talk!" Jimmy leaned forward and licked my ear. "Confess to being a witch and the pleasure will stop."

Jason slipped a finger under my panties, wet the tip, and let it slide up the sensitive skin between my opening and my ass, letting it swirl around before pressing against the closed flesh. Involuntarily, my hips bucked, and my knees banged against the front of the desk.

"I think you found her weak spot, Seaman Jay! Keep probing."

"Aye aye, Cap'n." The finger slid inside me up to his first knuckle while I shot daggers at Jimmy.

Jimmy grinned back at me and put one foot up on the desk beside me, slowly unzipping his fly and pulling himself from the front of his jeans. My eyes fastened to his beautiful cock as he slowly started stroking it barely a foot from my face. "Better make sure this stake is well polished before driving it into you," he muttered and masturbated while his cohort pulled my overly wet panties from my lips and slipped his tongue inside me.

It took me only a few minutes to come. I thrashed and pulled against my bonds as I wordlessly screamed in pleasure.

Jason pulled away and wiped his mouth against my thighs. "She's ready, Sir."

"Impale the lass!"

Jason's hands gripped my hips as he drove himself inside me. He slid right in and I felt his hips spread my legs even further apart as I arched my back, finally breaking my staring contest with Jimmy. He chuckled and kept stroking his cock while Jason pulled himself free and drove back inside me.

"Should we hear her confession?" Jimmy looked over my head at Jason.

"No. She's enjoying this. A confession might take a while."

"Good lad. You're learning the ways of these wicked witches."

"Would you like a turn, Sir?"

"Indeed, I might." Jimmy stood and walked around the desk. Jason pulled away and I silently whimpered as the full feeling left me. Jimmy stepped up and filled me back up and I sighed in relief.

"You're definitely right. She is enjoying this." He slammed into me repeatedly. My eyes widened in shock as I got the fucking of my life. "Make her taste herself."

Jason walked around and offered me his glistening cock. Without hesitation, I opened wide and took him nearly all into my mouth, my nose brushing against his curls.

"Oh, fuck," he groaned.

"Do not fill the witch's belly! If you are going to spill your seed, fill her here," Jimmy growled as he pulled free, just shy of my orgasm. I pounded my wrists against the desk in frustration as Jimmy and he switched places again. A moment later, I was filled again and Jimmy grinned as he sat back down in my chair.

"You tell me when you're about to come, Seaman Jason."

"Yes, Cap'n."

Jimmy started stroking himself, using my wetness as lube as his hand glided over his silky smoothness. Jason's hand slapped my ass as he started competing against Jimmy as to who fucked me harder and faster. The skin tingled as the slap echoed in the office. I came immediately, the stinging setting me off like the fuse of a cannon.

"Holy shit," Jason grunted.

"She liked that?"

"I'm not kidding. She gushed and damn near ripped my dick off."

Jimmy chuckled and leaned over. "You like to be spanked?"

Not being able to answer him, I just nodded as I pressed my forehead against the desk as the orgasm continued to rip through me, unending.

"I'm going to come," Jason said through jagged breaths.

"Do it. Fill her."

His hips slammed against my ass and I felt his shaft throb as he emptied himself inside me, grunting in time with his spasms. "Holy fuck. Holy fuck."

Jason collapsed atop my back, kissing my shoulder as he caught his breath.

"You're done, Seaman. Send in the next recruit."

"Aye, Sir."

Next recruit? What?

Jason zipped up his pants and I heard the door unlock and open. I sent a silent prayer to the goddess that nobody was walking past the door as it opened.

"Hi, Mrs. Rogerson," Jimmy said with a smile and a wave. The lights above dimmed as panic surged through me. Jimmy chuckled. "I'm kidding. I don't even know a Mrs. Rogerson."

My eyes narrowed in anger.

198

"It was some guy I've never seen before."

He was toying with my love of exhibiting myself and my fear of being seen by a customer, getting me caught up in a roller coaster of fear and excitement. A large glob of liquid slipped from inside me and clung to my thigh as it slid slowly down my leg. I wasn't sure if it was from Jason's deposit or my own excitement.

The door clicked closed behind me. I turned my head to look, but Jimmy put his hands on either side of my face. "No. Don't look. Let's see how well you know your lovers." He looked up and nodded.

The head of one of their cocks slipped inside me. I knew in a fraction of an instant that it was Chief. Nobody else filled me nearly as much. By the time he was fully buried inside, there wasn't a doubt in my mind. I wanted to scream but couldn't. His calloused hands gripped my hips as he slowly started to move.

"Well? Who is it?"

I mouthed the word, "Chief," and closed my eyes.

"You're right. But that was kind of an easy one, wasn't it?"

I nodded without looking.

"Are you surprised he dove in for sloppy seconds?"

Again, I nodded, smiling at the pleasure that was radiating from inside me like a Chernobyl meltdown.

"How does she feel, Chief?"

"Fucking incredible."

Jimmy kissed my closed eye. "He's the one who turned you in, you know. He told us you were a witch and came up with a fitting punishment. Told us *all* about your fondness for desks..."

I was too happy to care. Grinning, I opened my eyes and smiled at Jimmy who was still stroking his cock.

"I don't think I care for your silence, wench. I want to hear your grunts and moans of pleasure! *Bruidhinn!*" His canting timed with Chief's thrust and I grunted as I was filled for the hundredth time.

"Fuck you, Jimmy," I moaned in ecstasy.

"Not yet. You still have three more inquisitors.

Wait. What?

"I told you payback was a bitch." He winked at me and then looked up at Chief. "Hurry up, Bill. There's a line for this attraction, you know."

"Oh. It won't be long…" He wasn't lying either. Chief had a mellow voice, silky smooth. When he was excited…it dropped a few octaves and took up resident in his throat, almost a rasp.

"Oh, fuck. I'm coming," I screeched and started convulsing, trying to drag my ass over the top of the desk and get Chief's cock out of me. His hands held me firm as he pulled back and thrust into me as hard as he could. It didn't amplify my orgasm, it exploded it. And me. I managed to throw one leg up over the desk as I ground my clit against the rounded edge of the desk as Chief unleashed a torrent inside me. My hips bucked and ground my poor little clit into oblivion as I accidently smacked the side of my head against the wooden surface while I convulsed and panicked. Nothing should have felt that good. Ever.

"Woah. Easy there, Chief. Don't kill her," Jimmy said amusedly as Chief held my hips and caught his breath, twitching inside me.

"The fuck," I managed to whisper and moan, pulling against my restraints in an effort to bury my face in my hands and weep.

"Next!" Jimmy called out jovially.

Chief chuckled and stroked my ass lovingly before zipping himself up and straightening his uniform. I watched him from the corner of my eye, flashing him a happy smile as he turned and left.

"That was a good one, eh!" Jimmy rubbed my shoulders.

"Fuck off. You're so dead."

"Oh, shush. You can stop this anytime you want. Just admit to being a witch."

"Never!" I chuckled and braced myself for the next contestant.

The door opened, and once again Jimmy turned my head. "Let's see if you guess this one right."

As soon as his hand touched my ass, I knew it was Shea. I could feel him in my head before I felt him dip inside my sopping insides. "Shea," I said with a lazy smile.

"I think you're cheating."

I nodded. "I can feel him in my head."

"So unfair." Jimmy pouted as Shea pulled himself free of my pussy and pressed the tip of his cock at the entrance to my ass.

"Ooh," I grunted and braced myself.

Compared to the others, he was positively gentle as he slowly worked himself inside me. I flattened myself out against the desk and let the different sensations of ecstasy fill me completely. Jimmy's hand was moving a little faster than before. His eyes even had that glazed look of getting closer.

"He's in my ass," I whispered to Jimmy.

"I know. Everything this night is well orchestrated to optimize the finale."

"Oh?" The conversation was helping to edge the overwhelming orgasm building up inside me.

"You bet your ass."

"I can't. It belongs to Shea right now."

"He's worried about hurting you. Do you want him to go harder or faster?"

"He's perfect right now. It feels sooo good. Thank you."

"You're welcome," Jimmy answered and his face lit up.

"I was talking to Shea."

Shea's giggle behind me doubled my smile.

"She said to go faster, Shea." Jimmy chuckled evilly.

"What's that, Lady? Jimmy wishes to trade places with you?" Shea's evil chuckle was almost creepy. A shiver, that had nothing to do with pleasure, raced up my spine.

Jimmy actually groaned a little.

201

"I think he likes that idea, Shea," I managed to stammer as my orgasm got a little closer.

"Perhaps next time, Lady. I am about to come."

"Do it. Fill me even more."

His hips bucked a little faster, almost curling against me as he fought to drive himself a little bit further inside me. He swelled inside me as his cum fought against the constricting of my muscles as it finally escaped inside me. His movements picked up speed as he slipped in and out of me with ease. It was enough to push me over the edge and I brought my knee up on the desk while we both rode out the sensations overwhelming us.

"Next!"

Shea fastened his leather pants and slipped out the door. Ellis came in and stared in shock for a moment before freeing himself and taking Shea's place. "Are you sure, my Aiqua?"

"Fuck me, Ellis. Fill me."

"As you wish."

He slid right in as squishing and slapping noises filled the small office. Leaving my knee on the desk, I turned and grinned at Jimmy as he continued pleasuring himself. "Want me to suck that?"

"No. I'll come."

"Isn't that your goal?"

"No. I'm saving this for you."

"I could take it in my mouth. Then I'd have cum in all my holes."

"Is that what you want?"

"Yes. Let me taste you."

He groaned and stood, unable to stop himself. As soon as his head touched my bottom lip, I sucked him into my mouth. If there were a way to bring Dar into the office and have him fill my ass, I would have. Sex with the guys was almost getting out of control and I loved every fucking sticky moment of it all.

Ellis pumped my pussy full of cum with a loud groan of pleasure, pulled himself out wordlessly and left. A minute later, Dar came in and plunged himself inside me.

My thighs and calves were dripping with the evidence of our lovemaking. I had a demon cock inside my canal and a cock in my mouth. Life couldn't have possibly gotten any better.

"Do it, Dar," Jimmy managed to grunt.

I got him out of my mouth and had just managed to stammer, "Do what?"

I felt Dar swell inside me

"What the fuck?" I stretched around him as I fought to take his girth.

"You know he can shift. Bet you didn't know he could shift just parts of himself, did you?"

"James Duncan. If I have a hellhound cock inside me, not only will I kill you, I will make it painful. And slow." I looked up at him angrily.

"What? No! Ew. He can just make...parts...bigger. Longer. Et cetera."

"Oh, thank fuck. Carry on." I sighed and took his cock back into my mouth.

Dar was having difficulty fucking me through the laughter. "Shame on you, Master. For even thinking that."

"Well, you're uh... You're bigger than Chief right now."

"Do I get a prize?"

"You're partaking of it right now," Jimmy answered proudly.

"First place. Grand prize. I could not ask for more." He leaned over me and slid a hand beneath me, cupping one of my breasts as he swirled his hips behind me, churning my insides like butter. I grunted with each thrust, focusing on sucking the cock in my mouth. I pulled back and left just the tip of him in my mouth, swirling my tongue around and under the head.

"Oh. Don't do that. I'm going to—"

Jimmy exploded in my mouth. I nearly coughed at the force of it as he splashed against the back of my throat. Without thinking of the consequences, I pulled him from my mouth as the second wave painted my face.

"Holy fuck." Dar grunted and started pumping another load inside me.

Dar and I collapsed, practically crawling on the desk while Jimmy fell to his knees, hanging on to the edge like the final scene of Titanic.

"Just when I think I couldn't possibly be fucked any more than I already was..." I chuckled at my own joke.

Dar pulled himself from my abused insides and ran his fingers through the mess they had all made. "I would suggest not standing up." He laughed softly.

"I won't. I need a shower," I answered and let the shadows take me home.

Chapter 19

I walked out of my bedroom scrubbing my hair dry with a fluffy white towel. It had taken me nearly an hour under the hot spray of water before I felt clean again, but as soon as the grin split my face, I felt dirty again and frigging loved it. There were musicians, composers, and maestros. Jimmy was definitely a maestro and his favorite instrument was me. Sighing happily, I put a mug in the coffee maker and set it to brew.

By the time I was sitting on my couch in my robe and happily sipping on my cup of coffee, Yuki came out of her room and stretched gingerly.

"Don't tell me you're still hurting?" I set the mug down on the coffee table and motioned her over.

"That thing kicked my fucking ass."

"You hit that wall at about ninety." I turned her around in front of me and lifted her shirt up over her back. "No marks. I'll take that as a good sign."

"I think it shattered every bone in my back."

Unsure how well it would work, I pushed a bit of power into my hand and ran it over her skin. "Better?"

She did some over her head arm stretches and nodded. "Yes! Thank you, Master."

"Anytime."

She plopped down on the couch next to me and leaned against me. "So…"

Whatever she'd been about to say was interrupted by the sound of the front door opening and closing with a woosh and giggles of laughter. I turned my head and smiled at Josie and Candace arm in arm as they walked around the kitchen into the living room. I cocked an eyebrow. "You're home early."

Candace beamed at me. "The vampires kicked us out."

"What?"

Josie smiled and waved a hand, sensing my unease at Candace's words. "Our night crew. They're finally ready to be left alone." She stopped and smiled at Yuki. "I can't thank you enough."

Yuki just smiled and nodded and turned back around.

They both fell into the love seat across from us. "Who's first?" She looked at Candace.

"I am, but you can go if you want."

"Go where?" I tilted my head, confused.

"Shower," Josie answered and pushed Candace toward the bathroom.

"You both reek of coffee. Go together," Yuki said and pinched her nose.

"Not only did you hook me up with the best employees on the planet, but you're a genius, too!" She winked and followed Candace toward the bathroom.

Yuki and Josie got along like nitro and glycerin. For her to suggest Josie and Candace take a shower together when she would be able to hear every giggle and squeal through the thin wooden door meant she wasn't done with our conversation. As soon as they were behind the closed bathroom door and the sound of running water caressed our ears, she turned to me, her knees pressing firmly against my thigh.

"You need to deal with my uncle."

"I will."

"No, Master. You need to deal with him *now*. He has broken trust and the incident from last night it just the start. Even my mother could be involved." She frowned even more at the mention of her mother.

Reaching out, I put my hand on her shoulder. "We will, but honestly I don't see how much more damage they can do. All of the vampires who were loyal to him are dead.

For him to cause any more harm, he'd have to come here himself."

"That's what scares me."

"What if we split the clan?"

"What?" Her voice cracked in astonishment.

"Split the clan? He takes Ashville, and I keep everyone and everything in Cedar Falls?"

"You don't understand how vampires work…"

"Pretty sure I do." I smiled and ruffled her purple tinged hair.

"No. You don't. They're…territorial?"

"Yes? He'll have his territory, and I'll have mine."

"No. You don't understand. Not territorial, it's more of a pack mentality? Kind of like werewolves. He wants to be the head of the pack."

"Yes. He can be. Of his pack. I'll be alpha bitch here."

"That's just it. It's all one big fucking pack to him. The vampires here, the blood bank. His son. He thinks it all should be his and he will not rest until it is. It's kind of like an obsession. To relinquish a part of it to you… It would be like him admitting a weakness. That you're stronger than he is. That you deserve all of it. He won't rest until either you, or he, is dead. The strongest rules and that is that. It's why he never challenged my father."

"But I beat your father." I didn't feel guilty about doing it, but I felt guilty about saying it to his daughter. Even if he was an asshole.

"Which he probably sees as some sort of fluke. Like you cheated. You're not a vampire. He'll never see you as his equal."

"Are you telling me I have to kill him to end this?"

She nodded without an ounce of hesitation.

"And what will that prove?"

"That you are, in fact, our lord."

"Lady."

Yuki chuckled. "I think that's the first time you've ever wanted to be called Lady."

"Well, it's better than *Lord*. Jeezus, Lady is pompous enough."

Her smile faded. "Either or, it's what needs to be done."

"So, what? Do I challenge him to a duel or something? You think he'd come if I called?"

"He would. But it would be better for you to go to him and squash the...rebellion, for lack of a better word. Show them that you won't tolerate it."

"That's just it. I will. I don't want to kill your uncle. Not if I can help it. You're telling me there's no possible way that he won't back down?"

"He won't."

"But I'm not a vampire."

"Even if that were true, he still sees you as similar. We all do."

"I'll think about it. That's all I can promise you." I lowered my face and moved it closer to hers, staring at her eyes for emphasis.

She graced me with another small smile. "I should be happy."

"But you're not?"

"I'm happy that you're a kind Master that we can all love and adore. I'm sad that you won't listen to reason."

"Oh, I listen to reason when it's reasonable. Doing something when there has to be a better way, not so much. I'm happy here. I'll police the vamps in Cedar Falls, but damnit, Yuki, I don't want your father's property or the vamps in Ashville. I didn't even want my mother's coven. Here is my home, and here is my family."

She nodded in understanding. "Sounds like your mother's doing a bang-up job. Maybe you *should* take over that coven, too." She rolled her eyes.

"Her role is to guide, not to govern," Candace said somberly in an otherworldly voice from the hallway outside the bathroom before shaking her head, blinking, and scrambling her towel covered nakedness into her bedroom. Josie shot us a questioning look as she followed her.

Yuki sighed and shrugged, letting it go.

"Methinks the Lady doth put a little too much faith in her red-headed minion."

"Minion?" Yuki scoffed and took a sip of my coffee.

"Hey! Get your own." I took my cup and winced. Our conversation had lasted long enough for it to cool off and hit that tepid bitter stage. I grimaced and gulped down the rest. "Make me one, too?" I grinned.

"Yes, Master." She took my mug and headed to the kitchen.

A minute later, Josie and Candace slipped out of the room and settled back down on the loveseat wearing matching pink T-shirts and little, if nothing, else. I couldn't help but smile at their adorableness. "How are you not cold?"

"Who could be cold next to this little ball of sunshine?" Josie scrunched Candace a little closer.

"Speaking of little balls of sunshine, what the hell was that this afternoon?" I narrowed my eyes at Candace until she squirmed uncomfortably in Josie's arms.

"What was what?' Josie's curiosity was piqued.

I pointed at her fiancé. "While we were getting our asses kicked, she yells at an angel and it flies off with its tail feathers tucked between its legs."

Josie looked down at Candace for confirmation and Candace stared at the floor. "Did you?"

"Yes."

"That was very brave of you…"

"And stupid. Now they know where I am. I was foolish."

"Uh…what's going on?" I was so far out of the loop that I couldn't even see the loop.

Josie looked up at me and gave me an imperceptible shake of her head. For the first time in my life, Josie was privy to information that I wasn't. It was kind of refreshing.

"You're fey blooded, but your father wasn't elven," Yuki answered for her.

Judging from how Josie's eyes widened to the size of saucers, she had hit the mark on the head. "What?" I looked at Yuki.

"Today was the closest I'd ever gotten to one of the angels. Want to know what they smell like?"

"What?"

"Sunshine. Just like Candace."

I looked over and Candace had her face in her hands, shaking visibly. Josie practically snarled at Yuki and tried to comfort Candace by rubbing gentle circles on her back.

And it all clicked in my head. All the subtle clues, everything that she'd been hiding, her troubled past. "Candy?"

She pulled her hands from her face and looked at me forlornly with red rimmed eyes.

"Is it true?"

She nodded, ever so gently. I held out my arms toward her and she didn't waste a moment before she crossed the distance and jumped into my lap. "Do you hate me?"

"Hate you? What the hell for? Look at my mother. We're like sisters. You're the child of angels, and I'm the child of demons."

She pulled back and raised an ironic eyebrow. "Yes. Just like *sisters*." She pursed her lips, but I could see them trembling with laughter.

"Okay. Maybe cousins." I winked conspiratorially. "Why are you ashamed of being sired by an angel?"

"You've seen them. They are not nice." She frowned. "They're corrupt."

"Yep. They're a big bag of dicks. Doesn't change who you are, though." I ran my fingers through her hair, pulling some of the stray strands out of her eyes. "But why are they afraid of you?"

She shrugged. "I've met only one. It was nearly four hundred years ago in a church in Sweden. My master had left me with the priest when she was called off to battle."

My heart sank. No story of being left with a priest ended well.

"Father Mikel." She laughed at the memory. "Was a gentle soul who taught me much of what I know about healing. Then one day the angel appeared, and I wasn't surprised. The priest was as close to the angels as a human could attain. Then it started tearing apart the church and Father Mikel tried to stop it… He was cleaved in half by its sword." She gulped and started crying. I felt like an asshole for assuming the worst about the priest. "Something inside me broke, and I ran out from where I'd been hiding. I shoved it back from where it stood over his body and it watched silently as I tried to heal him."

I stared incredulously. "Did you?"

"No. You can't heal the dead, but I tried."

I rubbed her shoulder. "The angel left you alone?"

She shook her head. "It called for others, singing that it had found me. It was in a language I'd never heard before but understood completely. Fear filled me and I *knew* they were coming for me. The angel sneered but wouldn't come near me. It dodged when I tried to attack it with my dagger. Then I felt them. A choir of them were coming for me. So, I ran and barely managed to escape. It took me two years to find my master. When I told her what had happened, she didn't seem surprised. My mother told me my father was an angel, but I never believed her until that moment. I was an abomination in their eyes. Something to be destroyed, nothing more."

"You are so much more." I hugged her and looked at Josie over her shoulder. "You knew?" I mouthed my question and she nodded. I smiled in response, proud that she had kept her secret.

Candace went rigid in my arms. "What if they come back for me?"

"Then every witch, vampire, shadow, and dark elf in this city will stand between you and them."

"What if they come during the day?"

"Then we'll just have to hide until it gets dark." I winked at her reassuringly, not really feeling the bravado I was trying to project. Just one of the damn things had mopped the floors and walls with us under the midday sun. I wasn't kidding when I'd said we'd hide, but one thing was for certain. It would be over my dead body before they took Candace away from us. "Besides, I think they want my ass a little more than yours. Even though yours is cuter."

She shook her head, taking me seriously. "You have a glorious ass, Lady."

Josie was dying on the loveseat, using every ounce of power she had not to bust out laughing.

"It's nice that you think Josie is glorious." I ruffled her hair again. All of us couldn't help but grin when Candace unleashed her musical giggles.

You have the key, find your map... The words whispered in my ears as warmth flared inside me that had nothing to do with the ball of sunshine in my lap. When the goddess spoke through Candace, it was creepy. When her voice echoed in my head it was worse.

Chapter 20

It was kind of comical. The moment my hand touched the brass handle of First Moon Books, my stomach growled and twisted into a knot before it began chewing on my backbone. While I wanted to check on things at the store, the smell wafting from the diner was too irresistible. Jason had been successful on his own thus far, he could live without me for another hour while I fueled up. Plus, if I drank another coffee at the bookstore, Marge might put me up for adoption.

Sighing, I looked both ways before crossing the street and headed to get some breakfast.

The door chimed and Marge smiled at me from the table closest to the door. She set down the older couple's plates of eggs, toast, and bacon. "Coffee?" She asked me, not them.

"You bet."

"Decaf," the elderly gentleman answered, too.

I chuckled and sat in my spot, glancing at my watch and trying to decide if I was closer to lunch or a late breakfast. With as much as my stomach was twisting in hunger, I probably would have to settle with both. A hamburger and an omelet *did* sound quite delicious…

"Hey, Darlin'. Know what you want?" She set a cup of steaming brew in front of me and put her hand on her hip.

"Hamburger, rare."

"Rare?" She cocked an eyebrow, not that I could blame her. I usually liked my steak rare and my burgers burnt.

"And an omelet. With ham."

Her other eye widened in response. "Somebody joining you?"

"Nope. Just me."

"You're eating a burger and an omelet?"

"You think Herb could make it a steak and omelet instead of plain eggs?"

"I'm sure he could. So, you want a steak and eggs, but omelet instead of eggs and skip the burger?"

"The burger, too."

"Oh, honey!" She grinned, set the pot of coffee on the table, squealed, practically knelt on the floor beside me, and grabbed my hands, shaking them excitedly. "Congratulations!"

"Huh?"

She leaned in closer. "Which one?"

"Which one what?"

"Is the father?"

An icy shard of fear slithered down my veins. "I'm not pregnant!"

"What?"

"What do you mean what? I'm not pregnant?"

"You're not?" She got up off the floor.

"No?"

"You sure?"

Since witches couldn't get pregnant unless they *wanted* to, I was pretty fucking sure. "Hell no."

"Oh. You're hungry?"

"Very?"

"Steak, omelet, *and* hamburger hungry?"

"Yes?"

"And you're sure you're not pregnant?"

"Positive!" I held out my hands in exasperation.

"Positive?"

"Yes!"

She eyed me dubiously one more time. "Kay. I'll have your order out shortly."

"Hey, Marge?"

"Yeah?"

"Extra rare on the steak, please. Sear it."

"You sure you're sure?"

I just sighed and pinched the bridge of my nose between my fingers, praying to the goddess the headache that had come out of nowhere would leave just as quickly. Tomorrow I was getting a fluffy coffee and a Danish.

"Herb! Steak sushi and an eggroll and a burger still mooin'"

"Roger."

I sought solace in my mug of coffee, ignoring everyone and everything around me. It was probably the reason I missed the chime of the door and the warm hand on my shoulder. His aftershave broke me out of my reverie. "Mornin', Chiefy."

"Chiefy?"

"Shut up. It's cute."

"Okay, Dotty." He slid into the booth across from me.

"You didn't stay over last night."

"You noticed." He chuckled and waved at Marge.

"Yep. I'm super observant like that. You went home?" I raised an eyebrow, curious to how that went.

"No. I was busy getting the good doctor admitted and getting Judge Reinhold to sign off on it."

"Judge Reinhold?"

"Yes?"

"You're fucking kidding me, right?"

"No?"

"Never mind." The day was getting weirder by the minute and I wanted nothing to do with it. If I ignored it, it might just go away.

Marge set a cup of coffee down in front of Chief and then settled the three plates of food she'd managed to balance on one arm in front of me. She looked to Chief. "You hungry?"

"Uh. Too early for lunch, I just came for the...show." He was staring at the mountain of food in front of me.

"We got a pool going in the back. You want in?"

"On whether or not she finishes?"

"Boy or girl." Marge giggled and walked away. I stared at Chief with a horrified expression on my face.

"I'm not fucking pregnant."

He looked at Mount Saint Burgersteak and raised his eyes, cocking a disbelieving eyebrow at me.

"Not another word."

"Wouldn't dream of it."

"Smart boy. So, if you weren't at my place and you didn't go home…"

"Slept on a cot in cell seven."

"Ouch. Not the most comfortable accommodations."

He just stared deadpan, not having the courage to mention that I would know because he had made me spend the night in one of them when he arrested me. He was truly getting wiser in his old age. "Nope." Marge saved the situation by depositing a piece of pie in front of him. "This for me or her?"

"You. She'll probably want one with ice cream. And by one, I mean one whole pie."

I picked up my empty burger plate, snagging one more French fry, and handed it to her. "Nope. No pie for me. Gotta watch my figure." I grinned and cut a piece off my omelet with my fork.

"Watch it do what?" Marge rolled her eyes and walked away.

"Well, I was going to offer to pay, but I think I might have to wait until payday." Chief grinned.

"Okay, you can stop picking on me now. I was actually going to skip brunch, but my stomach was gnawing on my backbone. Think I've been using too much juice lately and my body is having trouble keeping up. Kind of like when I go all vampy and have to feed off Yuki."

"Ew."

"Shut up." I tore off a piece of steak, not having realized I'd picked it up with my fingers instead of using my fork and knife.

The shockwave hit first, blasting out the front windows out of the diner. The pain of shards piercing the skin of my neck and back registered before I heard the sound of the explosion. Then the searing heat instantly warmed the blast of cold air that filled the diner from the gaping hole in the plate glass.

Chief's face immediately started dripping blood before he got his arms up to protect himself. The rest of the diners dropped to the floor, but thankfully we were the only ones sitting by the window.

"What the fuck was that?" He got up and ran to the door.

Whatever it was had been far enough away to spare the diner any *real* damage. It had to have been one of the closer stores. I tossed the steak on the glass filled plate and gingerly got up, not wanting to slide my ass across any shards on the seat.

"Dot…"

"What?"

"Bookstore," he said morosely and ran through the door.

My heart throbbed in my chest and I followed, glass crackling beneath my feet as I slipped trying to gain traction.

The front of the store was concealed by a cloud of black smoke as fire poured out of the massive hole in the front of my building. Throbbing in my chest ceased when my heart stopped beating. Putting one foot in front of the other, I forced myself to cross the street. "No…no…nooo…nooooooo," I wailed.

By the time I got there, the fire was out, and the smoke drifted away from the building. Closing my eyes, I prayed that the store wouldn't be littered with bodies. In the distance, I could already hear the warble of the fire engine sirens as they started.

The smoke cleared enough for me to see Chief run through the front door into the store. Panic overwhelmed my dread as I took off after him.

The store was filled with people. People and undamaged books and shelves. People staring at the glowing wall of magic inside the store separating the smoke, fire, and damage. My ward wall. I choked out a sob of relief. "What the hell happened?"

Jason shook his head, standing next to the two new cashiers.

"Is everybody okay?"

He looked around the store. "I think? What the hell was that?"

"You tell me. I was across the street."

Chief was walking closer to the wall, slowly reaching out his hand and pressing it against the magic barrier. As soon as he touched it, it sizzled and faded from view. There was a blast of heat, but it quickly dissipated as the damage came into view.

Something had blasted a hole through the front window of my store. Some of the display materials in the window were still smoldering, but that was the extent of the damage.

"Well, I think we can rule out a gas leak." He rubbed the toe of his shoe over the fire blackened floor at the base of the window, flipping a metallic ring covered in tiny fins over. There were several other mangled pieces lying around the site of the blast. "And that's something you don't see every day."

"What is it?" I moved closer and stood next to him.

"Looks like the tail piece of a rocket, but I'm no expert." He looked over at me, giving me a questioning glare.

"Somebody shot a rocket at my store?"

"That's what it looks like."

"Who the hell would want to blow my bookstore up with a rocket? The OWLs?"

"You know how much one of those costs?" Jason had moved closer to survey the damage.

I looked at the customers inside the store. Normally, a scene like that would have caused people to scream and scramble for safety, but there they all stood, too shocked to move. "Uh…folks? We're going to be closing early today.

Take what you have and just head home. My treat. Sorry for the...boom."

An elderly lady closest to the register nodded, smiled, and headed for the front door, pausing to rub her hand over my shoulder before she left. "Thank you, dear. And thank you for saving all of us."

"Wasn't me. It was the store."

She winked and headed out the front door, the rest of the customers slowly following her lead. More than a few of them offered words of thanks and comfort as they passed. I waited to do or say anything until only my family and staff were left. The two newbies at the register looked like they needed to change their underpants. "You guys can go, too if you want."

The taller guy looked ready to bolt but stood his ground when his shorter female counterpart made no motion of leaving. "Well, at least go grab a coffee."

I looked up to see Josie and Candace standing at the entrance to the coffee shop from the bookstore. Josie raised her eyebrows at me and tilted her head. "What the hell happened?"

"We got blowed up."

She just shook her head and led the kids into the coffee shop.

"That's an RPG," Jason said as he bent down to inspect the piece of explosive on the floor.

"RPG?"

"Rocket-propelled grenade."

"And you know this how?"

"Video games."

"Seriously?"

He nodded solemnly. "Somebody wanted to turn this place into Last Moon Books."

"Funny." I rolled my eyes, anger overshadowing the fear that had been weighing me down like a wet blanket. "Who the fuck would blow up my store?"

"My uncle," Yuki said disapprovingly from the door. I hadn't even heard her open it.

"Uh. It's almost noon. Couldn't have been your uncle."

"You think he would shoot a rocket himself? Hell no. He'd hire some dumb human to do it."

She had a point.

"He's lucky he didn't do any real damage."

"Thanks to your wards and shields. Holy shit, Dot. I don't even think I could stop a bullet, let alone a rocket." Chief had a tinge of awe in his voice as he looked around. "If you hadn't had that strong of a shield over this place…"

"Yeah. Let's not think about it. I kind of want to throw up." I started breathing heavy and leaned against the counter, bracing myself with my hand and trying not to hyperventilate. Things could have been exponentially worse. A rocket launched into a building with that many people in it… The death toll would have been tragic.

He rubbed his hand over my back and the rest of the guys moved closer to support me. "Your shield is probably why we felt it so bad at the diner. The explosives didn't have anywhere to vent but out. Hence the gigantic shock wave."

"Shit. I need to go make sure everybody is okay over there."

"I'll go," Yuki answered and took off.

"I'll go fix the windows and give your apologies," Jason said solemnly and followed her.

"Pay my bill, too!"

He waved over his shoulder while I tried to get my breath back.

"Well, first thing's first. Let's get this place fixed up," Chief said and gently let me go after he made sure I had my balance. He frowned at the damage and knelt as close as he could without jamming his knee into a pile of broken glass.

Putting his hand on the floor he whispered the word of his canting and my legs prickled as he poured his magic into the foundation. Blue tendrils of power fanned out and crept over the debris and shattered frontage. Everything blurred as the shards slowly rolled and tumbled back into their original position as the cracks slowly sealed shut. Within a few minutes, you couldn't even tell someone had launched an incendiary device into my place of business. The only irreparable items were the poster board promotions that were burnt beyond recognition. As the damage faded, so did my heavy breathing.

"Thanks, Chief."

"My pleasure." He smiled as he nodded.

I poured even more power into the shields and wards, expanding them outward a smidge. *Next* time, if there was one, the rocket wouldn't even make it *through* the window. Smiling as I finished, I managed to stammer, "Everybody take the rest of the day off," before passing out.

∞ ∞ ∞

At least someone had taken me home and put me in my own bed and not left me passed out on the carpeted floor in front of the registers. So, I had that going for me. A splitting headache was the other.

"Welcome back," Yuki whispered from behind me.

"Ow, my head."

"I thought witches didn't get headaches?"

"We don't. Hangovers, sometimes, but headaches no. This is the second one this week. What the hell." I rubbed the bridge of my nose as I rolled over on my back.

Yuki propped her head up on her hand and gave me a worried look. "When was the last time you fed?"

"This morning. I had a burger and a bite of steak before bookstore went boom boom."

"I didn't say ate, I said fed."

"Tomato, tomahto."

"Damn it, Master. You need *blood* now, too. I thought you figured that out."

"Liquid diets are for when I get dentally challenged. I used my witch power at the store."

"We need to get you a supernatural nutritionist or something." I heard a soft crunch and then she held a

221

bleeding finger over my lips. "Does that make you hungry?"

I looked at the ruby red drop hanging from the tip of her index finger and nodded. It was almost seductive in its allure. Without thinking, I lifted myself from the mattress and licked the drop from the source, nearly whining as the flavor exploded in my head.

Yuki sighed and snapped her fingers.

To my surprise, a shirtless Ellis entered my room.

The hunger that had been momentarily filled by diner burger instantly expanded and demanded to be filled again by *sangreal du noir elf.*

Ellis crawled into the bed, pulling me on top of his rather chiseled chest, and offered me his neck. My fangs pierced his flesh and his blood splattered across my tongue. Inhaling his scent, I pressed my forehead against his silky hair and pulled my meal from his vein, refusing to stop until he started slamming his open palm against the mattress between Yuki and me.

"Master," she warned softly.

I let go and rolled off him, letting him catch his breath.

Preparing to be sated, I rubbed my tummy and smiled happily until the pain twisted in my gut again. "More," I groaned.

"Shit." Yuki offered me her wrist.

Grabbing it frantically, I sank my fangs between her tendons and guzzled her blood. She had a completely different flavor from Ellis. He was spicy, she was sweet. When she frantically pulled her arm from my mouth with a twist and a wince, I cried out for more.

Shea and Dar stepped from the shadows and looked at the three of us worriedly. Without thinking, Shea stripped off his shirt and crawled atop me, offering his shoulder. If he had been three times his size, he wouldn't have filled my hunger. When he tapped out, Dar took his place.

Shea was a side dish, but Dar was a meal. Wrapping my arms around him, I drank and fed and drank some more. He was endless. When his hips started bucking against me and he cried out with a shudder, I was full.

"Houston, we have a problem."

I looked over at Yuki. "What?"

She sighed and let her head fall to the pillow beside me. "Think about who and what you just ate."

I looked at the men spilled across my bed and the vampire beside me. "Shit."

"Yeah. Your belly needed to be filled by all your domains. Let's just hope your hunger is sated long enough for us to recoup what we lost."

"I hope to goddess it is." I frowned, not wanting to contemplate the implications if it wasn't. I could barely feed from my friends. The thought of strangers opening a vein for me turned my stomach. Just not in a hungry way.

"Now we need to talk about my uncle."

I couldn't roll over to face her as I was covered in hunk, but I turned my head and almost frowned at the seriousness etched upon her face. Yuki was many things. Broody, comical, angsty, and even snarkastic, but serious wasn't one of them. It was kind of scary. "Do we have to?"

"No. You can wait until he launches a rocket at someplace without wards and shields. Like the diner or the vampire's house."

"He wouldn't do that…" I trailed off. Judging by the look on her face, he would. He might even enjoy it. "But they're innocents?"

"And you love them. And it would wreck you."

"It would," I answered thoughtfully.

Yuki put her hand on my cheek. "Bring the war to him before it spirals out of control."

"So, what? You just want me to pop over to Ashville all willy-nilly and assassinate your uncle?"

"Yes! That's exactly what I want you to do."

"Yuki…"

"Please, *master*, for one time, just please listen to me."

I silenced her with a finger to her lips. "I hear you, and on some level, I agree with you. I have no problem killing in self-defense. I have no problem killing when there is no other option. But as long as the thought that there *is* another option is in my head, I can't do it. That's not who I am and that's not who I want to be."

"But he almost killed innocent people in your store!"

"And if he *had*, this conversation would not be happening."

"So, you're going to wait until he does?"

"No. I'm going to scare the fucking shit out of him. I'm going to make him understand that he is *nothing* compared to me. Want to know why? Because I have all of *you*." I poked her in the forehead.

"Never bring a gun to a Yuki fight." Dar chuckled against my chest.

Yuki blushed and it was the cutest thing ever.

Chapter 21

The sound of the end credit symphony woke Yuki up. She hadn't even lasted half the movie before putting her head on my thigh and interrupting the quieter parts of the movie with soft snores and mewls. Yuki's dreams were apparently scarier than her real life, and she only quieted with a soft touch on her shoulder or face.

Josie and Candace hadn't even made the attempt at a late-night movie. They snuck off to their room as soon as it started. Even Chief hadn't been tempted and wandered off for a shower and bed as soon as he walked through the door. With all the energy coursing through my veins, I knew better than to try to sleep.

"Why didn't you wake me up?" Yuki *humphed* from my lap.

"Because you're so damn cute. When you're sleeping."

"Well, I'm going to my room to be cute. I donated too much blood tonight. Can't keep my eyes open."

"Sorry, sweetie."

"No worries, Master. I'll see if I can get one of the other vamps to donate, too. Amir would probably be happy to take one for the team."

"Yeah. Now I just need another demon, shadow walker, and dark elf." I rolled my eyes.

"Probably not. Vampires are anemic by nature. We don't produce blood, we consume it. You don't feed enough to bother the others."

"We'll see." The thought of having to feed off another vamp bothered me more than it should have. I could barely accept Yuki's sacrifice. To feed off someone who wasn't close to me… It wasn't a pleasant thought at all. "Night, Yuki."

She leaned and looked out the front window. The subtle glow of pre-morning illuminated the street in blue. "Closer to good morning, but whatever. Night, Master."

I smiled as I watched her retreat into her room, listening for the subtle *click* of the lock. Once I heard it, I let the shadows swallow me into the couch.

Dreading what had to be done, I walked through the realm of shadows slowly, playing voyeur along the way. Most people were asleep, some were getting ready for the day, some were still in the throes of passion. Whatever they did, I smiled as I passed, getting a tiny thrill at the ability to peer into everyone's life as I strode by, feet soundlessly padding over the shadow stuff beneath me.

As I roamed, the shadows began their subtle song. Pinpricks of gooseflesh crawled over my arms as the sibilant symphony wrapped me in warmth. Then the chorus of shrieks and snarls joined in as the shadow demons crawled closer.

For the first time, I didn't panic. I even halted my journey as they circled around me, red glowing eyes cutting through the darkness. They ventured closer, but not within touching distance as they slowed, stopped, and lowered their faces to the ground. The song continued, but the shrieks morphed into a bass line of their muffled whines of joy. Without fear, I stepped toward the ring of shadows, knelt, and caressed the head of the nearest.

Lifting its head, ecstasy rolled from it in waves. Smiling, I stood and continued my journey.

It had been the biggest mistake of the Abernathy line to ever bring me to the mansion in the hills surrounding Ashville. I'd even been there as a child, accompanying my mother on coven business. It made the journey from Cedar Falls almost effortless as I traversed the shadow realm. With one last sigh, I stepped from the shadow of a tree just inside the gate.

My original intention had been to go with a sneak attack, appearing behind him and subduing him in a show of power, but he wouldn't have respected that. Feared, yes. Fearful enough to stand down? No. It would be much better to show him how utterly powerless he was against me.

Unfortunately, I didn't even make it across the expanse of grass separating the wall and door before being attacked by vampires. With almost shadow walker ability, they melted from the shadows and were on me before I even registered their presence. I mentally cursed myself for not looking before leaping.

However, once in my field of prescience, their movements became almost comically slow. Batting two of them aside, I turned the third to ash. It was a combination of a jab and fire spell that worked out exponentially better than I'd imagined. The first two were hesitant to attack after the display, and I couldn't blame them. I used my shadows to leave them in the dust of their fallen comrade.

The front door of the mansion fared as well as the vampire I turned to ash. It sent a strong message to the two guards inside. There were few things in the mortal realm that vampires feared more than fire. One of them kowtowed, but the other merely shook as he looked up to the landing above.

"Where is Abernathy?"

The one standing snarled when he turned back to face me. The one at his feet pointed toward the stairs without looking up from the floor. I turned and made it to the first step when Lady Abernathy stepped onto the landing with a sigh.

"Lady Dorothea," she whispered softly and bowed her head.

"Hey, June. Are we going to have a problem?" I spoke steadily, more confident than I felt, as I walked up the stairs and stopped halfway.

"Since I am not in line for succession, only bound to the clan through marriage, absolutely not."

"Even though I killed your husband?'

Darkness passed over her features for a moment before she schooled her countenance and the smile returned. She might not have agreed with the former Lord's actions and methods, but she did love him, that much was certain. "No. He challenged you and you were victorious. In fact, I should be thanking you for saving my daughter." She might have loved her husband, but she loved her daughter more. I could hear it in her voice.

"She's my pride and joy. Of course, I'd save her." I winked and continued up the stairs.

"Are you here to kill him?" She didn't sound concerned, merely curious.

"Only if he won't see reason. He tried to incinerate what is mine."

"I warned him not to."

"Are you telling me he can't be reasoned with?"

"I am. But he might be bullied. I wish you luck. Last door at the end of the hall," she answered coolly and stepped past me, heading down the way I'd come.

Husband and daughter aside, she held nothing but disdain for her brother-in-law. I chuckled and headed down the carpeted runner filling the length of the hall Stopping at the double polished oak doors, I kicked them open without so much as a knock.

The vampires had a fucking throne.

Abernathy was sitting on it, chin on his fist, sneering at me as I burst into the room.

That close to dawn, I had assumed he'd be alone. I had assumed so very, very wrong. A kiss of at least twenty vampires stepped from the shadows and rushed me *en masse*. Fearlessly, they swarmed me, confident in their numbers. In the space of a heartbeat, I was gripped and pushed to the ground at their feet. One of them grabbed a fistful of hair and lifted my head to face their lord as they parted before him.

"What? Did you truly think you were a match for me?" He lifted his chin from his fist and started laughing. The vampires around me joined him and stopped when he trailed off.

When he finished, I started and ended it with a single word. "Fidget."

Abernathy tilted his head and scrunched his eyebrows in confusion. I smiled as I felt the shadow slither down my sleeve and crawl over the flesh of my hand, dropping to the polished wood floor between me and the vamps.

Soundlessly, he grew and then bellowed a screech as he stood and towered over the semicircle of undead around me. They began hitting the walls around us, thudding twice as they fell to the ground wetly after.

A wave of fear washed over me as the shadow demon started tearing their flesh and limbs. I stood slowly and let the fear change me into exactly what I needed to be at that moment.

Snarling, I walked toward the mediocre throne as my fangs ripped through my gums, my nails tore through the flesh of my fingers, and a burning bloodlust boiled through my veins. For nothing but effect, I ripped the broom charm from my neck and swung the scythe. I led with the dull edge as I charged, stopping short just as the metal pressed his neck against the high back of his chair.

"Call this pointless war off."

"You're not even a vampire!"

I hissed and bared my fangs at him. His eyes bulged even more. "No. I'm more," I lisped around my overly large teeth and let the shadows rise up around him and bind him to the chair he'd been so proud of the moment before. "Are you done?"

He nodded, quickly and emphatically.

Fidget roared behind me. I turned my head and sent a mental command to him, sparing the lives of the handful of vampires cowering on the floor.

The squeal of the shadows binding the vampire to the throne were the only warning I had. He had been bound, but with silver daggers hidden in his hands, blades turned toward him. I caught the glint of their gleaming surface as he raised them after severing the bindings. In a blink, he stood and plunged one in my chest and the other into my heart, the other through my back, its tip nearly nicking the other between my ribs.

I looked down at the grizzly wound as pain blossomed through my chest. My vision darkened as the edges faded away into nothingness.

Abernathy's laughter filled my ears as he lowered me to the ground at his feet. With an evil sneer he twisted the blade in my chest and yanked it from my chest.

I didn't scream, I didn't call out, the pain was already too intense for rational, or irrational, thought. The wounds weren't enough to kill me, but I was fighting to remain conscious. If I passed out, it was over. He could *really* kill me at his leisure.

Abernathy made one horrid mistake.

Without my reins, Fidget was free to flee or feast. He might have been a shadow demon, possibly just a baby, but he loved his mother. His shriek of anger blasted the laughter from my ears and Abernathy's lips as he hurtled over the bodies of the vampires between us and smacked Abernathy across the room with an elongated shadow claw. Blood sprayed over my field of vision in a crimson bow and splashed down over me in liquid fire. Three more shadowy figures joined my shadow demon as they flew across the room and ended Abernathy in screams of pain and rage.

∞ ∞ ∞

A cool cloth wiped across my brow and the smell of wet blood wafted to my nose. Blinking, I stared at a very worried looking vampire hovering over me. "Yuki?"

She pulled the cloth away and frowned at me. "If you were in better shape, I'd roll you over and kick your ass. Master," she added almost as an afterthought.

"We would, too," Dar chimed in angrily, hugging a scared looking Shea to his chest behind my vampire nurse. They had been the shadowy figures I'd seen beside my angry looking Fidget. He chirped in my ear to let me know he agreed with all three of them.

Turning my head, I smiled at the little shadowy fluff beside me on the unfamiliar pillow. "You, too?"

Another angry chirp, but he quickly favored me with a wispy cuddle shortly thereafter.

"How is she not dead?" June asked from the doorway. I guessed we were still in Ashville.

Yuki turned and looked at her mother, eyes narrowing in distrust. "Do you really think a couple of daggers can kill a god?"

"God?" Quickly she strode across the bedroom floor and hovered over me as she stared at me. Gingerly, she held out her hand and lightly ran the tips of her fingers over my still damp skin. Power flared between us. She gasped and knelt at my bedside. *The* bedside, not mine, as I didn't have a fucking clue where I was.

"My old room," Yuki answered with a sad smile. "She needs blood," she said over her shoulder to Dar and Shea.

"We have some in the vault?" June answered questioningly.

"Not human," Yuki answered.

Dar stepped forward, but without hesitation, June offered her wrist. "She doesn't smell like a vampire," she said thoughtfully as my fangs grew again and pierced her flesh. I fed without gripping her, letting the blood fill me, and the holes her brother-in-law had left in me before he died. She gasped and braced herself against the bed as I fed.

"You're grounded," Yuki said to me, uncharacteristically motherly.

I let it go for a few moments while I fed. Finally feeling a little better than shit, I let go of June's wrist with a nod of thanks. "Because I didn't kill him?"

231

"Because you tried to do things *your* way without *us*." She motioned toward Dar and Shea.

"Where's Ellis?"

Shea frowned. "When the blade pierced your heart, he felt it. Worse than any of us."

I started to sit up, worried about him, but Yuki pressed me firmly down against the overly hard mattress. "He's alive. We were all about to shadow walk here when he collapsed. He begged us to leave him and save you."

"How did you know where I went?"

June blushed and looked away.

"You told them?"

She nodded. "I didn't doubt you would beat him, not after you destroyed Philipe, but I know what a devious, sneaky bastard Jules can be."

"He surprised me with those knives… I thought it was over and I was calling my shadow off the vampires before he killed all of them. Fucking sneak-attacks get you every time."

She nodded, looking like she had witnessed more than a few of them herself.

The sounds of explosions outside shook the walls. "What the hell is that?" Even Yuki's hand couldn't keep me from sitting up, but I stayed still as pain lanced through my chest and Dar ran to the window. He pulled the curtain, stared for a moment, and began chuckling softly.

"What is it?" I debated ignoring the pain in my chest and looking for myself.

"Your mother," he answered with a bark of raucous laughter.

"Great." I groaned and leaned back against the bed. "The pain in my chest moved to my ass."

"One of us should go down there and let her know the fight is over. Little vampires are flying through the air and landing rather abruptly."

Yuki giggled and was gone in the blink of an eye and a *whoosh* of air. I desperately tried to rest for a few moments and heal before my mother made an appearance. With the

232

hole Yuki had made with her vacancy, Shea took the opportunity to fill it, gently caressing my arm as he sat beside me.

"Are you all right?" He looked down at me sheepishly.

"I'll live."

A single tear rolled down his cheek. "You had better. I do not know what I would do without you."

"What any of *us* would do without you," Dar added as he came back to the bedside.

"I was never in any real danger."

They both scoffed.

"Seriously. I knew you would be here in an instant if I needed you." I winked. "Look at you. You both ran out of the house in the middle of winter without even putting on a shirt." I *rawred* and ran my finger down Shea's chest, watching in rapt fascination as his tattoos lit wherever our skin touched.

"Well, your safety outweighs our modesty," Shea answered with a smile as June backed away, not wanting to be a part of our tender moment.

"I'll make some tea for your mother, but I fear I must depart for the day shortly thereafter. Yuki can show you around your home when you feel up to it." She bowed her head.

"Your home. I'll continue living in Cedar Falls, thank you very much."

"You do not intend to…"

"I never intended to. That's what I was trying to tell your brother-in-law. I am where I'm needed."

"Well, that is a discussion for another time."

"Yes. Best to keep my mother caffeinated." I rolled my eyes and earned a smile from June.

"You remind me so much of her."

"And here I thought we were friends," I said half-jokingly. And half-indignantly.

June laughed. "In the area of formidableness, you, your mother, and your grandmother are all cut from the same cloth." She bowed and backed out of the room.

Just as Yuki returned with a very angry looking banshee in tow, with red-hair and answered to the name Mother. Crying, the banshee ran across the room and fell to the floor beside me. "Are you okay?"

"Yes?"

"Oh, thank the goddess." She bowed her head and pressed her forehead against my arm, sobbing silently.

"What are you doing here?"

She lifted her head and stared at me incredulously with red-rimmed eyes. "You were hurt! Of course, I would come."

"I mean, how did you know?"

She gulped and stared at me. "Your father…"

I smiled. "You saw him, too?"

She nodded, seeming almost frail. "Daughter…"

"Yes, Mother?"

"I am sorry. Truly sorry."

"For?" The list was so long, I didn't know where she was starting.

"Treating your human…with such disdain."

"Marge?" Again, the list was too long, and I needed clarification.

"Yes. Midge."

"It's not me you need to apologize to," I said sternly.

"I know, and I will."

"Why do you hate her so much? She's the sweetest woman in the world?"

Mother shifted in embarrassment. "That is just *one* of the reasons."

"Huh?"

Mother sighed. "I'm jealous."

"Of her?"

She nodded.

"Why?"

Taking a deep breath, she thought about her answer for a moment before speaking. "Because of how much you adore her. You treat her more like a mother than you have *ever* treated me."

234

I nearly slapped her upside the head. "Because you never *let* me!" Enough was enough. I sat back up and stared down at my mother, fighting the urge to throttle her about the head, neck, and ears. "You and Nana both treat affection like some sort of disease! If you weren't belittling me, you were teaching me how to be a bigger, badder witch!"

"Sweetie, belittling is *how* we show affection."

"So, you love Marge?" I cocked an eyebrow in disbelief.

She swallowed. Hard. And nodded. The answer I was *least* expecting.

"What?"

"How could I not? You move across the country, start a new life, and from the moment you rolled into that dinky, dingey little town, she made sure you were fed and loved! I owe her a great debt."

I blinked. Looked up at Dar, over at Shea, and back down at my mother, waiting for the punchline. "Seriously?"

"Yes?"

"Well, okay then. Apparently, I've slipped into the Twilight Zone." I pushed myself back against the headboard and sat up straighter, pulling Shea into the space between my legs and hugging him like a teddy bear. I needed an anchor.

My mother blinked as the tattoos on him flared into life, tilting her head and gasping. "What is that?"

"I am tattooed," he said simply and held out his arm.

She reached out and touched his arm, but they were lifeless beneath his fingers. She started tapping them.

"They only light with your daughter's touch," he said by way of explanation.

"He's my nightlight," I said with a chuckle.

"That is the most...*unusual* thing I've ever seen. What language is it?" She looked at Shea instead of me. I barely spoke English, sometimes.

"I do not know."

"Doesn't matter," I answered and hugged him a little tighter, causing them to flare just a little brighter.

"Daughter?"

"Yes?"

"Pour a little power into them…" She stared at the arm in her hand.

"What?"

She finally looked up, huffing in frustration. "Pour. Magic. Into. Them," she answered slowly, for us slow kids in the back.

I shrugged and smiled, letting my love, warmth, and magic flow into the embrace.

The room flared a brilliant blue, and I had to blink a few times to let my overly light-sensitive eyes catch up. The script on his arms, shoulders, and chest was scrolling like a computer monitor, rearranging themselves and blending together until the brush strokes began to form constellations and swirls.

"What the hell is it?" I pushed him forward, keeping my hands on him to keep the magic flowing as some sort of map finally coalesced over every visible ounce of flesh above his waist.

"It would appear as if you have found your map," my mother answered in a voice that wasn't her own.

Chapter 22

"Can you keep this between you and me?"

Candace looked up at me, almost fearfully. Her bottom lip was trembling and she looked like she was on the verge of hyperventilating. "They'll be there, won't they?"

"Those angel thingies?"

She nodded.

"Probably, but you don't have to be there, just get me there. As soon as we're in Tartarus, I want you and Shea to get somewhere safe."

Candace blinked. "You would go alone?"

"Rather than risk either of you? Absofuckinglutely."

"How will you get home?" She looked like she was about to completely lose it. It had been hard enough getting her alone to have the conversation I didn't want to have with her to begin with. Actually saying the words was ten times harder.

"This is my job. He's *my* father. I'm not going to risk losing anybody else," I said steadfastly.

"Everyone will be mad at you. Again."

"Everybody can suck it. They'll be alive to be mad. That's more than enough for me." I grinned at Candace to hopefully lighten the mood.

"You still didn't answer my question. How will you get home?"

"I'll try to use the shadows. If I can't, I'll call Shea and you guys can swoop in and pick me up when I'm sure there's no danger."

It was the first time since I'd met Candace that she doubted what I was telling her. I could see it on her face and in the shrug she gave me.

"Is that a yes?"

She didn't say a word, just gave me a single curt nod and opened the door to Charlotte's bistro. To coax Candace into going someplace we could be alone, I'd promised her lunch at her favorite place. Desperate times called for desperate measures. Especially when I saw Charlie smile and wave at Candace, and borderline scowl at me.

"Welcome back," Charlie managed to get out.

"Thanks. Good to see you again."

"I'm sure."

Without ordering, she brought our teas and set them on the table we had just settled ourselves at by the window. "The usual?"

Since there was basically nothing else on the menu I'd eat other than her attempt at a hamburger, I nodded. I *really* didn't want a turkey burger, I wanted a steak, but it was definitely the time of sacrifices, and a turkey burger wouldn't kill me. Maybe.

"You need to tell Josie."

"No. If I tell Josie, the whole coven will know what I'm planning and either try to stop me or go with me."

"That is not what I am talking about."

"Oh." I opened my mouth to protest, to tell her I would keep my promise to tell Josie at the wedding, but Candace was right. This might be a one-way trip and if I didn't make it… "I will."

"Today."

"Fine, Mrs. Pushypants. I will. Right after lunch." Before I could say another word, the door behind me opened up and two hands gripped my shoulders excitedly. I could feel Sherry's excitement. "Hey, Miss Mayor," I said and turned my head to smile.

"How'd you know it was me? Oh, never mind!"

"Pull up a chair. What's got you all excitable?"

238

She grabbed a wooden chair from the table beside us and sat down. "He proposed!"

"Huh?" My heart stopped beating.

"Derek! He asked me to marry him!"

Best day ever. "Oh, my goddess! That is amazing! Congratulations!" If I could pretend a turkey burger was the real thing, I could pretend I was happy for my friend. On some level, I was. On the other eight levels of hell, I wanted to scream in rage, claw his face off, and possibly destroy the planet. I didn't love him. I didn't want or need him, but something primal inside me was still screaming, 'Mine!' I shut that bitch of an inner voice up and took a sip of my iced tea. "When's the big day?"

"Since the bar is opening in two weeks, we're going to Vegas!"

"Awww, I was hoping for a small-town wedding!"

"I know! I was, too. But this will be better. We're going to leave Friday, spend the weekend, and then we'll have a party when we get back to celebrate. I'll fill you in on the details when we make them!" Sherry stood, and leaned over, awkwardly hugging my hand before turning to pet Candace on her head. "I'll call you later!" Grabbing the basket off the counter, she headed back the way she came and left me sitting there with less of an appetite than I already didn't have.

"Gosh. That was exciting."

Candace just snickered.

∞ ∞ ∞

I stood in the shadows of the First Moon Café. Technically I was in the shadow realm and not the shadows, but I wasn't going to correct myself. I didn't move, I didn't step out, I just stood there staring at my sister and watched her work. In just a few short months she had grown from a flighty best friend into a shrewd, hard-working business savvy woman in a serious relationship and I didn't think I could have felt any more pride in who she had become. Even working, you could see the love flowing between her and Candace. Nothing overt, just subtle smiles, glances, and touches. They were going to be together forever, you could tell just by looking.

Business was at the point, just after the rush of everybody leaving work and just before the sun setting and drawing in the nocturnal coffee drinkers looking for a fix before perusing the bookstore. It wasn't slow, but it wasn't slammed either. The vamps would be there soon to relieve the day shift. It was time. Candace could handle the store with the younger humans while I kidnapped my sister.

Somehow, Candace knew I was there and nodded in my direction. "Josie? Could you grab me a couple sleeves of twenty-ounce cups? I'm getting low."

"Sure thing, Sunshine." She winked at her fiancé and headed for the door into the kitchen, right toward me hiding in the corner where the recessed lighting afforded a nice corner shadow. As she passed, I reached out, grabbing her arm, and tugging her into the shadows with me.

She screamed. Thankfully, sounds in the shadow realm were vastly muffled or I might have had to go to the hospital for ruptured eardrums.

"Holy shit, Dot! What the hell. Don't do that to me!" She huffed and covered her heart with her hand while she tried to get her breathing under control.

"Sorry. Didn't mean to scare you."

"Bullshit."

"Okay, maybe a little." I chuckled.

"What's going on?" She looked around, trying to calm her nerves. It wasn't her first trip into the realm of shadow, but one didn't exactly ever get used to it. Unnerving was a good way to put it.

"Needed to highjack you for a bit. We need to have a talk."

"Oh fuck. What did you do?" She shifted her weight onto one leg and put the opposite hand on her hip.

"It's nothing I did, or you did. Just have something to tell you," I answered and grabbed her hand, pulling her away from the café. If she were going to go ballistic or have a meltdown, I didn't want her to do it any place public.

It only took a few heartbeats to traverse the distance to Ashville. Since we'd moved, she hadn't been back, and I thought she might want a bit of familiarity for her conniption. We stepped from the shadows of the pines of the grove used by the Coven of the Black Well. When we were younger…hell, right up until we moved to Cedar Falls, whenever we snuck out to drink, make out with guys, or just get away from our mothers, we always went to the grove. I couldn't think of a better place to drop the bomb on her.

"Oh, my goddess!" She squealed and ran to the rock, the one we always sat on, and hopped up to sit in her usual spot. Then her face darkened. "Oh, shit. This is bad, isn't it? It's really, really bad. For you to bring me all the way here…"

"Not bad. Kind of awesome actually, but I won't lie to you, it's *big*."

"Big as in epic or big as in you're about to crush my heart and tell me something completely life altering like Candace is my sister and I can't marry her." She frowned and scrunched her eyebrows.

She gave me the perfect lead in. "No… Not Candace…"

"Oh, thank the goddess. I can't even begin to tell you how gross that would be. Sister…shudder. Wait, what?"

"*Candace* isn't your sister…"

She stared at me blank faced for a moment while she processed the words. I was fully prepared to give her a few minutes, but it sunk in. "She's not? Who is? Princess Leia?" She scoffed. "Juke, I am your father," she raised her arm and pinched her fingers together while making heavy breathing noises.

"Josie, focus."

She let her hand drop slowly and cocked one eyebrow at me. "What? Don't tell me *you're* my sister!" She scoffed.

241

I remained silent.

"Dot..."

"Josie... I *am* your sister."

"Oh, come on. Quit joking around." She slid off the stone and started walking toward me. "We've known each other our whole lives, shared almost a hundred birthdays. Lived through depressions and wars and... I mean it's just not possible. You're not being funny, you're being mean." She frowned as she stopped in front of me. "I mean, we can't be sisters. You're perfect. You're beautiful, funny, powerful. You're a fucking Blackwell for goddess' sake. I'm just me. Josie. With a mom from hell. Okay, we kind of share *that*, too, but stop kidding around, Dot."

"I'm not. And I won't say I wish I wasn't. You know I've always *thought* of you as a sister... Well, it turns out we *are*."

"That's not possible. You're telling me we're twins and I got adopted off..." She was starting to get angry.

I put both my hands on her shoulders. "No. We have different mothers, but the same *father*."

"You're telling me my dad is your dad. A god? Sorry, Dot, try again. The only godly thing about me is my ability to screw up."

"You're not a screw up, Jose. Knock it off." It was my turn to get angry.

"You're telling me that *your* dad cheated on *your* mother with *my* mother? Nobody's that fucking stupid, Dorothea Blackwell."

"Not cheated on... See, your mom, my mom, and my dad went to a party..."

"Oh, gods. I'm going to be sick." She dropped low, crouching down in front of me and wringing her hands through her hair as she stared at my kneecaps. "No...no...no. That's just fucking wrong." She started shaking her head, not letting go of her hair. I couldn't blame her, either. I kind of wanted to put bleach in my eyes when I had my first visual, too.

I crouched down and gave her a crooked smile. "Try not to think of the deed, just the result. It helps."

She lifted her eyes. "How long have you known?"

"Not long. I was just trying to figure out how to tell you."

"I'm never going to be able to look at your mother again. Or mine. Oh, goddess…"

"I know. Kind of hard to believe, but I'm glad they did."

"How can you be glad? I may never have sex again."

"Yeah, right. And what do you mean how can I be glad? Josie Barton, you're my *sister*. My flesh and blood sibling. How can I *not* be glad? That's fucking awesome!"

She smiled for the first time and nodded. "That explains the same age and birthday, huh? We've always wondered about that."

"Yep. Mystery solved." I laughed and hugged her.

"Dot?"

"Yeah, Jose?"

"Thank you."

"For telling you?"

"No. Well, yes, but thank you for never succumbing to my hitting on you. Oh, goddess, I'm going to be sick again."

∞ ∞ ∞

I slipped the seven letters stuffed into seven envelopes into the pen drawer of my desk and pushed it shut. Well, it *used* to be my desk. It was Jason's now. And after the night I was about to have, the whole store might be his, too. A single tear fell and landed on the already worn surface of the wood surface. Quickly, I wiped my eyes and stood up, nearly shaking with fear. Reaching in my pocket, I let the warmth of the giant gem holding my father's power warm my skin. If everything went *right*, it would be his again soon.

243

Opening the door, I squeaked and caught my breath after nearly colliding with Jason. "Sorry, Dot! Didn't mean to scare you."

"No problems, Love. I'll see you later," I managed to mumble and tried to walk around him.

"Want to grab some dinner?'

"Uh…can't tonight. Taking Candace wedding dress shopping," I lied smoothly. After telling Josie that I was her actual sister, I used it as an excuse to steal Candace away from her for the night. Dar, I had told that I nearly shadow walked myself into a tree and that I would be kidnapping Shea to take us to the mall in Syracuse until I could control my power better. He had bought it, but I wasn't sure it was a hundred percent after the strange look he had given me. Not that it mattered. He would know the truth soon enough and it wasn't like he could follow us to Tartarus.

"Oh, that's cool. And sweet." He grinned at me and gave me a chaste kiss. No snogging in front of the customers. I didn't want them getting jealous or getting any ideas. "How about tomorrow?"

Sure. If I survive, I'll take you all out for dinner. "Sounds good. See you later, Sweetie." I returned his kiss, but this time on the lips and a little longer. "I love you."

"Woah. You feeling okay? I love you, too."

I needed to leave before I started crying. "Yup. Peachy keen. I'll see you tomorrow."

"Okay. It's a date." He grinned.

Without looking back, I headed for the coffee shop. Candace was still making coffee, but when she saw me, she sighed, stopped, and wiped her hands on her apron. "Is it time?"

I nodded.

She turned to Josie. "We are leaving. Do you need anything before we go?"

"Nope. Have fun! Pick out a winner." Josie grinned and waved to me. "Thanks, Dot. Best sister *ever*."

Sure. Write that on my tombstone. "My pleasure." I returned her smile, a little half-heartedly and waited for Candy to walk around the counter. When she was close enough, she reached out and took my hand and we headed for the back room, nodding at Shea along the way. The plan was for Candy and I to go back to my house and change, Shea would meet us there.

As soon as we went through the door, I pulled the shadows to me and stepped out into my living room.

Chapter 23

The shower felt divine. I let the hot water beat the anxiety out of me before I finally shut it off, dried off, and stepped out into my chilly bedroom to get dressed. I'd laid out my war gear on my bed before I hopped in the shower and frowned at the jeans, sweater, and tank top. I would have felt better with a suit of armor and a flaming sword, but the rugged gear was as close as I was going to get. It was harder than it needed to be pulling the jeans over my wet skin, but we were in a hurry.

Stomping my feet into the walking boots, I opened my bedroom door and gasped at the crowd standing around angrily.

"Hey, guys," I stammered. "Whatcha all doin' here?" I asked, but I had a feeling I already knew. Somebody had ratted me out. Chief, Jimmy, Jason, Dennis, Dar, Yuki, Nana, Josie, Ellis, and even my mother were standing behind Shea and Candace, with nothing but contempt on their faces. Shea and Candace were looking *everywhere* but at me. The little snitches. I narrowed my eyes at them.

"Snitches, even witches, get stitches," I said to the two of them.

"Forgive us, Lady, but we could not let you do this."

"I'm doing it."

"Not alone, you're not," Chief answered for the group.

"Huh?"

My mother stepped around everyone and closed the distance between us, stopping in front of me with a sigh. "You're too fucking stubborn to try and stop. You're too fucking stubborn to ask for help. These two angels realized that and sounded the alarm as soon as you headed into the bathroom and gathered your family to help you on your absurd quest." She put her hand on my face. "You get your stubbornness from your father. I hope you know that."

"Sure, I do." I chuckled softly. Looking over her shoulder, I stared at the group behind her and started crying. "Damn it. I didn't want to get you involved because this is going to be *dangerous*. If anything happens to any of you… I couldn't handle that."

"And how do you think we would feel if something happened to *you*? If you're going to do this, you're doing it with *all* of us," Jimmy answered and looked at the group for affirmation. All of them nodded, leaving absolutely *no* room for argument. To go, I needed Candace and Shea. The odds of getting them away from everyone else wasn't possible. Not with the death grip that Josie had on Candace and the grip Dar had on Shea.

"Fine. You win," I answered and let out the breath I'd been holding.

Smiles and nods graced their faces, but only for a moment. "So, what's the plan?" Chief stepped forward.

"We go, get in, find my father, and hopefully get home in one piece?" I shrugged, letting everyone know I was open for suggestions.

"Sounds like a plan," Chief answered. "So, how exactly do we get there?"

"We shadow walk into the depths of hell. We have a map and a key." I smiled at Candace and Shea before looking around at the others. "Is everybody armed?"

Some nodded, most didn't. Jimmy grinned as he held up a tire iron. Chief pointed at the gun on his hip. The gun he never carried. Candace produced a wicked looking dagger while Josie made claw gestures with her hands. Ellis was the only one with a sword. Hopefully, we wouldn't get our asses handed to us, but out of the thirteen of us standing in my living room, eight of us were witches, one was a demon, and one a vampire. We weren't exactly helpless without weapons, but it would have certainly made me feel better if somebody had thought to bring a crate of assault rifles to the party.

"Guess we're ready as we can be," I muttered and motioned for Shea.

He pulled away from Dar and removed his overcoat and shirt before he stood in front of me.

"Let's see if we can figure this out."

"I am sure you will, Lady," he said and turned, exposing the largest group of tattoos on his back.

Remembering to breathe, I put my hands on his back and poured power into him. The entire room lit like a blue star as they began to wiggle and dance over his flesh.

Everyone moved closer, but Nana and my mother moved closest. "Try moving them," Nana suggested, pointing at the randomly scrolling tattoo.

Keeping on hand on him, I touched the lowest point of his back and pushed upward, mesmerized as they swirled upward.

"There! That is Gehenna. Each plane is bordered with that archaic text. I recognize the mountain in the center," Dar said excitedly.

"So, keep going," I said and scrolled some more.

"You went too far. I do not know how I know, but that is the highest material plane. Home of the winged ones," Candace chimed in, fear tinging her voice.

I pushed the tattoos down until a warped plane wrapped in angry text took its place. At the point farthest from the bottom a mountain stood with twisted rivers feeding from the base, crisscrossing the rest of the plane. "Sure, that looks like hell. Let's try that one," I said more cheerfully than I felt.

"We have the map and the key, did anybody bring a bus?" Dennis looked around the gathered. "How do we actually get there?"

I sent another flare of power directly into the exposed plane on Shea's map and wrapped the room in shadow.

We fell at least a foot to the spongy shadowstuff beneath us, but it was unlike any I'd ever seen before. Even the landscape was different. Usually we were surrounded by shards of light that led back to the mortal realm. This time, we were on a road. A road that looked suspiciously like water. We were standing on a frozen river leading through the night sky. Tiny pinpricks of light above us did little to illuminate the expanse around us, but it offered some comfort from the complete blackness.

"There's people down there," Candace said shakily, pointing at the frozen river beneath us.

Sure enough, souls floated by, lifeless eyes staring up at us through the frozen surface as their bodies drifted by.

"It's the River Styx," Nana said with a bit of awe.

"Well, I'm glad it's frozen since we don't have a boat," I answered drearily.

"It is not frozen," Shea answered. "It is covered in shadow…"

"Maybe we should just get going." Jimmy looked around nervously, jumping at things that weren't there.

"There's no song. I don't think we're in the shadow realm," I muttered to myself.

Shea reached back and patted my thigh. "I would suggest not taking your hand from the map, Lady."

"Good call." I nodded at the back of his head.

We all started shuffling forward, the river moving beneath us impossibly fast. It felt like an hour later that we halted before a wall of stone with a double doored gate standing twenty feet above us. It would have been impossible to climb even on its own, but the downward pointing spikes of obsidian didn't help either.

"Never in my day," my mother whispered as she looked up.

"Your day had tyrannosaurs until the big meteor put a stop to that."

"Really, Mother?"

"Well, that is the popular theory. But if those scientists had bothered to ask you, we wouldn't be having this conversation."

"Little less quibbling? How do we open the gate?" I looked at Candace.

She just shrugged.

"Maybe just have her give it a push?" Josie offered meekly. "She *is* the key."

Candace shrugged again and stepped to the seam between the giant doors and put her hands on either side. It was almost comical to watch her struggle and make little groaning noises as she put all her weight behind it. "I do not think this is going to work," she called out when a resounding *thud* that echoed in our chests filled the darkness. She squawked and backed away.

The doors split and red light filtered through the crack between them as they pulled inward, stone grinding on stone. It wasn't a pleasant sound. The teeth in the back of my mouth started to ache in sympathy.

"Little WD-40 would clear that right up," Jimmy said, mesmerized as he watched them slowly grind open.

I finally had the courage to let go of the map. Uncharacteristically, the tattoos didn't dim when I pulled my hand away, either. At least the gate would remain open without me running around keeping one hand on Shea. As fun as that sounded, there was a time and place for everything.

"Let's go," I said with more determination than I felt and stepped through the gate and into hell.

The landscape was barren of everything except dust. Red rocks littered red sand beneath a red sky. Rivers, that had been apparent on the map, were trails of liquid fire leading northward.

"Which way do we go?" Jimmy scanned the horizon.

"Follow the river," I answered him.

"Which one?"

"Any of them. They all lead to where we're going."

"You're the navigator." He tested the trail with a foot with a shrug. "Seems safe enough. Just red dirt."

"Did anybody bring any water?" Mother passed me and followed Jimmy. It was going to be a long walk.

It turned out to be longer than I'd imagined. We ended up camping for the night, even though the sky never changed from its brilliant red hue. We were exhausted from walking, and for the first time in my life, I agreed with my mother. We should have brought some water.

"Maybe we can shadow walk," I suggested after we were rested.

"I would think not." Shea looked around and dusted off his overcoat. Thankfully, the fiery realm was fiery only in appearance. The temperature was quite chilly actually. I didn't, however, wish to dip my hand in the burning fire of the river.

"Why? You don't think the shadow realm extends to Tartarus?"

"Look around, Lady. Do you see any shadows?"

I spun in a circle, looking for the shadow of myself that should have been there under the bright sky, but there was nothing. I wasn't half as creeped out being there as I was at that moment.

"Never mind. Good call." Another thought quickly nagged at my brain. "Fidget?" I called his name softly and looked at the sleeve of my sweater. A full minute passed before I accepted that he wasn't there. "Shit. I hope he's okay."

"I am sure he is. He was probably left in the mortal realm when we passed through."

"Are your tattoos still lit?"

He pulled his collar away from his flesh and I sighed in relief when it looked like he was hiding a blacklight under his shirt. "Yes."

"Good. If you notice them dimming, let me know."

"Why?"

"Because they're our ticket home, I think. Best to keep the lines of communication open."

"Wise."

We set out and continued our trek over the sloping hills. Two hours later, and the fiery mountain was finally visible in the distance.

"I feel like a hobbit," Jimmy murmured. "Nobody said Mordor was in Tartarus. Who has the ring?"

Dennis chuckled beside him.

"You doing okay?" Chief bumped my shoulder with his.

"Yep. How you doin'?"

"Thirsty as hell."

"I don't see how there can't be any water *anywhere*. How could anything survive here?"

"Look around. Do you see anything surviving?"

He had a good point. "Anybody have a bag or something waterproof?" I looked at the rest of the group.

"I have a pair of rubber gloves?" Dennis stepped closer and pulled a pair out of his jean's pocket. Leave it to the paramedic.

"You kinky fucking bastard." Jimmy slapped him on the back.

"I'd just left work. Bite me."

I stopped reaching for them. "They're not…used, are they?"

"No. I usually keep a pair in my pocket just in case."

"Well, you're the new boy scout. Sorry, Chief. You're fired."

"I can live with that."

I opened one of the gloves and stuck my finger inside, whispering, "*Uisce,*" and praying that my spell would work. Slowly the glove filled with water and started expanding. "Okay, everybody drink some," I said and passed it around.

My mother took it first and punctured a hole in the middle finger with her nail before drinking some. "Ugh, it tastes like rubber."

"I don't know whether to make an 'udderly disgusting' joke or an 'I'm sure that's not the first time you've had that taste in your mouth' joke first." Nana cackled.

"Well, I'll be sure to make an 'I'm surprised you can't fit all five of them in your mouth at once' joke when it's your turn." Mother huffed and handed the glove to Candace.

"Remind me to slap both of them with the glove when we're done," I whispered to Chief.

"Make sure it isn't empty when you do."

"A glove full of water might hurt."

"Water? I was going to tell you to fill it with sand," Chief said with a throaty chuckle.

A shriek pierced the otherwise quiet. Yuki took a couple of strides forward and peered at the mountain. "Uh…that mountain is surrounded by angels."

"What? Where?" I stood next to her, putting my hand on her shoulder. That was the first words she'd spoken since we'd left.

"Flying around the mountain," she answered curtly.

"You can see that far?"

"You could too if you'd try. But it just goes to show you, you do need us." She *humphed* and walked away.

Pissed off I was going to go off on my own again?

Lord forbid you ask for help instead of leaving us to pick up your pieces.

Yep. She was pissed. Not that I could blame her. I'd done exactly what I'd promised I'd never do again.

I'm not too happy with you, either. Dar wasn't angry, more disappointed. I felt it more than heard it.

Nor I. Shea seconded. Technically, he thirded, but the list of people who were pissed at me was usually pretty long.

I'm not angry. Just confused.

Thanks, Ellis.

You are welcome.

Jimmy cuffed me in the back of the head. "So, what are we going to do?" He motioned toward the angels.

"Hide if we can and try our best to be sneaky bastards."

It took nearly four more hours and two gloves of water before we were close enough to make out the details of the

254

mountain that wasn't a mountain. It was a giant castle carved from stone. It might have been a mountain at one time, but Mephistopheles had made it into a big ass fortress.

"Two in front of the door and another twelve circling overhead like righteous buzzards. Think there's a back door?" Chief asked as quietly as possible. Even whispering, I was watching the angels warily. Who knew how good their hearing was.

"Doubt it. Wouldn't be much of a fortress. I don't see any sewer grates either. Think we only have one option."

Master?

I looked over at Dar.

I have an idea.

What?

He shimmered for a moment before growing two feet, gaining rows of razor like teeth, and sprouting a pair of wings. I stared at him in disbelief.

I thought you could only assume a form of something you've consumed?

I can't.

You mean?

He shrugged.

That's disgusting.

Tell me about it. I had indigestion for a month. Can you conjure some chains? He stared at me hopefully.

I can.

Then you are now my prisoners.

Only when I, and everybody else, was shackled behind him did I realize how stupid of a plan it was. *This never works out well in the movies.*

You watch too many movies.

From the rocks where we'd hidden, we marched as Dar dragged us along in tow. The angels circling above us continued to do so, keeping their distance, but focusing their attention on us below, slowing their lazy spirals.

At least they're not attacking, Dar said proudly.

They're a couple of hundred feet above us. Let's see how well we do with the two guarding the door.

"They do not appear to be arch angels, at least," Candace whispered behind me.

"No, they don't." The arch angel in the town square had been more human looking in its beauty. The two ahead had the same shark-like grimace as Dar. It was a shame he hadn't munched on one of their more powerful cousins.

When we made it to a short distance away, they came to life and crossed their spears, barring entry. One of them said something in a language I'd never heard before and hoped to never hear again.

Dar answered in English. "The child of Aodh."

Both angels tilted their heads and took a step forward, keeping their spears crossed and muttering something else.

"They are confused. Lady Belenus didn't say anything about more prisoners. Tell him to say, '*Vicna nao Belenii mith vorath.*'"

I relayed Candy's message to Dar, who repeated it. It would have been so much easier if Candace had telepathy, too. I sucked at repeating things. I needed to pick up a copy of Angel as a Second Language for the store.

"How do you know what they're saying or what to say?" I whispered my question to Candace.

"I do not know. I am just grateful I do."

The guards uncrossed their spears and stepped apart, reaching out with their free hands, and pulling the doors open for us. I thought we were home free until they pulled them shut behind us and brought up the rear.

Which way? Dar hissed the question in my mind, panic tinging his mind speech.

I don't fucking know! Left! Go left! We had a fifty-fifty shot of guessing right.

The angels shouted angrily behind us. I chose poorly.

The sound of gunfire echoed in the stone hallway as Chief fired off two rounds, one in each of the angel's faces. It didn't drop them, but they screamed in agony for a moment while their wounds healed. Their silvery blood stopped spreading across the front of their white garments. Long enough for me to pluck my scythe from my neck and slash them from shoulder to hip in two swings.

Blood splattered the walls beside us, but still they didn't fall.

Aim for their necks! Dar managed to shout before a hell hound leapt over all of us and encircled one of their heads in its massive jaws. Ignoring the crunching going on, I took another swipe with my scythe. It went in, but it didn't come out, getting hung up on its spine. Growling, Yuki circled around it and latched onto its back, finishing the job with her hands, and throwing its head against the wall with a frustrated snarl and a dull *splat.*

Their bodies kept quivering even as the blood from the rest of their bodies poured out onto the floor. It was kind of pretty in an obscenely morbid sort of way. "Drinking unicorn blood will keep you alive, even if you are an inch from death, but at a terrible price," I whispered.

"Shut up, Firenze," Yuki giggled and shook the blood from her hands.

Dar shifted back into his more angelic form. "So, keep going left, or go the other way like we were supposed to?"

I almost said right, but something was tugging me in the opposite direction, something in my heart. "Left," I said blankly and pointed.

Hugging the walls and wishing for shadows, I led the way until the narrow hallway opened into a giant cavern complete with pits of flame and scattered bones. And two more angels guarding the door at the opposite end of the cavern. Two angels who had seen us before we had seen them. There was no time to redon our shackles and pretend to be prisoners. Screeching like banshees, they swept across the room, spears leading the charge.

The fireball that Nana set off right in front of them filled the cavern with fire, knocked us all on our asses, and singed off my eyelashes.

"Holy fuck," Chief groaned as he stood slowly.

I was quite content lying on my back against the cool stone beneath me. It felt like I had opened the oven door to grab the brownies and forgot to give the heat a second or two to dissipate. Times a thousand.

"Everybody okay?" I swear I saw smoke come out of my mouth when I spoke.

There was a chorus of disgruntled affirmations.

"Oops," was all Nana offered by way of apology.

"Holy hell, Mother." My mother stood and put out a few smoldering spots on her silky black wrap.

I just stared at the two charred heaps that hadn't even made it halfway across the cavern, reminded once again why I never wanted to piss off my Nana.

"Now I want chicken wings," Jimmy said as we moved closer, starring at the crisp stumps protruding from their backs.

"There is something *really, really* wrong with you. I hope you know that." Yuki stared at Jimmy, shaking her head.

"Oh, come on. Who doesn't like chicken wings?"

"Me."

"You don't count. You'd like them if you could eat them."

"I could just eat you."

Jimmy paled and backed away.

"Come on. Let's find your father," Nana said and moved toward the door. "I really want a nice cold shower."

"Cryogenics isn't safe, Mother."

I just shook my head and followed the two most dangerous weapons in our arsenal and *tried* to ignore their banter.

The staircase led down, and I decided to take that as a good sign. Every castle had a dungeon. Every dungeon was down. Dungeons were also where they kept prisoners. Hopefully, the castle wasn't inverted, and he was in the highest room of the tallest tower, waiting for his true love and his true love's first kiss.

I looked over at Jimmy. At least we brought our donkey.

After one spiral, the circular staircase opened into a pit going down and down and then down some more. It wasn't completely black more of a deep purple. The staircase continued as far as the eye could see, the bottom lost in the abyss.

"Nobody fall," Dennis said solemnly as we peered over the edge.

"Nobody push Jimmy," Jason added as an afterthought.

"Wow, the love is real." I chuckled and continued down the stairs.

"I'm going to scout ahead," Yuki said as she passed us on the outside of the stairs, disappearing in a gust of wind as she practically flew down them.

Be careful, I said as I took the steps one at a time.

Like you do when you go off on your own?

Touché.

Her mental sigh was a real thing. I heard it. *I'm sorry, Master.*

Don't be. I kind of deserved that.

You just make me so angry when you do self-righteous, self-sacrificing, stupid, ignorant, never-learning, stubborn bullshit every damn time. Trust us. We're here to protect you, not the other way around.

Gosh, don't hold back. Tell me how you really feel.

She gave me a light mental chuckle.

I have no problem with that, Yuki. If the shit we were facing were normal shit. But vampire lords, gods… Come on. You are protecting me by not putting yourself in stupid amounts of danger. I love you guys so fucking much, and it would devastate me if anything ever happened to any of you.

And that's exactly how we feel. Stop. Doing. Stupid. Shit.

Yes, ma'am, I mentally muttered and kicked a stone over the edge as I continued down the steps. It was a full few seconds before the clatter of its impact reached our ears.

You at the bottom yet?

No. Quit throwing shit at me.

Sorry.

Now I am. There's another door and more guards. Have Nana drop another fireball.

Doesn't work like that. She needs to see it to set it off.

Fine. I'll take care of these two.

Yuki? Yuki! No! Negative! Stand down! Heel!

Unfortunately, I felt the impact of her against the unforgiving stone wall at the base of the cavern. With a scream of pain and rage, I launched myself over the edge, ignoring the shouts of the rest of our party. I fell most of the way before plucking my broom from my neck and floating down the rest of the way. With one hand, I clung to the broom and landed in the middle of the circular cavern behind the two angels almost on Yukina. Rage burned through me as I swung the broom, feeling it thicken in my hands and slow as it shifted into my wicked looking scythe. That time, I managed to sever the head of one as the blade sunk into the shoulder of the other. One was silenced, the other shrieked in anger as it rounded on me.

Laughing maniacally, Yuki ripped its head from its shoulders.

Standing over its corpse, tossing its head from one hand to the other, she sneered at me. "There. See how fucking stupid it is *now*?"

"Wait, you did that on purpose?"

She shrugged.

"To teach me a fucking lesson?"

She shrugged again.

"You're a fucking asshole. I just jumped from like two thousand stories up!"

Her sneer turned into a smirk. "And did we learn our lesson?"

"Maybe. But you're fucking grounded!" I couldn't help but laugh and ruffle her spikes.

"Good. We can be grounded together and Netflix and chill."

I stared at her for a moment.

"What?"

"Yeah. I don't think that means what you think it means, Yuke."

"Huh?"

"It means watch a movie and fuck."

"No, it doesn't."

"Yes, it does. Ask Jimmy."

"Everything means fuck to Jimmy."

"Good point."

Chapter 24

Judging by the number of metal doors with bars lining the hallway on the other side of the door being guarded by the angels, I would have guessed we were in the right place. I'd actually wanted to wait for the others to catch up, but Yuki had talked me into seeing what was on the other side of the door. Cell by cell, we peered through the bars. Finally, I gave up and shouted my father's name.

"Dorothea?" My name was croaked through the bars of the very last cell at the end of the hall.

Stopping the search, I put one foot in front of the other until I was running the rest of the way, using my vampiric speed without realizing and leaving even Yuki in the dust. Slamming against the door, I gripped the bars and peered inside.

My father hung from burning hot chains against the far wall, his flesh smoking in the manacles. "Oh, my goddess," I whispered and kicked at the door. And kicked again. I was pounding and screaming in an effort to get to my father when Yuki pulled me away. "Together," she reiterated.

We backed up as far as we could and hit it together, blasting it from the hinges and jumping over it as we fell into his cell.

"I told you not to come," he groaned through the pain.

"And I told you I would," I answered and looked at his bonds. His flesh was burning, but healing just as fast, keeping him in a constant state of pain. "*Bheith fuar,*" I canted, watching the burning hot chains freeze against my spell. They were already warming as I canted, "*Fuascail,*"

Frantically pulling them off his wrists before they burned him again. He fell into my arms.

"Thank you, Daughter."

Lowering him to the ground, I leaned him back against the wall. For being imprisoned for over ninety years, he looked surprisingly well. His clothes were tattered, his flesh drawn, and his beard nearly to his waist, but he was alive. "We need to get out of here."

"No. You do. I thank you from releasing me from my chains, but I cannot leave."

"Why?"

"Because, Daughter. If I were to take my power from you, you would not survive. It is why I told you not to come!" He smiled at me sadly.

"Funny story about that," I said with a small chuckle and reached into the pocket of my jeans, pulling the stone and tucking it into his hand without showing it to him.

"A receptacle? How?"

"Gift from Delron."

"That dastardly elf!" He chuckled, but then looked at me again sadly. "Then you no longer have my…"

"Godhood? Nope."

He tilted his head and stared a moment, looking between Yuki and me. "But…"

I sighed. There was so much to tell him. Once we were back in the mortal realm. We would have all the time in the world. "Long story. Tell you later."

There was a flash of brilliant red light and he let the dust of the gem fall to the ground beside him. Shimmering, his beard disappeared as his skin filled, his clothes mended, and he radiated black power. The power of the night. He lifted me to *my* feet.

"So much better," he said and stretched, sounding much stronger. And then he hugged me.

The smell of the father I hadn't seen since I was a child wrapped around me, comforting me, soothing me. His chest pressed against my face as he kissed the top of my head and held me close. The tears started falling, soaking his shirt, as the sobs began wracking my body from the depths of my soul. The man I had thought I would never get to meet was real. And he was holding me.

Yuki just smiled and leaned back against the wall beside us, her hands folded behind her.

"I cannot believe how beautiful you are," he whispered and pushed me back to arm's length, getting to look at me with his own eyes. "Nor how strong. You look just like your mother."

It was funny, coming from my father's lips, for the first time, it felt like a compliment. "Thank you, Father."

"Oh, shush. Call me Dad, or Aodh, if you prefer. You're all grown up now."

"Lady of her own coven, Lord of the vampires, Master of the dark elves, and Lady of the shadows, too," Yuki chimed in proudly. "Just like her father."

Aodh stared into my eyes, put his hands aside my face and shifted his gaze to the air around me. "I see. That is why you no longer needed my power. You have your own." His face split in a grin. "Just like your father. More even. Since you have witches behind you, too." He sounded almost...proud.

I sniffled and rubbed my nose against the sleeve of my sweater. "Well, this is a conversation better left for home. Let's get the hell out of hell. I need some coffee."

We slipped out of the cell and down the never-ending hallway, breaking out into the bottom of the circular cavern just as the others dropped off the last of the stairs.

My mother fell to her knees. Nana smiled happily. Ellis, Shea, and Dar bowed to the floor, taking a knee. The rest of my boys looked at my father nervously. But Josie... Josie stared and didn't know what to do.

"I see you told her?"

I looked up at my father, smiling proudly. "Yep."

"Kids. They never listen." He chuckled and let go of me, taking a step closer to my sister. "Hello, Daughter."

Josie didn't run, but she didn't walk either, towing Candace behind her as she crossed the cavern and stopping short. "Uh… Hi. I'm Josie. Your other daughter…"

Aodh hugged her just as hard as he had hugged me. "I am sorry for not being in your life," he said sadly and pulled back.

"It's okay. I know you were…uh…busy." Josie smiled.

"And who is this?" He leaned around his daughter and smiled at Candace.

"This is Candace. My…fiancé. We're getting married."

He smiled again. "My, how times have changed. I have a lot of catching up to, I see. It is a pleasure to meet you, Candace." He held out his arms for her, too.

Shyly, she hugged him back.

"You smell like," he started.

"Sunshine," Josie and I finished.

"Yes! Welcome to the family, daughter of the light."

"Thank you," Candace managed to whisper.

"Shall we go?" He offered her his arm.

∞ ∞ ∞

We ran into two more groups of angels, but with my father's power, we didn't even slow as we headed for the front door of Mephistopheles's castle. Kicking it open, we stepped out onto the plains of Tartarus and landed onto green grasses under an endless sky of bright blue without a sun.

"Uh. This doesn't look like Tartarus," I stammered and spun in a circle, having a very horrible feeling. "Or earth."

"No. It's not," Aodh agreed and frowned.

"You know where we are, don't you?" I did, too. The sunless sky was a *huge* hint. I just wanted to hear how much trouble we were in straight from my father's lips.

"Yes. You do, too."

"Shit."

"Double shit," he said and let go of Candace's arm with a soft pat of assurance. "You and your friends get back. It's

266

me she wants." He pushed me behind him with an outstretched hand.

I moved behind him, but stayed close, urging everyone back with my own hand gestures while we waited for the attack to come.

"Come on out, Belenus. You know we're here." He was looking toward the sky, but dropped his gaze to the plains before him as the blue curtain of the sky parted and the goddess Belenus stepped through.

"Well, well. I knew putting that portal on the inside of the door would be a good idea. Beautiful piece of work, don't you think? My angels can come and go as they please and anyone foolish enough to infiltrate the castle would be stuck there for all eternity or dumped in my lap for a proper punishment. Or quick death. You should have stayed in your hole, Aodh. It's where you belong."

"In your hole? That seems like too harsh of a punishment to me," I chided from beside my father. More of behind, but a little off to the side.

Aodh turned his head and shook it, telling me to shut up and leave the banter to him. She was his mirror power. She couldn't be any more powerful than my father. I was confused as to why he was worried. The odds were fourteen to one.

Until the choir of archangels landed behind her, flaming swords at the ready.

"Oh."

My father nodded.

"If keep me you must, I surrender. Let the rest of them return to the mortal realm."

Belenus cackled. "Another human has emerged as a god against the decree of the All. And you wish me to simply let her go?" Belenus took a step closer. "No, Aodh. She will be joining you. Maybe I'll be sweet and give you adjoining cells so you can have company until her mortal coil finally withers away. Then you can spend eternity together as daughter and daddy gods." She chuckled again at her own joke.

"Let her go, Belenus." *Daughter. I will fight her. Flee. Circle around her, find her castle, and use the portal inside to go back to your realm. Do not worry, she will not kill me. And this time, leave me be. She is crazed and will not relent until I am broken.*

I'm not leaving you.

Go! Use the child of the light to get past the archangels.

How he knew Candace could do that, was beyond me. I was *almost* prepared to listen. Until my mother and grandmother took up the spaces beside me.

"No, Aodh. Enough is enough," Mother answered. "She is punishing you for leaving her, nothing more. There is nothing righteous about her decree or imprisonment of you. We will fight. The three witches of Blackwell stand beside you."

"Together," Nana added and grabbed my hand. Mother took the other.

"All of us," Yuki and the rest strode closer, witch hands ablaze, fangs bared, and talons at the ready.

Aodh just chuckled. "Well, I had thought to surrender peacefully, but my daughter's family wishes for a fight. What say you, Belenus? Last chance to let us go?"

"When Tartarus freezes over."

"It was pretty cold there. I'm just saying," I said to Nana and Mother.

"It was. Kind of surprising actually. You'd think it would be hot with all that fire and redness? Really kind of strange." Nana shrugged.

"I was thinking about a nice summer home right by the fire springs," Mother answered Nana.

Belenus fumed and the angels attacked, command unspoken.

"Wall of fire," Nana said calmly as the three of us focused our power and canted the words together. A wall of fire the likes of which even the goddess had never seen sprang up behind Belenus, separating her from her choir.

Belenus snarled in fury and attacked Aodh, curved flaming swords appearing in both hands as she tried to separate his head from his body. Tendrils of earth sprang from the ground beneath her feet as my coven casted spells with the sole intention of helping my father. Ice cracked off her arms as she swung her blades, severing vines, and clashing against the matte black blades of my father. The sky shuddered with each strike.

"Help Aodh, Daughter," Nana said calmly. "Dorothea and I will keep the angels at bay."

The wall of flame diminished for a moment as Mother let go and strode behind Aodh, casting slowing spells, binding spells, and everything and anything she could to aid his battle.

The first angel skirted the crest of the wall of flames and attacked Nana and me from above. It was almost upon us when Candace's scream of fury stopped it in its path, dropping it to the ground and leaving it staring at her in bewilderment.

"You have a child of light," Belenus sputtered.

"My future daughter in law," Aodh answered proudly.

"Child! Quell your song. I command it!" There was a momentary rumble of thunder and Candace shrieked, falling to the ground. Letting go of Nana, I almost beat Josie to Candace's side.

"Are you okay?" She opened her mouth to speak but nothing emerged. The goddess Belenus had silenced her. By letting go of Nana, the power fueling the fire wall diminished, and it continued to shrink. Archangels started to pour over and around it. Calling the shadows, I nearly cried in frustration. Just as in Tartarus, there were no shadows to be found. Light illuminated everything above and below, leaving no room for darkness. Not in the realm of Belenus.

If we were going to win, we needed the night.

Turning, I ran back to Nana. I needed her power. Putting both hands on her shoulders, I whispered into her ear, "Forget the fire, we need to blot out this damnable day."

"Huh?"

"I need shade!"

"What do you have in mind?"

"Darkness…"

"*Dorchadas,*" we canted together.

It started slow, a mere sphere before us. Reaching over Nana, I plunged my hand into the heart of it, feeling its coolness against my skin, reveling in its familiarity. Turning his head, my father blinked in surprise and took a blade across the bicep. Ignoring the pain, he reached behind him and added his power to our own.

It swelled to double its size, but it wasn't nearly enough. Until Yuki, Ellis, Dar, and Shea put their hands upon me as I had mine on Nana. The night swirled through me, darkness caressing every inch of me like a familiar lover teasing all my most tender of places. I took all of that, all they had offered me, and forced it through my grandmother and into our budding bubble of night.

It groaned as it fought against the day, swelling and enlarging until it covered us. Stars twinkled above as the grass beneath our feet turned blue under the nighttime sky.

"No!" Belenus did a double strike against my father but two splotches of red blossomed across her chest as Chief fired twice. Candace shrieked once more and drove the host of angels to the ground. With almost practiced ease, Aodh batted her blades away as Belenus dropped to her knees, stopping herself from collapsing face first into the ground. It was over.

My father turned and raised his hand toward me, a smile as brilliant as the sun on his face. Time stopped. Belenus lifted her head, a wicked smile on her face as she called a spear of light to her hand and drove it up under my father's ribs and into his heart.

Screaming his name, I reached out and tore through the fabric of her realm, just as I had done in the lands of

270

Faerie, with a clawed fist. Almost like black water, the shadows poured in through the gaping wound as I ran.

Ran to catch my falling father.

The shadows swarming behind me didn't stop as my arms wrapped around him and stopped him from crashing to the ground. Blackness completely enveloped the bitch as she cackled in the success of her deathblow. Wordlessly she died as the shadows tore her into pieces no bigger than my Fidget.

"Dad. Dad! Aodh!" I whined pitifully as his labored breaths came slower and slower.

"It is okay, my daughter."

"No. No, it's fucking not. Hang on!" I pulled the slick spear from his wound and tossed it away even as it severely burned my hand. "Heal!"

He shook his head. I poured my power into him, holding my hand over his gaping wound and moving it up to his heart. Back and forth, trying to get the wound to heal and his heart to keep beating. Candace plopped to the ground across from me and lent him her power, too. Josie just knelt by his head, soundlessly sobbing. He reached up and took her hand in his.

"It is okay, my daughters. You're both safe now. Be good to each other. Take care of each other. And your mothers." He winked.

I poured every ounce of power I had left in me into him, and still it wasn't enough. "No. No. You fight, damn it!"

He just smiled and closed his eyes. "I cannot. I may be a god, but I am a god of the night. A spear of the day… Even I can't fight against that," he whispered. And stopped breathing. "I love you both. All of you," he said to my mother, nodded once, and I watched in horror as the light left the god of night's eyes.

"No. No. No, no, no." Pain gripped my chest. Everything we had worked for…everything. It was for nothing. He was gone. Truly gone and *nothing* would ever replace the hole in my heart I had just filled.

271

I wailed.

Josie sobbed.

Mother closed her eyes. Tears fell down her cheeks. It was the first time I'd ever seen my mother cry. I never wanted to see it again. The three of us touched him, and beneath our hands, he faded away.

"I am sorry, my sisters."

We all looked up to stare in shock at the goddess herself standing where the shadows batted around the remaining pieces of Belenus.

Reaching down, she smiled and whispered, "Shoo." They scattered before her moonlit presence. The remaining pieces of the goddess of the day, she scattered to the wind. As she stood and stepped forward, her husband coalesced behind her. His antlered head twinkling in her light like exquisitely crafted silver. She was the moon, he was the sun, but in darkness even his bronzed skin was pale.

"We were so close," I said forlornly, sobbing before her, my lip quivering.

"And now you must move on. It is what my brother would want."

"And that was what my sister deserved," the Lord said solemnly. Day and night, moon and sun. They truly were two sets of siblings, married to their opposing forces. But now we were truly without half the gods.

"No. You are not," the goddess said with a smile, reading my thoughts.

Gently she reached out and caressed Candace and Josie, closing her eyes in rapt pleasure.

Josie and Candace looked at each other as power filled them. I smiled as I realized what she had done, imbuing my sister and her lover with power that needed new hosts. Night and Day couldn't have found better avatars. Much better than my father and his insane ex-wife. Hopefully, my sister and her love would bring a little more balance to the world. One day.

"Well, since the night has a new goddess, can I give up my power and go back to being just a Dot?"

The goddess laughed. "You stopped being the goddess of night when you came into your own power. No. Things are going to become much more interesting in the future, goddess of *darkness*." She winked.

"Oh, come *on*."

"Well, the creatures of darkness need *someone* to look out for them. Who better than that which they already adore?" To reiterate her point, the shadows began to swirl and dance around me.

"Well, that hardly seems fair. The sun and the moon. The day and the night. There can't be darkness without light, and I don't see myself getting married anytime soon."

The goddess chuckled. "Your guide back to the mortal realm has arrived." She nodded behind me.

I turned to look and groaned. Jaeren was sitting astride a unicorn of the purest white, bowing in homage to the goddess.

"Fuck me."

"What was that, Sister?" She smiled at me warmly.

"Nothing." I just shook my head. "So, what do we do now?"

She crouched in front of me, smiled, and kissed my forehead. "Now, you live your lives. For as long as you can or want. When it is time to move on, you shall join us." She reached up and took the hand of the lord. "And then we shall all dance together." She paused for a moment and grew solemn once again. "I am truly sorry for the loss of your father."

"Can I ask one more question?"

She nodded.

"What happens when a god dies?"

"That, I do not know. I would like to think there is something more beyond death for even us, but that is a mystery only two know the answer to, and they are not here to give us the answer."

"Wait and see?"

"Wait and see, Sister."

Epilogue

"I don't think I've ever been more nervous in my life," Josie whined and lowered the veil over her face.

"Well, just think of it this way, Sister. Even if you weren't getting married today, you're still going to spend an eternity with her. So, there is absolutely nothing to be nervous about. You're just making it official." I smiled at Josie over her head, into the mirror we'd hung on the wall of the tent.

"An eternity, huh? With Candace. That does sound like heaven." She grinned back at me. "I still can't believe–"

I shut her up with a hand over her mouth, trying hard not to smear her lipstick. That was one thing I refused to talk about. "Remember the rule."

"No god talk," she muttered behind my hand, but it came out more like, "Vo gov tavk."

"You got it. The less you talk about it, the more normal things stay. And I'm very fond of my normal," I said and took my hand away.

"You've never been normal, weirdo. You ready to hitch us up?"

"You betcha." I offered her my hand and helped her up off the stool that had settled in the grass of the grove.

"Have you seen Candy? Is she beautiful?"

"Even if she weren't dressed in a gown of pure white silk, she would be beautiful, but yes. She is."

"Oh, my goddess. The butterflies in my stomach!"

"I told you, you have nothing to be nervous about!"

"I meant from seeing her!" She grinned and practically ran to the flap of the tent, peering outside.

"Stay here. You know the drill and no peeking! Come out when the music starts."

"I know. We did it like three times yesterday."

"I know you know, but this is you we're talking about." I kissed her cheek and ducked through the opening, smiling at Chief and Jimmy standing by the huge oak next to the red runner leading into the grove and altar on the far side.

"She ready?" Chief motioned toward the tent I'd just come from with the beer in his hand.

"As she'll ever be. You're not supposed to start drinking until *after* the wedding."

"Well, I was getting nervous. We only have an hour left."

I shaded my eyes with my hand and stared up at the sky. He wasn't joking. The moon and the sun were still in the sky, but the sun wouldn't be for much longer. We'd thought it fitting for the ceremony but had a narrowed window of execution. "Tell Shea to start the music."

Jimmy lifted a radio and keyed up the mic. "Perv One to Shadow Boy, come in."

"Shadow Boy here. Over."

"Cue the gather music."

"Roger."

The elven quartet inside the grove started playing the cue music to let the guests know to gather and that the wedding was about to start. People from the tented area and the parking area started heading into the grove.

"Afternoon, Lady," David Stevens said as he and his wife Connie passed. She looked beautiful, even three months pregnant.

"Hi, Dave. You look radiant, Connie!" I smiled as she grimaced. Since I'd taken over the coven, they'd been so busy and things had been so crazy, we hadn't had much time to socialize. It was nice to see faces I hadn't seen in a while. It added to the normal.

I felt the coolness that was Yuki in my mind a moment before she slid up to my side. "The vampires are all set. My mother is so happy!" She grinned up at me.

276

I looked over at the special section of the grove we'd set up for them. I'd woven shadows over the seated area, not a single ounce of sunshine could touch them. It would be dark by the time the ceremony was over and they would be free to join the reception. It had all worked out nicely for once. "I'm glad they could all come."

"They are, too."

"They should be. You're their new Lord, after all." I ruffled her spiked hair.

"Still can't believe you did that to me." She stuck her tongue out. "And I prefer Lady to Lord."

"Hmm. That sounds kind of familiar. And you know, my role is to guide, not to rule."

"Yeah. Yeah. You still make a better scarier vampire than I do."

"Oh, shush. You're very scary, Sweetie."

Yuki giggled and wandered off to join the other vampires, even though she didn't need to sit in the dark. I just wanted to pinch her cheeks. She looked adorable in her red dress. It wasn't often that she let me doll her up, and I *fully* took advantage of the situation.

"You look beautiful, Master," Dar said as he snuck up behind me and planted a kiss on my cheek.

"You really do, Dot." Dennis reiterated as he stepped up beside Jimmy.

"You do," Derek said as he walked past our little group, Sherry grinning like a fool as she hung from his arm. "Why thank you, Mr. Flynn. Looking mighty beautiful yourself, too, Mrs. Flynn."

"Thanks, Dot!" Sherry grinned even more.

Nana and Mother walked by, both affording me with a nod. Miranda, Josie's mother, was surprisingly practically clinging to my mother. The three of them would be sitting with each other in the front row, too. I'd made sure of it. I chuckled softly to myself.

"You glad to be back home?" I asked Chief.

"A little. Not that I minded sleeping in your bed every night. Even when it was a little crowded." He winked and pulled me into a hug. "Thank you, Dot."

It had been a little over a week since I'd *finally* laid the ghost of his wife to rest. It had taken me almost two weeks to figure out *how* to do it. She'd smiled as I did, too. No ghost wants to be a ghost. I still had a sinking feeling that it had been my fault she'd been brought back to begin with. After she was laid to rest, I found the little girl in the park and sent her on her way, too. I was looking into purchasing a proton pack for the more unruly ones that had popped up wandering around town.

"Well, I'll be at the altar. Don't forget the brides, guys." I gave Jimmy and Chief a stern look. They were walking Candy and Josie down the aisle, after all.

"Who's got the rings?" Jimmy started patting down his suit jacket.

"I do." Ellis handed the two bands to Jimmy and Chief, respectively.

Not only were they walking them down the aisle, they were the maids of honor and the best men, too. When Candy and Josie asked them, they both cried. Then I cried. Then we all laughed. It was very cute. I threw up a little.

I waved at Marge and Herb as I walked down the aisle to the altar. They looked ragged. I'd offered to cater the wedding from *any* restaurant in the state, but the brides had insisted on diner food. Herb and Marge had been *flabbergasted* and honored. The only condition was that they, themselves, attended the wedding and the reception, not serve food. Tabby and the other crew were doing that.

"Looking good, Dot!" Dwight whistled as I passed.

I smiled when I recognized him. Gone was the scruffy witch who had been Jason's boss at the factory he used to work at. He was clean shaven, his hair was styled, and he had a bounce in his step that had *never* been there before. "Not so bad yourself, Dwight." I winked at Cedar Falls' newest police officer, still kind of mad that Chief hadn't said anything while Dwight attended the academy. He'd kept the whole thing a secret, "Just in case it hadn't worked out," he'd said. I hated surprises that weren't of my planning. At least I understood why he turned down the job at the bookstore.

Jason stepped out from behind the altar and handed me the ancient leather tome that had come straight from the museum in Ashville. Every Blackwell that had ever been married or handfasted had done so to the rites inscribed in the tome. Mother had mentioned it, Miranda insisted on it, and Josie loved the idea. Who was I to argue?

"Thanks, handsome." I slipped him a quick kiss after checking to make sure nobody was watching.

"Showtime," he said and wiggled his eyebrows.

I nodded to Shea.

The elves started playing The Wedding March and everybody drew silent. Candace and Chief were first, and they glided down the runner elegantly. Chief looked a little nervous but held it together quite nicely. Once they reached the altar, Chief bowed low and lifted the veil to kiss Candace on the cheek before settling beside her and crossing his hands.

The tempo of the music changed, and I stared in shock as the elves stood and proceeded to pound upon their instruments. The drummer pounded the bodhran and twirled the beater over his head between beats. It took me a moment before I recognized it as the opening to Thunderstruck, and my jaw dropped open as Jimmy and Josie stepped onto the runner. There was absolutely *nothing* elegant as they danced merrily down the runner in time with the music. It was gawdy, it was funny, and it suited them *perfectly*. Josie was laughing and crying as he danced her down the aisle. Even Candace was giggling beside me. Just before they reached the altar, their dancing died down, and they returned to a normal march as the music switched gears and once again the elves played the traditional wedding march.

Just as I was about to start the ceremony, the Lord and Lady appeared by the entrance to the grove and a dome of golden light sealed us inside. A spring breeze wafted through dragging the scent of flowers through the air, pushing away the chill in the air. Everybody sat straight as the magic coalesced around them. I bowed in thanks.

"Ladies and gentlemen, we gather today to join these two together in matrimony. If there is any here who thinks they should not be joined, please speak now or forever hold your peace."

It was the only concession to normal tradition in the entire ceremony. The rest would be held in Irish. Every person in the audience was holding a printed translation in their hand to follow along the ceremony. I'd practiced every night in the mirror for two weeks until I felt comfortable enough to do it. It had been beyond nerve wracking, but if it was what my sister and Candace wanted, I was sure as hell going to do it. I spoke Irish fluently, but the ceremony was *archaic*. But it was beautiful.

I opened my mouth to start, but Jaeren caught my eye standing beside Shea. He smiled and blew me a kiss.

Reacting without thinking, I caught it with my hand and pretended to stick it in my pocket. A few resounding coughs around me brought me back to reality and I blushed harshly as I looked back up and winked at Jaeren.

But that was a story for another day…

THE END

About the Author

A late comer to the writing game, Jacquelyn had always been a fan of romance novels and lately become addicted to the reverse harem category. I mean seriously, who wouldn't? Sitting alone one night she flipped open her laptop and said, "I'm going to give this a whirl." And thus, the Lovin' the Coven series was given life. She has designs on other series as well, but only time shall tell.

As for her, she is five-foot-something, with graying hair, wicked eyes, an eager smile, and an annoying laugh. She lives at home with her dog, a cat, and that is about all she is comfortable sharing.

Other Works

Lovin' the Coven Series
(Reverse Harem– 7 book series)

First Moon
Second Blood
Third Charm
Fourth Rite
Fifth Essence
Sixth Sense
Seventh Seal

The Fox and the Hounds
(Reverse Harem– trilogy)

A Tail of Woah
A Tail of Two Kitties
The Tell Tail Heart (Coming Soon!)

Other

GirlFiend (Standalone YA Paranormal Romance)
Succubus Soccer Mom (Reverse Harem Standalone)